THE FRENCH FOR
MURDER

BOOKS BY VERITY BRIGHT

The Lady Eleanor Swift Mystery Series

THE FRENCH FOR MURDER

VERITY BRIGHT

bookouture

Published by Bookouture in 2022

An imprint of Storyfire Ltd.
Carmelite House
50 Victoria Embankment
London EC4Y 0DZ

www.bookouture.com

ISBN: 978-1-80314-322-4
eBook ISBN: 978-1-80314-323-1

This book is a work of fiction. Names, characters, businesses, organizations,
places and events other than those clearly in the public domain, are either the
product of the author's imagination or are used fictitiously. Any resemblance
to actual persons, living or dead, events or locales is entirely coincidental.

To the latent Francophile in all of us.

France has neither winter nor summer nor morals – apart from these drawbacks it is a fine country.

$\sim$ Mark Twain

1

'I apologise for delivering news of an inconvenient nature, my lady, but there appears to be a dead body in the wine cellar.'

Lady Eleanor Swift laughed briefly before dragging her gaze away from the endless sparkling blue Mediterranean. She turned to her butler standing by the unlit fireplace and shook her head at his appearance. Despite the fierce August heat that had her repeatedly fanning her face, he still sported his customary morning suit tails.

'Nice try, Clifford.' Her piercing green eyes glanced over his shoulder at the clock. 'We only arrived at our villa an hour or so ago. The suitcases and trunks aren't even unpacked and I'm still in my twill travelling trousers. And yet it seems you're already teasing me.' She ran her hands through her fiery-red curls and then folded her arms. 'Well, it will do no good. I came here to recuperate and not get caught up in anything unpleasant – like murder – again. I intend to do the ladylike thing for a change and lounge about the pool and dine in elegant restaurants. After all, we are on the Côte d'Azur, only a few miles from Nice. So,' – she unfolded her arms and waggled a finger at her butler – 'you'll need to try a lot harder than that to catch me out.'

'If you say so, my lady.'

She turned back to the view, ruffling the ears of her bulldog, Gladstone, who was sprawled out on the low window seat beside her.

Positioned on a rocky promontory above the village, the imposing villa was built of pink stone in the Italianate style. The set-back central section was porticoed in ivory white, with four floors of arched full-length windows giving stunning views over the sea.

A full minute passed as she became lost in admiring the myriad white-stone buildings that tumbled down the steep hillside to the azure water below. Finally, she tuned into the uncomfortable feeling that, unlike the sailboats zigzagging across the bay, her butler hadn't moved an inch. She spun round.

'Clifford?'

He arched one brow in reply.

'Rather a protracted joke, even for you, wouldn't you say?'

She'd known Clifford since she was nine, and he'd been her beloved uncle's butler, batman and friend before that. Over time, she'd got used to his dry sense of humour.

Consulting his pocket watch, he closed the casing with a snap. 'Not especially. However, my lady, on this occasion I am afraid there is no joke.' He held up his leather pocketbook, lined in his meticulous copperplate writing, and tapped the page with a white-gloved finger. 'My interrupted inventory of the wine cellar most definitely contains the unusual addition of a dead body.'

She stared at him in disbelief, mouth agape. 'Clifford! No! That can't be. I mean... Genuinely?' At his nod, she groaned. 'Well, you'd better show me. But I'm certain you must have made a mistake.'

'My lady, if I might suggest—'

'Thank you, but no, you may not. I can only think that,

uncharacteristically, you've been on the port early. But even if by some horrible chance you aren't hallucinating, I'm not some fainting violet! Or is it wilting violet? Either way, I've seen enough bodies in my years as a war nurse, and, unfortunately, since then, as well you know. Anyway, imagination is usually worse than reality. If I don't see for myself, I shall inevitably conjure up all manner of troubling images. And then I won't be able to sleep and you'll have to answer your bedroom door to me in the small hours, in your pyjamas...'

With a horrified look, he gestured towards the stairs. 'Shall we?'

In contrast to the rest of the villa, the stone steps down into the cellar were positively mediaeval. Clifford lighting their way with a flickering silver five-branched candelabra only added to the dungeon-like atmosphere.

'Please watch your step, my lady. To ensure the best possible conditions for the contents, the cellar is cut into the rock-bed foundations themselves and thus the steps are hazardously steep and uneven in parts.'

Eleanor steadied herself by sliding one hand along the cool wall. 'Well, at least it must have electric lighting like the rest of the villa.'

Clifford shook his head. 'Electric light has many benefits over traditional gaslights, I am sure, which is why your uncle had Henley Hall converted entirely to electric light. The first major home in the county to do so. However, its impact on wine has yet to be properly documented.' He shuddered. 'Harsh light and the accompanying increase in temperature caused by the heat given off could damage a vintage bottle irreparably.'

At the base of the steps he pulled out a large ring of keys and paused with his gloved hand on the arched iron grill covering the thick oak door. 'Must a last entreaty fall on deaf ears, my lady?'

She nodded, still sure that there had to be some other explanation. Maybe their previous investigations had taken more of a toll on her butler than she'd imagined? He resignedly unlocked the door. She took a deep breath and stepped hesitantly over the threshold.

The vaulted brick ceiling lit only by a few gaslights made the shadowy space feel even more forbidding than she had expected. Myriad alcoves were filled with rows of dusty bottles cradled in conker-brown wooden racks, while two lines of oak barrels ran down the middle of the flagstone floor.

She stepped forward and turned in a slow circle. 'Where is our poor *monsieur*? Or,' she said with a shiver, '*madame*?'

'It is indeed a *monsieur*, my lady. He is this way, between the champagnes and the dessert wines.'

'Oh, Clifford,' she breathed a moment later, staring at the motionless figure lying on his front on the flagstones, one arm stretched out as if grasping for something. It seemed she owed her butler an apology.

The man's face was hidden from view by the outstretched arm, but as she knew not a soul in the area there was little chance she'd recognise him. She shook her head in bewilderment. How had he got there? And how had he— The first question remained unanswered, but the second died on her lips as she spotted the long blade jutting out from the man's back.

She shuddered. 'Clifford, is that a...?'

'A sword. Yes, my lady. From its sweeping inward curve, I would say possibly a sabre. I feel, perhaps, awaiting the police upstairs might be the best course of action? I hope you do not mind, but I called them before I informed you as I felt it was most important they arrived speedily, given the... nature of the gentleman's death.'

'You mean because he was obviously murdered?'

'Unfortunately, yes.'

She stared again at the curved blade sticking out of the man's back. 'It does seem unlikely that he fell on... *that* by accident. And from those thick swathes of ebony hair poking out from his cap and his vigorous build, he doesn't look to have been much older than me.'

Clifford glanced at her in concern and held out a pristine handkerchief. 'I concur, my lady. The gentleman's hands also show little signs of ageing, other than the unsympathetic effects of time spent in the sun.'

'He was quite the dapper gent by the manner of his rather theatrically patterned jacket and mismatched trousers.'

Clifford looked at her as if she'd declared the world was flat. 'My lady, this is the French Riviera.'

'Yes, but it is totally out of season, which is why we came now. It's mostly deserted and closed up and therefore peaceful. Although that doesn't seem to have been the case here, does it?'

'Regrettably not. My apologies.'

'Hardly your fault, Clifford. But he is either a very flamboyant local or a very lost tourist. Whichever, how he ended up in my wine cellar we shall have to leave to the police to find out.' She sighed and willed her legs to move. 'Rest in peace, *monsieur*.'

As Clifford went to lock the door after them, Eleanor felt a doubt jab into her thoughts. She tugged on her butler's jacket sleeve, which drew a disapproving sniff in response.

'You're absolutely sure that he is, you know... dead? I'm not questioning your infallible judgement, it's just...'

'Would that I could say otherwise, my lady. But I checked his pulse immediately on finding him. Sadly, he is most definitely no longer with us. It would have taken a gentleman of exceptionally robust constitution to survive a blow by such a weapon.'

She felt another wave of sadness for the lost soul they were leaving lying alone on the cold flagstone floor. 'Probably don't really have to lock him in though, do we? Feels a bit... final, as it were.'

'It is as much for the scene to be preserved for the police as for the security of the cellar's contents. The agreement is we pay only for what we use. Hence my making an inventory, the agent singularly having failed to turn up with one. Or indeed turn up at all.' He rolled his eyes.

She nodded. 'I know. Hardly the done thing just to leave the keys on the doormat and not even put in an appearance!'

His lips pursed. 'Perhaps the gentleman was aware that the cellar is woefully inadequate in one area at least.'

'How so?'

'At the risk of delivering more bad news, my lady, having completed my inventory of the reds before finding the deceased, there are no sufficiently robust reds for Mrs Trotman's beef daube Provençal.'

'Our Mrs Trotman? My cook? The best cook of *English* food ever?'

He nodded. 'The very one, my lady.'

She threw her hands out. 'But she's never even been abroad before. Where did she get the idea of cooking something so quintessentially French as beef daube? But, dash it, what are we thinking, Clifford!' She jerked her head toward the now locked cellar door. 'A lack of the right wine is hardly important at the moment.'

His ever-inscrutable expression turned to horror. 'My lady, forgive my overstepping the mark, but while we are here, a word of advice: Never say that in front of a Frenchman!'

'Mr Clifford, sir?' The anxious voice of Eleanor's housekeeper stuttered down to them.

'Mrs Butters,' he called up, 'her ladyship and I will be with you in just a moment.'

'Oh, thank the stars because it can't be right, but there's a bunch of foreign gentlemen up here. And the one who speaks a bit of English is insisting as they're the police!'

2

As they reached the top of the stairs, Eleanor was greeted by the sight of her four staff huddled in a line, flanked either end by a po-faced police officer. Despite standing to sharp attention, to Eleanor's mind their uniforms belied their authority, designed, as they appeared to be, for aesthetics rather than practicality. Dark-navy silver-buttoned jackets, embellished with red piping to match the scarlet cuffs, pillbox caps and bright cobalt-blue trousers made a vivid fashion, if not authoritarian, statement.

She smiled reassuringly at her anxious staff, as a middle-aged man with a glowing complexion stepped forward. He was dressed head to toe in an oyster-grey and olive-green linen striped suit, the colours mirrored in his hatband and loosely looped cravat. His entire look was far more suggestive of an afternoon jaunt around Nice than a murder investigation. As he addressed Eleanor with an unmistakably strong French accent, his neat black moustache twitched.

'Inspector Jacques Jean-Baptiste Damboise. And you are, *mademoiselle?*'

'Lady Eleanor Swift. But surely a *"madame"* at the ripe age of thirty-one?'

'*Mais non.* Since the lady wear no wedding ring, she has not yet the privilege of being a *madame.*'

She noted his ring finger sported a wide engraved gold band. 'Well then, I suppose I am Mademoiselle Lady Swift, if that works. Thank you for coming.'

Damboise studied her face. 'Hmm, perhaps it is not wise to thank me so quickly. But we will see.' He pointed at Clifford. 'And by the look of the much-too-hot suit, this man is your valet?'

Eleanor shook her head. 'He is my butler. And a great many other things besides. It was he who telephoned the police station.'

'Ah!' The inspector strode over and addressed Clifford. 'Then it was you who found the body, *monsieur*?'

Eleanor's four staff gasped and said in unison, 'Body?'

Her youngest maid, Polly, jiggled nervously and shuffled closer to Lizzie, Eleanor's second and older maid.

'Ladies.' Clifford held the inspector's gaze. 'I will explain later. Until then, her ladyship has company.'

'Yes, Mr Clifford, sir,' they chorused in barely more than a whisper.

Damboise smiled in amusement. 'Ah, the English politeness. How delightful. Yet we are not here to enjoy the ceremony of tea taking.' He indicated to the two policemen to lead the ladies away.

Eleanor watched them go with concern.

'Inspector, with the exception of Clifford here, none of my staff speak a word of your wonderful language. Might I request—'

'Many things, once I establish who is responsible for the dead man in this villa. Until then, please, let me work my business, *oui*?' He produced a slim notebook from the breast pocket of his waistcoat and slid out a pencil from under the leather band, which served as a clasp. He checked the sharpness of the lead point and, seemingly satisfied, smoothed open a new page. 'Now. When did you arrive?'

'Only this afternoon. About...' Eleanor realised she'd been far too excited to note such things. 'Clifford?'

'Seven minutes past three, my lady.'

'So precise.' Damboise's voice had an edge of suspicion. 'Normally, witnesses are very cloudy about these things.' He frowned. '*Non, excusez-moi*, I mean foggy.'

Eleanor shrugged. 'Clifford is the walking definition of precise.' She peered sideways at her butler. 'Which is both invaluable and irritating, on occasions. So, yes, we arrived exactly then.'

'And you discovered the body at what time, *monsieur*?'

'Thirteen minutes to five,' Clifford said. 'I was taking an inventory of the wine cellar.'

Damboise's eyebrows rose. 'In a moment, will you try to have me believe you listed the deceased among the Bordeaux and the Beaujolais?'

'No, Inspector. For two reasons. Firstly, I found him between the Sauternes and the champagnes.'

The inspector narrowed his eyes. 'And the second reason?'

Clifford pulled out his leather pocketbook and flipped it open, the black silk ribbon marking a particular page. 'You may see for yourself.'

Damboise took it and cast an eye over the entry, before pocketing it. 'Lady Swift, what did you do while your valet... your butler, was being so strangely precise about the contents of the cellar?'

'I was sitting in the drawing room, captivated by the view.'

'I see. Then he comes with the news of a dead man and – what? You fall to the floor in a faint?' He fixed her with a hard stare. 'Or perhaps another response?'

'I'm not the fainting sort, actually.' Her cheeks coloured. 'To be completely honest, I... I laughed.'

The detective's eyebrows met. 'So,' – he took a slow walk around Eleanor and Clifford, staring between them – 'the mistress and her butler find death amusing, *non?*'

Clifford gave a quiet cautionary cough, halting the flippant response burning on Eleanor's lips.

'No, Inspector.'

'Perhaps,' he said without conviction. 'Now we go see the body.' He looked pointedly at Eleanor. 'Together.'

Clifford's brows flinched. 'Inspector, if I might request that Lady Swift not be exposed to such unpleasantness.'

'Another *non, monsieur.*' At Clifford's pursed lips, Damboise raised a finger. 'But I say this not only because the lady herself says that fainting is not a habit she has need of. But also because you have already given your mistress the full tour of the body, *non?*'

Eleanor jumped in. 'Well, we might just have come from that direction but it doesn't necessarily mean—'

Damboise gestured to Clifford's now wrinkled handkerchief, which she still held. 'Your butler does his duty worthy of a medal, I think. And he has not the conceit to go against the command of his mistress. So he aids her in doing what he wishes she would not. Look upon a dead man.' His eyes narrowed. 'I am interested to find out precisely how far he aids you in unpleasant matters!' Clicking his fingers, he waved Eleanor forward. 'After you, *mademoiselle.*'

At the locked door into the cellar, Clifford held out the ring of keys to the inspector.

'No, please. I watch.' But far from scrutinising her butler's every move, he busied himself checking each of his jacket pockets until he found a small metal tin. Gesturing that Eleanor should open her palm, he lifted the tin's lid and dropped a black pastille into her hand. After insisting that Clifford and the other policeman take one too, he popped one into his mouth and closed his eyes.

Eleanor stared at hers.

'It is liquorice, my lady.' Clifford tipped his into his pocket.

Damboise nodded. 'First you help me not eat too many so that my heart does not thunder like the train. Too much liquorice does that to the heart.' His tone hardened. 'And then you tell me why the man in there is dead!'

'But we don't know!' Eleanor turned the pastille in her hand. 'We've only been here five minutes.'

'Ah, *non*! An English expression I know, but also an untruth. You have been here...?' He whipped out a silver pocket watch from his waistcoat and held it up to Clifford.

With nothing more than a flick of his eyes at the timepiece, Clifford said, 'Three hours and forty-six minutes, Inspector.'

'Ah!' Damboise re-pocketed his watch. 'Precision can be the good friend, *non*?' He led them over to the body. 'So you decided he is dead because?'

'Aside from the gentleman having bled extensively over the cellar floor, I noted he had no pulse,' said Clifford.

'It does not upset you to touch a dead man?'

'After many years in the army, no.'

The inspector sucked on his sweet thoughtfully. Holding his pencil up like an artist peering around the side of his canvas at his subject, he said nothing for several minutes. He stared at the dead body, intermittently jotting notes and gazing into space. Finally, he called to the policeman.

'Pierre, *à gauche, puis à droite, s'il vous plaît.*'

This prompted the young man to pace out distances from the door, the cellar's perimeter and then the various wine racks, calling them out as he went. Eleanor stole a look at the inspector's page, marvelling at his detailed sketch of the scene with the measurements neatly noted at key intervals. *Worthy of Clifford's obsession with the meticulous, Ellie.*

'What do you think so far, Inspector?' she asked.

He didn't look up from his page. 'I think, *mademoiselle*, a great many things.'

Dissatisfied with the obvious brush-off, she stepped to Clifford's side and spoke under her breath. 'It's unthinkable that here we are again caught up in another—'

Her butler cleared his throat loudly, his arched brow cautioning her not to finish her sentence. He tapped his ear and gestured at the inspector, who still appeared deep in his notebook.

A moment later, Damboise spun around. 'What is the word in English for the weapon selected for this man's death?'

'A sword,' Eleanor said.

'Or to be more precise, Inspector,' Clifford said, 'a sabre.'

'Ah! Same in French. You are knowledgeable of the particulars of unusual weapons, it seems.'

'Inspector!' Eleanor said. 'Are we done here?'

He shook his head. '*Mais non*, how could we be done, since we have not identified the person who is deceased?'

'Well, I can't help with that. And neither can Clifford.' She waved a sad hand at the body. 'We don't know a single living soul here.'

Damboise nodded. 'But he is not a living soul, of course.' He tutted. 'It is a shame you did not think to put the honey.'

'What?' She stared at the inspector, then at Clifford.

'It is a superstition, ahem, I mean belief, in some parts of France, my lady. A pot of honey is often placed near the deceased to draw flies in which it is believed souls reside.'

Damboise made an appreciative face. 'Is there much you do not know?'

Clifford held his stare. 'About this murder, everything.'

Damboise waved at the policeman, then gestured for him to move the body so they could see the man's face.

'*Oui, Chef.*' The young man saluted, but swallowed hard. He sunk to his haunches and reached out tentatively to the dead man's shoulders. With a deep breath, he turned the man's head to face them and then jumped back in astonishment. '*Mon Dieu!*'

3

With its elegant white marble balustrading and fluted columns, the villa's expansive main balcony offered the outdoor escape Eleanor needed. As she paced up and down, staring out to sea, Gladstone padded beside her, clearly unsure of what was happening. On such occasions, his default behaviour was to stick close to her side.

'How much longer is Damboise going to keep us all apart, boy? I'm worried about each of the ladies being interrogated alone. Polly, especially, will be terrified, bless her. And Clifford is no doubt as concerned about me as I am him after that awful scene he came across. And there is still an unexplained body in my wine cellar!'

She changed tack and walked up the three wide curved steps onto the second, smaller, circular balcony suspended above the lower one. Gladstone huffed up beside her. She stared out over the tops of the poplars rising from the garden below. The early-evening sun, low in the sky, made the deep-blue Mediterranean water shimmer and sparkle. Gladstone leaned against her legs, closing his eyes, the warm air making him dozy. She stroked his ear distractedly.

'I can't make out that Inspector Damboise, you know, boy. In some ways, he seems as relaxed as this holiday on the Riviera was supposed to have been. Informal suit, polite to his junior officers, dishing out liquorice as if we were children on a jolly. And yet behind all that, there's something in his manner that feels so...' She paused, trying to find the right word. 'So quietly discerning.' She glanced at her bulldog, who had succumbed to the balmy weather and was snoring away, still propped against her leg. She decided, despite appearances, that he might still be listening. 'Hmm, the inspector is definitely more intelligent than he is letting on. In fact, I think he may be disconcertingly astute.'

'*Merci, mademoiselle.*'

With a start, she spun around to see Damboise tilting his head at her from the first step. 'This is a compliment, *non*? Forgive me, my English is still the apprentice.' He stepped up and came over to join her. 'Some minds always are so busy with questions. Like mine.' He studied her face as if trying to peer into her soul. 'And like yours.'

She returned his stare. 'So, is it my turn for your questions now?'

'It is.' He waved a linen-clad arm back towards the rattan chairs halfway along the main terrace. 'But, *mademoiselle*, you might prefer to sit in comfort?'

'This is fine, thank you.' She perched on the edge of the balustrade's rounded stone capping rail. 'I'd really like this to be as quick as possible.'

'*Naturellement,*' he said drily, pulling out his notebook. 'Everyone I have ever interviewed wished the same. But this I cannot promise. What I request first is that we discuss only the truth.'

She shrugged. 'I have nothing to hide. But before you begin, I have a question for you. How are my ladies? They weren't too upset when you questioned them, were they?'

'*Non, mademoiselle.*' As her shoulders relaxed, he held up a hand. 'But I have not interviewed them yet.'

'What!'

'The honour of answering the first questions I have saved for the lady of the house. So, please let us start. You have come to Garbonne sur Mer for how long?'

'For this month only. I have to be back at the beginning of September to attend a wedding.'

'Yours, *mademoiselle?*'

'Oh, gracious, no!'

He looked momentarily surprised at her reaction but did not remark upon it. 'Why are you here? Not just a holiday, I think?'

'It is purely for a holiday, actually.'

As he peered at her intently, she flapped a hand of surrender.

'Well, I admit, more a... recuperation, really. I finally gave in to all the repeated insistence that I needed to have some time away from—' She bit her lip. *This is not the man to confess to that you've recently been caught up in a raft of murders!* She hurried on. 'I realised that he was right. I did need to get away.'

'Hmm. And who is this "he" who is concerned about you, *mademoiselle?*'

'Hugh, my, um... sort of beau.' The image of Hugh's deep-brown eyes and chestnut curls topping off his tall, athletic frame made her blush.

'*Quel dommage.*' Damboise jotted down a line in his notebook. He looked up. 'What a shame, I think you say in English? He wishes for your happiness, yet this gentleman does not accompany you here. Because it is not correct?'

Despite her anxiety over recent events, she laughed. 'You mean would it have been improper? You've met Clifford, Inspector. My butler is the ultimate chaperone. A lady's honour and reputation are beyond safe with his unbending sense of propriety. Not that Hugh isn't the perfect gentleman. It's that, well, to be honest, he and I... well, it's early days. And, besides, he could never have got the time off work. He's always so busy, forever being called here, there and everywhere because he's a senior... person in the organisation he works for.'

For some reason, she felt uneasy at telling Damboise that her awkward beau was a chief inspector with Scotland Yard. *He definitely spotted your hesitation though, Ellie.*

'Your... er, assistant recognised the dead man in my cellar. I confess I looked away.' She'd feared he might have had some other disfiguring injuries from the sabre. 'Who is he?'

'All in good time, *mademoiselle*. So this boyfriend suggests that you come to the Riviera?'

'No. That was Clifford's idea. Ever the unfathomable fount of knowledge, he knew it wouldn't be crowded, as the season doesn't start until September. He was right too. I was easily able to rent a villa for a whole month at the last minute.'

'This is true. The English ladies and gentlemen with the titles do not come before September or after April.' He held her gaze. 'But you decided to come at the opposite time, *n'est-ce pas*? And alone.'

'I'm far from alone, Inspector.' She frowned. 'I have brought my staff with me.'

'Who are all very...' He paused. 'What is the word I wish for?'

'Trustworthy?'

'*Non*. Ah, loyal. Always they do as their mistress say, *non*?'

'Well, naturally.'

It felt like a loaded question, but scrutinising his face told her nothing. He closed his notebook carefully and slid the leather band into place. 'But the most loyal, I think, is also the one who is the most precise. He knows many things. And he suggested you come. And you say you were able to rent a villa here? But I think it is your butler who actually made the booking, *n'est-ce pas?*' He nodded as if to himself. 'Your butler will be an interesting man to question. But first, the ladies.'

It was less than twenty minutes later that Mrs Trotman appeared carrying a tray of coffee and some divine-smelling pastries, her white apron swinging over her English pear hips. She smiled as Eleanor hurried over to her, looking anxious. ''Twasn't too bad at all, m'lady. No need to fret. He has a queer way of talking, that inspector, mind.'

'I imagine that's because he's, er, French?'

'Ah!' Her cook nodded. 'That'll be it. But I understood him well enough. And he'll be gentle with young Polly, I'll warrant.' She set the tray down on the wall.

'Thank goodness.' Eleanor patted her cook's arm. 'I have been fretting for you all, in truth.' She eyed the tray's contents. 'But how have you managed to conjure up these delectable-looking fellows during it all?'

''Taint just an empty saying that the way to a man's heart is through his stomach, m'lady. Even a foreign one. I learned that early on when I started working for your late uncle, God rest his soul. When a bunch of trouble barged in, be them in suits, uniforms or rags, nothing took the wind out of their sails like a plate of my specials. Same as these have with him.'

'You've had him eating in the kitchen?'

Mrs Trotman nodded. 'And asking me to carry on so he could watch me cooking and poke his nose into it all. Honestly, he asked me that many questions about what meals I make for you, m'lady, you'd think as I'd poisoned that poor dead man in the cellar! Hardly asked me much about anything else 'cept when we arrived and why you brought us with you.'

Mrs Butters bustled out through the French windows. 'Oh, my stars, m'lady. Fancy that inspector making you stay on your own all this time. I told him as you would want Mr Clifford with you but he wouldn't have it.'

Eleanor smiled at them both. 'Thank you, ladies, but I'm fine.'

'Maybe.' Her housekeeper's face was etched with motherly concern. 'Good job Mr Clifford packed his chess set. You'll be wanting to sit up late with him this evening and be properly distracted, I'm sure, m'lady.'

'You mean bend his ear into the small hours while he listens patiently and pours me one too many glasses of port, while pretending I'm a worthy opponent.'

'I mean, like his lordship always found when summat crooked his plans in the neck, Mr Clifford is good company. And never more than when the mistress needs help relaxing after some nasty business has crept in uninvited.'

'A nasty business, indeed.' Eleanor sighed. 'Did the inspector ask you much, Mrs Butters?'

Her housekeeper glanced at her cook, then shook her head without making eye contact. 'Not so much at all, m'lady. Just the sort of thing you'd expect, seeing as he's got the strange idea that we're foreign.'

Her cook and housekeeper laughed.

'We are,' Eleanor said in confusion. 'We're in France.'

Mrs Trotman tutted. 'He's the one who's foreign, my lady. We're English. No matter what country we're in.'

'Ah, I see.' *Best to leave it there.*

A loud squeal heralded the arrival of a very flustered Polly. The young girl flew out of the nearest door, fighting the voile curtain caught over her head. She fell up the steps and then skidded to a stop and bobbed a curtsey. 'Sorry for running in front of the mistress,' she mumbled. ''Tis against the rules, I know, your ladyship.'

'It's alright, Polly. I understand you were probably glad your chat with the inspector was over.'

'Yes, your ladyship.' She stared at the ground. 'But he was really kind and spoke to me in English. But then...' Her young maid's eyes filled with tears. 'He... he shouted at me!'

Eleanor shook her head. 'Why on earth would he suddenly shout?'

Mrs Trotman rolled her eyes. 'Polly, my girl. Tell me you didn't pour him coffee while you were so nervous, did you?'

The young girl nodded through a sob. 'His cup were empty. And he asked me to fill it up, saying as he never thought a cook from t'other side of the water could make such good coffee. And... and I spilled it and he shouted.' She wiped her nose on her sleeve. 'He... he did apologise afterwards, though.'

Mrs Butters poked the cook in the ribs. 'Oh, lawks, Trotters! How the devil's biscuits am I supposed to get a lapful of coffee stains out of the inspector's pale suit afore he leaves!'

Mrs Trotman grinned. 'I don't know, Butters, but Mr Clifford will be sniffing all night if he gets wind you was so brazen as to ask the inspector to take his suit off!'

'Not now, Trotters.' Her housekeeper hurriedly pulled the tearful maid into a hug. 'Probably a good technique though, m'lady. Anything to hurry him up out of your villa, eh? Shame Lizzie isn't clumsy too. Might make her session with him even quicker. Oh, but looks like she's done already.'

'M'lady.' Lizzie curtsied from the top step, waiting for permission to come forward.

'Please join us, Lizzie. It's fine.' Eleanor beckoned the newest addition to her staff over. 'As I hope you are?'

'Och aye, m'lady. He was nae fierce.'

Lizzie's thick Scottish burr still enchanted Eleanor. At seventeen she was only two years older than Polly, but the gap seemed much larger.

Lizzie slid her arm through Polly's and dabbed at the younger girl's cheeks with her apron. 'Dinna worry, Polly. He cannae be that cross. He managed to ask his questions and munch a load of Mrs Trotman's pastry cigars at the same time.'

'Cigarillos, my girl,' Mrs Trotman said. 'On account of them being delicate and refined.' She turned to Eleanor and pointed to the tray. 'Them on the left is crab and them on the right is goat's cheese.'

Mrs Butters grinned. 'With chervil in the first and nutmeg in the second.'

Mrs Trotman huffed. 'Which the inspector insisted you had to try, m'lady, since you're here in his home country. 'Pologies. Didn't feel I could say no.'

Eleanor laughed. 'I'm sure they'll be delightful. However, until Clifford reappears, we should finish—'

'My lady.' Her butler's measured voice came from the doorway. 'With sincere apologies, I shall continue to be indisposed.' He turned to the inspector, who was rubbing shoulders with him. 'But briefly, I am confident.'

'I do not share this confidence, *mademoiselle*.' Damboise pulled his arm forward, dragging Clifford with him.

'Handcuffed!' At her raised voice, Gladstone jumped up and growled in Damboise's direction. She grabbed his collar. 'Inspector! What on earth do you think you're doing handcuffing my butler?'

Damboise looked at her as if she were a small child. 'What do you think, *mademoiselle*? I am arresting him for the murder of the man in your cellar!'

4

Eleanor tripped and dropped the keys to her rented Delage car onto the terracotta-tiled entrance floor.

'Dash you!' she muttered, feeling under the ornate mahogany carved chest that served as a telephone table. 'Dash you, Damboise!'

'M'lady?'

She straightened up with the recovered keys in her hand. 'Yes, Mrs Butters?'

Her housekeeper hesitated. 'Beg pardon for being so bold, but perhaps Trotters or me ought to go with you? 'Tis a foreign country and a very peculiar car. Even Mr Clifford himself said as it was ever so different to the Rolls.'

'I'll be fine, thank you.' In truth, she wasn't so sure. She'd never learned to drive until Clifford had given her a few lessons a year or so ago. And she couldn't exactly remember when, but his instruction had just petered out. Why, she couldn't fathom. 'And I only need to drive there. Clifford can drive us back once I've corrected this ridiculous error. The most helpful thing you can do is keep the other ladies from worrying too much.'

'I'll try. You know, m'lady, we'd all lay our heads on the block to prove Mr Clifford hasn't done anything wrong since he's the most upright man alive.'

'Absolutely! The grounds Damboise has hauled him off on are preposterous. But I will go and sort it out.'

Mrs Butters nodded. 'If anyone can bring Mr Clifford back, my lady, 'tis you. But, please, be ever so careful.'

Having dissuaded the ladies, Eleanor was still struggling to leave as Gladstone had become adamant he would join her rescue mission. All the usual tricks to defeat his mulish insistence failed to dislodge him from blocking her way out of the front door. And when even the lure of a bone with plenty of ham still on was ignored, she relented and grabbed his lead.

'Alright, old friend, you know when something is wrong, don't you? Come on then, we need to hurry. I've no idea how the French legal system works. Damboise might already be halfway to court with Clifford by now!'

With Gladstone lumbering on her heels, she ran down the curved drive to the lower level, where four spacious garages made up a section of the villa's ground floor. In the second, a gleaming open-top, cherry-red car sat haughtily, its long running boards bashing her shin as she reached for the door handle. Having jostled Gladstone onto the bench seat, she scooted him across the deep-seamed leather to grab the steering wheel.

'Gah! It's on the other side, of course.'

She ran around and slid in the driver's side, using her body weight to shuffle the obstinate bulldog back to the passenger side. Having no idea what any of the dials or switches on the dashboard were for, she simply ignored them all. With a great roar, the engine jerked into life. And then stalled as she rammed the gear lever into a position it apparently wasn't intended for.

'Slow down, Ellie,' she said aloud. 'Less haste, more speed.'

After a string of hideous graunching noises, she coaxed the

car out of the garage but only to have it leapfrog and judder up the steep drive. She stroked the dashboard soothingly.

'We need to be friends.'

Having finally got the car to move without it imitating a kangaroo, she drove out of the villa's gates.

The narrow road down the steep hill to the town was a series of switchbacks, the navigating of which caused Gladstone's bulky form to slide across the stitched leather seat, bump into her and then slide back at each one.

'Why are these corners so dashedly sharp, boy? Whoa, and the drop offs so dizzying? And why leave so much thick fleshy greenery everywhere! With all these giant cactus fellows sprouting so wildly out over every wall, I can't see if anyone else is coming.' Hunching over the wheel, she urged the car on. Progress, however, was slow, as she had to keep stamping on the brakes to avoid catching the bonnet on the stone walls lining the road at each bend. Above the screaming of the engine, she shouted to her bulldog. 'I'll have to get Clifford to return it to the rental company for a service. It didn't make that racket when he drove it here.'

As Gladstone slid across to her once more, he buried his head behind her back.

'Wishing you stayed behind with the ham bone now, huh?'

Hands gripped tight to the wheel, she cursed not bringing her sunglasses as the early-evening sun blinded her. She'd just concluded that if the current corner didn't straighten out soon, she'd be back where she started, when she felt a sharp gash to her cheek. The culprit was one of the many thorned tips on a colossal Agave succulent growing out over the road. She winced as she held her hand to the cut. *If Clifford were here, he'd force me to apply some of that spitefully astringent ointment he always has about his person.*

She wished he was beside her. She'd been brought up abroad by her bohemian parents until one terrible night when they'd disappeared. Aged nine, her uncle had arranged for her to come to England to attend a private girls' boarding school. She'd hated it. Her only escape had been her holidays at Henley Hall, her uncle's estate. However, her uncle had rarely been there as he was always travelling abroad. Her only companions had been the staff, particularly Clifford. And even though they'd had their disagreements, since the death of her uncle, he'd always been there for her.

She blinked away a tear and whispered to the evening breeze, 'I'm coming, Clifford.'

It seemed forever before the rutted road surface gave onto smoother tarmac. At the same time, the sparsely dotted buildings gave way to a collection of rambling stone houses, their terracotta roofs running up and down the hill like a series of giant steps.

By now her arms were aching from hauling on the steering wheel on the many bends, but she let out a whoop as she recognised the demure villa in front of her. The garden was bursting with tall cerise flowering shrubs Clifford had told her were oleanders, the local favourite bloom. At her cry, Gladstone pulled out his head.

'Now that's more comfortable, isn't it?' She rubbed the small of her back. 'For me as well. But look.' She pointed to the villa. 'We passed that on the way through the centre of the town.'

Gladstone hung his front legs over the passenger door and peered up and down. Having failed to spot anything edible or chaseable, he huffed down onto the seat.

As they set off again, exasperation soon replaced her relief at having found the correct route. All manner of donkey-drawn carts, small vans and even pedestrians seemed hell-bent on forcing her off the road.

'*L'autre côté!*' she heard for the hundredth time.

Finally, the few awake moments she recalled in French class penetrated her preoccupied brain.

'Ah, of course! Pardon!'

Easing back on the accelerator and steering across to the right-hand side seemed to appease the other road users. But the multitude of unsigned turnings soon had her baffled. No stranger to being abroad – she'd travelled half the world alone – she jerked the car to a stop. Leaping out, she accosted a group of bored-looking young men lounging outside a bar-cum-tobacconist. Pointing in every direction, she asked, 'Um, *le* police station, *s'il vous plaît?*'

'*Mademoiselle.*' The tallest of them flicked the end of his cigarette to the kerb and pointed straight down the road. '*Le poste de police est par-là.*'

She thanked him, jerked the car back into life and shot off to a chorus of '*Bonne chance, mademoiselle!*'

After only four wrong turns, she arrived at the station, a severe two-storied slab of grey stone.

'Come on, Gladstone, old chum.' She mentally rolled up her sleeves. 'Let's go get our Clifford!'

Inside, she marched over to the long bare counter; Gladstone's claws clitter-clattering on the black tiles. She recognised the dark-eyed officer behind the desk. It was Pierre, who had turned over the body in the cellar. He nodded, obviously recognising her as well.

'*Bonsoir, mademoiselle.*'

'And *bonsoir* to you. Inspector Damboise, *s'il vous plaît.*'

This seemed to amuse the policeman as his eyes crinkled at the corners. 'You make it here, *mademoiselle!*' His chest swelled at dredging up what was possibly his entire knowledge of English. 'This way, you, please.'

The dark stairs and the long bleak corridor he led her along were even less welcoming than the police station's reception area. Finally, he drew up outside the only smartly painted door she'd seen and rapped out a rhythm with his knuckles.

'*Entrez!*' a disembodied voice called.

The door swung back to reveal Damboise sitting behind a modest-sized desk, noticeably not littered by a thousand files and all the other paraphernalia she was used to seeing Hugh, her policeman beau, buried under. And unlike Hugh's drab grey office, Damboise's was painted a soft yellow, the walls sporting framed sketches of what she assumed were notable buildings of the town. In one corner, a coat stand stood beside an enormous potted palm.

'Ah, Mademoiselle Lady Swift.' Rising from his curved wooden chair, Damboise waved her in. 'Your coffee is cold.'

She shielded her eyes from the sun streaming in through the two long open windows. 'Pardon?'

He pointed to the lifeless cup of dark-brown liquid on the desk. 'My apologies. I anticipated you would arrive here sooner.'

'Well, I've never had need to visit the delights of Garbonne sur Mer's police station before, so it took a while to find. But it seems you imagined I had?'

'*Non.* But I think you are a lady of much intelligent thinking, so I think you will find me sooner.'

'Thank you for your confidence, however misguided.' She accepted the seat he held out for her.

His moustache quirked with amusement as Gladstone shuffled up against her legs.

'But,' she continued, 'delightful though it is to see you once more, Inspector, I am here purely to retrieve my butler.' She glanced at his suit, noting he had swapped it for a pale-blue one. 'And to offer to pay to have your other clothes cleaned after my maid spilled coffee on them, of course.'

'Ah. So kind, but not needed. Pierre.' He beckoned the officer forward. '*Un autre café, pour mademoiselle.*' Returning to his seat behind his desk, he smiled. 'An interesting thing you say for it is a brave sentence.' He checked himself. '*Non*. A bold announcement – since your butler is under lock and key.'

'Yes, I know. But, Inspector, you have no evidence against Clifford. You can't have, because he is entirely innocent.'

'Maybe. Maybe not.' Damboise looked at her earnestly. 'But he is the man who suggested you come to France, *oui*? And not just to any part of France, but to the Riviera. And he is the one who found you Villa Marbaise to rent from all that distance away in England.'

'But there's nothing suspicious about that. He's my butler. He makes all my holiday arrangements.'

'Of this I do not doubt. But are you not surprised by the last thing he did? Less than one hour and a half after you arrived, he found a body in your wine cellar!'

'I know, poor chap.' She shook her head sadly. 'He didn't need that any more than the rest of us.'

'Poor chap, you say?'

'Yes, Inspector, I do.' She tried to keep her tone light. 'What do you say, exactly?'

Damboise rose and stepped over to the first window. Putting his hands on his hips, he held her gaze. 'I say maybe he is responsible for the body there.'

She fought to control her voice. 'Why would you think Clifford...?'

Picking up on her anger, Gladstone let out a long, low growl.

Taking a moment to regain her composure, she forced a smile. 'Inspector, if I might repeat that, even with the different laws of France, I believe you cannot charge him with murder.' That thought stuck in her throat for a second. 'Not without proper evidence. All you have are the facts that he made our booking and that he stumbled across the body whilst trying to carry out his duties. If you had—'

'*Quoi*? Something stronger for evidence?' Damboise waited

as the door opened and Pierre strode in to furnish Eleanor with another coffee and a saucer bearing three ice cubes. As he left, Damboise gestured to the raised welt on her face. 'To fight with plants is not so much fun, *n'est-ce pas?*'

Eleanor shrugged and held the cold ice to her cheek as he perched himself on the edge of his desk.

'*Mademoiselle*, we take the fingerprints of your butler. You do not wish to hear, I know, but I am sure we find a match in the wine cellar.'

'Well, of course you will!' she said more forcefully than intended. 'He was taking an inventory of the wine.'

'But I see no evidence in the villa of you having unpacked. Or having dined. Yet your butler is so quick as to make the catalogue of all the wines available?' As he finished his sentence, he tutted to himself. 'Idiot, Damboise! *Bien sûr*. As a Frenchman, this I understand.' He tapped his forehead. 'How else does your cook know what to make for her mistress that evening if she knows not what wine there is to accompany it?' He smiled. 'How did you like the nutmeg with the goat's cheese I recommend? *Délicieux, non?*'

She shook her head in exasperation. 'I have no idea. Somehow, my appetite left me when you marched my butler away in handcuffs.'

'*Quel dommage*. Again, I have to say what a shame to you, *mademoiselle*. Not to savour the fresh pastry. *Sacré bleu!*'

Engaging though the inspector was, Eleanor had had enough. 'Inspector, can't I just pay the bail money and you release him? Even if only for the moment while you continue your investigation?'

'*Naturellement, mademoiselle*. This suggestion is fine by me.'

'Oh, thank goodness.' She fumbled to open her handbag.

But Damboise's next words made her heart still.

'However, your butler must stay in jail. You see, it is not in my hands.'

'Then,' – she rose as he stood up – 'tell me in whose hands it is!'

'Ah, now that, *mademoiselle*, is easy.' He savoured the last of his coffee, reached for his hat and offered her his elbow. 'But first, you must take a short ride with me.'

5

Despite her worries, as Eleanor and Gladstone shuffled into the back seat of Damboise's black sedan, she couldn't help thinking it was rather cramped after her luxurious, if unwieldy, rented car. The sombre grey interior made the outfit Damboise had swapped his coffee-drenched jacket and trousers for stand out even more. Somehow, he had also found time to come up with another matching hatband and cravat.

In the driving seat, an animated Pierre straightened his pillbox cap and rubbed his hands, before spinning around to Damboise.

'*Le maire, Chef?*'

'*Oui*, Pierre.'

On any other occasion, Eleanor would have delighted in an impromptu tour of Garbonne sur Mer with such an enthusiastic guide as Damboise proudly pointing out his beloved town's finer points. However, getting Clifford out of jail – and off a murder charge – hung heavily on her mind. Also, Pierre was urging the car round every corner as if he were in a Grand Prix. As Damboise adjusted his hat a fourth time, he reached forward and tapped his eager driver on the shoulder.

'Pierre! *Doucement! Doucement!*' He turned to her. 'The young man wants to be the champion of a race he is not in!'

Only half a minute later, they stopped at the base of two tiers of wide white steps, edged with giant palms. She shook her head, wondering why they had come by car at all as they couldn't be more than ten minutes' walk from the police station.

'We are here,' Damboise said unnecessarily as Pierre jumped out and opened the door for her.

'Wherever this is,' she muttered, staring up at the majestic four-storied building, resplendent in pristine ivory paint. An enormous gold crest emblazoned the front, the French national motto painted below in bold black lettering – *Liberté, égalité, fraternité.* Each of the seven windows on each floor had wooden shutters in the same pale blue as Damboise's suit.

Coaxing Gladstone to trot a little faster up the steps, she passed two policemen wearing what looked like ceremonial garb on either side of the door. They kept their eyes straight ahead, but nodded as the inspector drew level.

Inside, a sea of polished wood floors and cream-and-burgundy upholstery was offset by rows of oil portraits of important-looking uniformed officials. Damboise led her along several corridors before beckoning her into a palatial office.

'Mademoiselle Lady Swift. Welcome! Welcome!' A commanding, white-whiskered man threw his arms out in greeting. This caused his short-waisted black jacket with gold buttons to part, revealing a red sash worn diagonally across his chest. The sharp crease of his grey-striped trousers perfectly complemented the authoritative image he cut. 'Ah, and your fine dog too. So cordial that you accept my invitation.'

She shook his proffered hand. 'Thank you. Do forgive me, but you are?'

'The man so fortunate as to administer the affairs of this fine town and area. I am Alonse Gaston Bertrand Lessard. The mayor.' He gave a self-effacing bow and gestured around the opulently appointed room. It was graced with not one, but three ruby silk-upholstered settees, as well as a formal meeting table for twelve and a bookcase of red leather-bound tomes that surely constituted an entire library. In each of the six corniced alcoves sat an exquisite objet d'art.

'Delighted.' She hid a frown, now even more confused over why she had been brought there.

'As am I. *Enchanté, mademoiselle*, as we say. Please, you will sit. I understand you must have some questions. Well, I will tell you all you wish to know.' He gestured to the meeting table.

Intrigued, despite herself, she slid into the silk-upholstered chair Damboise held out. On each was an embroidered heraldic monogram of a castle's turrets, above a haughty-looking greyhound. Lessard waited for her to get comfortable – which involved untangling Gladstone's lead from between the chair legs – and then took a seat beside her, at the head of the table. She was surprised to see Damboise waiting until he was nodded into the seat opposite her.

It seems Mayor Lessard reigns supreme here, Ellie.

A young, chic-suited woman with an enviable figure and the longest legs Eleanor had ever seen appeared. She served each of them a long-stemmed wine glass, a third full of a straw-coloured liquid with a ball of ice floating alongside a slice of lemon. Between the three of them, she placed a wooden board filled with all manner of delectable-looking miniature wheels and logs of cheese. Eleanor's empty stomach let out an unladylike gurgle as she surveyed the spread. Half of the cheeses were covered in a variety of herbs, finely chopped nuts or apricot pieces, while the others ranged in colour from alabaster white to butter-rich yellow. A mixed bowl of fresh and dried figs, and another of baguette slices was added to the feast. Evidently furnishing each of them with an embroidered napkin and a cheese knife fulfilled the last of the woman's duties as she nodded to Lessard and disappeared.

Fearing she was missing a plate, Eleanor looked up to see Damboise discreetly shaking his head and waving his napkin at her to show she was to use that instead.

'*Mademoiselle*.' Lessard kissed his raised glass. 'This is Noilly Prat. The most supreme Vermouth in the world, made from grapes by our refined neighbours along the coast for almost seventy years.'

Taking a sip, Eleanor had to admit the delicate mix of herbs, coupled with a zing of lemon and a slightly bitter aftertaste, was delicious. Perfect for such a warm summer evening. Lessard watched her face, evidently delighted by her sincere appreciation of his favourite apéritif. However, she then had to wait until a great deal of cheese had been sampled and discussed before he would deliver on his promise to explain why she was there. All the while, her thoughts were of Clifford, fearing the conditions he was being held in and, worse, that he might already have been charged with murder.

Finally, the mayor sat back and steepled his fingers. '*Mademoiselle*, I will tell you a secret.'

She leaned forward, but was unprepared for the words that followed.

'The economy in our country is not good since the war. Especially here on the coast. My beautiful town dies every April when the rich and titled of Europe leave, not to return until September at the earliest.' He paused. 'But you. You come unexpectedly early. Or is it late?'

She restrained her natural impatience. 'That is because, as I told Inspector Damboise, I came here for a quiet time, away from the crowds. To rest.'

'If this is so, you chose well. We only have an American couple near here, no British, Italian or Russian. But you are not like your fellow compatriots, I can see.' He took a sip of his drink. 'And how do you find this part of the Riviera?'

She shrugged, unable to follow the thread of the conversation. 'I'm sure it's lovely, but I haven't really had time to form an opinion. And I haven't really seen any of France. In truth, I only know the area around Abbeville in the north where I was stationed during the war as a nurse for the South African Military Nursing Service.'

'I know.'

She stared at Lessard in surprise and then at Damboise, who merely smiled back in reply and spread some more fine white cheese on the fig he was holding.

'Monsieur Lessard.' She dropped her napkin on the table.

Damboise fixed her with a cautionary look. '*Monsieur le maire, mademoiselle.*'

She paused, summoning up all her limited diplomacy. 'Monsieur le maire.' Encouraged by the smile this drew, she continued. 'I am uncomfortably on the back foot here. Please explain why you asked me here. I wish to urgently retrieve my butler from Inspector Damboise's custody and I cannot but feel your invitation is somehow connected?'

Lessard ran a hand over his whiskers. 'Indeed it is, *mademoiselle*, but there is more of my story first.'

'Try the Roquefort.' Damboise raised his eyebrows, suggesting she would do better to listen than ask questions.

Lessard waited until she had taken some.

'As I say before, there are normally few foreigners here after April. Except this year, this American couple come. And, *mon Dieu!* They spend!' He threw his hands out and then seemed to deflate like a punctured balloon. For a moment he was silent, then he took a sip of his drink and sighed. '*Mademoiselle,* since the war, the French franc is not so healthy. The American dollar, however, is king! So, I tell all the people of my town to welcome these Americans with open arms. And, I confess, I let them do whatever they want without trouble. I tell Inspector Damboise and his men to let them be.'

'Unlike my butler,' she muttered.

'Ah!' He held up his hands. 'Unlike your butler. But patience, *mademoiselle*, I get there soon. This year I am excited to learn some more special visitors have come. Perhaps our American couple have spread the word? I do not know. But an American film company has graced our town!' His face lit up. 'Famous actors and lady stars of Hollywood have come here.' His shoulder twitched. 'Well, almost here. They are a few kilometres along the coast. But if their filming goes without problems, and the famous stars enjoy themselves, just think who will come next year! And the year after! How many other film companies!' He raised his glass. 'I have a dream for my town, *mademoiselle*, that many around me call foolish, but we will see. I dream Garbonne sur Mer will become the resort one must be seen in all the year round. It will be filled with the rich and famous.' His eyes glistened. 'Maybe we will even have a film festival each year!'

She tried to appear interested. 'And this has to do with me because?'

'Because if the film company find out the man in your cellar was murdered, they will leave. They will run back to America with stories that Garbonne sur Mer is the home of killers! That it is not safe. And then, my dream is dust! *Oh là là!*' He whipped out a handkerchief and held it to his mouth.

Eleanor winced. 'Um, perhaps they would have a point? Since someone was killed rather brutally in the villa's cellar?' A flashback to standing, staring at the body, made her swallow hard. She flapped a hand. 'But since the man was clearly a local chap, from the look of his clothes, and not connected to the film...' She broke off as both men shook their heads. 'Oh, gracious! He... he was one of the film crew?'

'*Mais non,*' Lessard said gravely. 'He was not an unknown member of the film crew.' He looked into his drink for a moment and then up at her. '*Mademoiselle*, the man found murdered at your villa was possibly even better known than our illustrious president!'

6

For a moment, there was silence in the room. Eleanor tried to think of anyone who could conceivably be more well known in France than the French president, though she guessed Lessard was possibly exaggerating for effect.

She held out her hands. 'I have no idea who you can mean.'

'The man was... Chester Armstrong.'

She gasped. *Even you've heard of him, Ellie!* 'The Chester Armstrong?' she asked. 'The famous American film star? The one who—'

The mayor nodded. 'The same.'

She whistled softly. 'I understand now why you believe it might put off more Americans from coming.' She laid her hands on the table. 'Gentlemen, I realise this is a big problem for you. But I did not know Mr Armstrong. And neither did my butler.'

'Perhaps,' Lessard said. 'You didn't recognise him when Damboise's officer turned his face upwards?'

Her nose wrinkled. 'I... I did not look at his face, as I told the inspector. I have seen enough—'

'We understand, *mademoiselle*.' Damboise shot Lessard an apologetic look. 'Please do not upset yourself.'

She let out a long breath. 'Monsieur le maire, since neither myself, nor my butler, killed Chester Armstrong, I have to ask again: What has all this to do with me?'

Lessard put down his glass. 'I will explain. Inspector Damboise here is supreme at his job. Always he deals with the visitors here with diplomacy. The English, Russians, and Germans, too.'

'And Greek, Monsieur le maire,' Damboise prompted respectfully.

Lessard nodded. 'But, *mademoiselle*, the inspector does not deal with the Americans. They are an unknown.'

Eleanor frowned. 'But his English is superb. Like yours. You have both amazed me over your command of the language.'

'So kind. But it is not the words he cannot understand.' He leaned on his elbows and tapped both temples. 'It is their thinking. You English, how you act, is arrogant. You expect France to bow down and become a little England while you are here on your holidays. This I can understand. You own half the world. But to the Frenchman, the American has surely fallen from the moon. What he does and how he acts is... *incroyable*! Impossible!'

Despite the situation, his emphatic tone and dramatic gesture made Eleanor smile.

'Are you suggesting I will understand them? Because, honestly, I've hardly visited America.'

Lessard gestured to Damboise to top up their glasses. '*Mademoiselle*, do you know who is the owner of the villa you have rented?'

'No idea. My butler used an agent to make all the arrangements.'

'Interesting.'

'But—'

He held up a polite hand. 'Please, we do not play games

together. Inspector Damboise checked all about you, *mademoiselle*, as soon as your arrangement for the villa was made.'

She frowned, staring at Damboise. 'But why?'

Lessard shrugged. 'It came to his ears, let us say. And to mine too.'

'I see.' *That's why they know you served in a South African hospital in France during the war, Ellie.* She tried to stop her annoyance from showing. 'Since you dug into my affairs, I hope you found something interesting to have made it worthwhile? Although I really can't imagine what. I—'

'Am not the stranger to death.' Lesssard took a sip of his drink. 'To murder.'

She groaned. 'It's not at all as it might look on paper.'

Lessard shook his head. 'Ah, but it is! The intelligent Lady Swift has been successful in catching a killer, how many times?'

She looked away.

'Nine, *mademoiselle*. Nine times you have got to the finish line before the police. A miracle of cunning and intelligence. You see, here at this table, we do not think less of the female intellect like the Englishman does. No!'

Damboise nodded in agreement.

Despite the praise, Eleanor felt she was caught in a bad dream.

'Monsieur Lessard... I mean, *le maire*, please understand I came here purely for a holiday, *not* to solve a murder.' A thought struck like an archer's arrow. 'But wait. If you want me to help Inspector Damboise find the murderer, then... then you can't believe my butler—'

'Is guilty of the crime? True.' He sat back in his chair, but kept his eyes on her.

She rose. 'Then I thank you for your gracious hospitality. Now, I wish to extract my butler from whatever cell the poor fellow is being held in.'

'Of course you do, but it cannot be.' Lessard waved her back into her seat. 'Let us talk openly. I think, like all English aristocracy, you do not wish to forever peel your own grapes. You must have your butler back by your side. And nothing would give me greater pleasure. But the fate of my beautiful town rests in your hands, *mademoiselle*. Only the director of the film company and Inspector Damboise and his team know Monsieur Armstrong has been murdered. All the other Americans they think he has died of natural causes. The inspector cannot interview the Americans without arousing their suspicions. And, as I said, he does not understand them. There will be a big row and they will leave in a rage. No, I must have this murder solved before anyone learns of it.' He finished his drink and carefully placed his glass on the table. 'So, you have two choices. You can help Inspector Damboise solve this murder. Or—' He held out a coaxing hand.

She groaned. 'Or I can leave my butler in jail to take the blame so the whole thing can be swept under the proverbial carpet.'

Lessard nodded. 'And your answer?'

She shrugged. 'My answer is, obviously, yes. But if you have checked my record carefully, you will know that I solved those murders with the help of my butler. So, until you release him from jail to aid me—'

Lessard held up an imperious hand. 'No, Mademoiselle Lady Swift. If we release your butler now, what proof do we have that you will help us and not just try to sneak out of the country back to England?'

She smiled coldly. 'Because I imagine you would have us arrested before we could leave the country and brought back here!'

He nodded slowly. 'Perhaps, but I do not want such publicity.' He stroked his whiskers. 'Mmm. I tell you what, *mademoiselle*. I will release your butler so he can help you discover the murderer once you have proven to Inspector Damboise and myself that you will help us.'

She frowned. 'How?'

'By finding one clue. One piece of evidence that Damboise's men have overlooked. Then – and only then – will I release your butler. Inspector Damboise will contact you tomorrow to arrange things.' He shrugged. 'What do you say?'

She looked from Damboise to Lessard and then sighed. 'What choice do I have? But you do know this is' – her jaw tightened – 'a gross abuse of authority!'

Lessard smiled and raised his glass. 'No, *mademoiselle*, this is gunboat diplomacy. You English invented it.'

7

Eleanor awoke the next morning as the hot fingers of the Mediterranean sun caressed her face. She rolled over, enjoying the distant caw of seagulls floating in on the pine- and herb-scented breeze. But the horror of seeing the murdered man in the cellar the day before and the hideous situation the mayor had placed her in flooded back, making her stomach clench. Grabbing her robe, she flung it over her silk pyjamas and headed down the swirling marble staircase. In the hallway, she met Mrs Butters emerging from the kitchen.

'Breakfast is ready to be served on the terrace, m'lady, if that suits you?'

'Breakfast, Mrs Butters? I can't think of breakfast at a time like this. I need to get Clifford out of that horrible jail. And I'm not going to wait around for Damboise to contact me!'

Her housekeeper nodded. 'I know, m'lady. We all want Mr Clifford back where he belongs. But there was nothing achieved on an empty stomach what couldn't have been done twice as well and in half the time as on a full one.'

'But—'

'But nothing, m'lady,' her housekeeper said in an unusually

stern voice. 'If it's not out of line to say so, of course. Now, Mrs Trotters has prepared you a breakfast as will give you plenty of ideas and energy to get Mr Clifford out of that there jail, and it's waiting on the terrace.'

Eleanor held up her hands in surrender. 'Then I suppose I'll be heading in that direction.'

Out on the terrace, the warm morning sun already hinted at the heat to come. Eleanor sat at the table and smiled at her housekeeper.

'I do appreciate you filling in for Clifford in his absence. His temporary – *very* temporary –absence.'

Mrs Butters smiled and curtsied. 'We've all got to pull together, m'lady. And as your late uncle was wont to say "Eat first, act after."'

Eleanor laughed. 'Well, it would be foolish to ignore Uncle Byron's advice. So, what delights has Mrs Trotman kindly conjured up for breakfast this morning?'

'A most creative continental twist, my lady.' She lifted the lids on the salvers, introducing the contents as if they were honoured guests. 'Scrambled egg soufflés with lardons made by Trotters, I mean Mrs Trotman, with local eggs and bacon. Grilled tomatoes served on local goat's cheese medallions. And slow-roasted Toulouse sausages with aromatic plum garnish. And, of course, French toast, as Mr Clifford would call it.'

'Or eggy bread as you and I would call it.'

Her housekeeper nodded and picked up a pair of tongs and indicated a delectable-smelling basket. 'And would you like a fresh-from-the-village brioche, croissant or pain au chocolat to start, with your coffee? A man brought them up this morning.'

They both turned at the slow click of a sleepy bulldog's claws on the tiles.

Mrs Butters tutted. 'Or perhaps best go with the Toulouse sausages so Master Gladstone can have his share?'

Half an hour passed as Eleanor did justice to breakfast.

Meanwhile, Mrs Butters busied herself keeping Eleanor's cup and plate topped up, clearing away the mountain of flaky croissant crumbs, and treating Gladstone to his own breakfast bowl.

Finally, Eleanor pushed her plate away. 'That was too divine, Mrs Butters. I shall go straight to Mrs Trotman and let her know.'

'Most kind, my lady.'

'And then I will go down to the cellar. I have to find a clue that Damboise's men missed or Clifford won't be coming back to us any time soon!'

Mrs Butters placed the empty coffee pot on the trolley and looked at her in concern. 'You shouldn't be going down there on your own. Not after what you saw. Me or Mrs Trotman can come down with you, m'lady.'

Eleanor shook her head. 'That's very kind of you, but the fewer people disturbing the crime scene the better.' Her hand flew to her mouth. 'Oh, gracious! Not that I was suggesting—'

Mrs Butters laughed. 'Don't you go worrying, m'lady. I know what you mean. Neither of us really have a clue when it comes to looking for clues and whatnot, not like you and Mr Clifford. Just be careful, that's all.'

'I will, Mrs Butters. But, first of all, I'll go and thank Mrs Trotman. Then I'll tackle the fatal scene!'

Before she had a chance to do either, Mrs Trotman hurried up to her.

'Oh, m'lady, beg pardon, but the telephone's been ringing for ages. I thought as you were in the garden and looked all over. It's that policeman—'

'Ah, excellent! It must be Inspector Damboise.' Without waiting, she rushed to the receiver and picked it up. 'Inspector!'

'Inspector?' A deliciously familiar deep voice rumbled out to her from the earpiece. 'Is that you, Eleanor?'

'Hugh!' She silently cursed herself for not asking her cook which policeman had called.

Seldon's voice cut in again. 'For Pete's sake, Eleanor, all I've done is telephone to see how you are. Does that warrant being addressed as "Inspector"?'

'Oh, gracious, no! I... I was just reminding... Polly that your correct title is "chief inspector", not just "inspector".'

Her heart skipped at the rich chuckle that tickled her ears.

'Now, listen. This is a flying call. I just wanted to hear...' He paused. 'Well, your voice actually.'

'Oh, Hugh. It's the most wonderful surprise. But how did you get hold of this villa's telephone number? I don't know it myself yet. Surely, even the long arm of the law doesn't stretch this far from England?'

'I can't say, but I definitely owe your scallywag butler something in return. Is he there, by the way? He normally answers the phone.'

For a moment she thought of telling Hugh that her butler was far from there. That he was, in fact, languishing in jail on a charge of murder! But what could Hugh do about it back in England? He'd only worry himself sick that she'd got herself mixed up in another murder investigation and Clifford wasn't there to keep her safe.

Before she could reply, however, Seldon's voice came down the line.

'Hang on a moment, Eleanor.' There was the sound of muffled conversation. Then he came back on the line. 'Oh, blast it, I have to go. Just tell me you're behaving yourself and not up to your neck in trouble?'

She hesitated. *How can I possibly answer that truthfully?* 'Well... don't worry, Clifford is... is close by to play his irritatingly fiendish terrier card to make sure I stay out of trouble.' *Well, the jail in Garbonne sur Mer is fairly close.*

'Good man. Then, Lady Swift, I shall leave you to languish in your pool or whatever it was you were doing before I interrupted you. And I'll bid you a fond adieu as they say around those parts.'

'Adieu to you, Hugh. Eat some proper meals, please.' *If you call cold toast and a piece of cheese proper meals!*

'Will do.' The line clicked off.

As she leaned back against the cool of the marble-clad wall, she closed her eyes. Her cheeks burned as much as her whole body ached to be with him. Equally stubborn and cautious in matters of the heart, he was, she admitted to herself, a perfect, and terrible match.

In her mind she heard Clifford clear his throat. 'My lady? Are you ready?'

She opened her eyes and shook her head, whispering to herself, 'To work out the next step in my relationship with Hugh? No! But to get you out of jail? Yes!'

At the head of the stairs to the wine cellar, Eleanor paused and took a deep breath. *Don't be silly, Ellie, there's no body there any more – Damboise's men took it away. So what are you afraid of?* She rolled her shoulders back and nodded.

Despite reassuring herself, her heart was beating so loudly that she was only faintly aware of a sound behind her. By the time she reached the bottom of the stairs, however, it was impossible to ignore. It seemed to be coming from halfway up the steps.

'Gladstone! What on earth are you doing?'

Her bulldog grunted in reply, his front legs on one step, his back legs on the one above. He'd obviously followed her, and as the stairs had twisted and steepened, he'd got himself stuck. It was plain there was no way to turn him around, so she put down the candlestick, heaved him up and deposited him by the cellar door. She straightened, holding her back.

'If you're going to make a habit of that, old chum, I'll have to put you on a diet!' She looked up the stairs and then back at the bulldog now sniffing the crack under the cellar door. 'Well, I'm not carrying you back up right away, my spine needs a chance to recover. So, you'd better come in with me. But remember, this is a crime scene. So, no licking or eating any evidence. Or stealing it and burying it later!' She gave him a stern look, even though, secretly, she was glad of the company. 'Well, Gladstone, as Mrs Butters stood in for Clifford at breakfast, you'll have to do the same here.'

She took his silence as agreement. 'Good. So, the first thing is, I suggest that Inspector Damboise and Mayor Lessard are definitely holding back on some things. Which is why we shall play the same game. Starting with our visit here to the crime scene. If we find anything, let's make sure it doesn't reach their ears unless it will help to free Clifford. Helpfully, Damboise believes he has the only key to the cellar, which he does. However,' – she pulled a long, slim roll of picklocks from inside her jacket – 'Clifford has been showing me how to use these!'

Gladstone watched in awe as she worked the lock like an expert safecracker. Well, he pawed at the door impatiently while she fumbled away, which she took to be the same thing. After a while, he sat down and looked at her with a bored expression. She glared at him.

'Look! I know Clifford would have had this open in a jiffy, but he had years of practice with my uncle.' She paused, wondering exactly what Clifford and her uncle had got up to that involved picklocks. She'd often asked, but somehow Clifford had always avoided the issue. She shook her head. 'Anyway, I—'

The door swung open. She turned to Gladstone with a smug expression, but he was already trotting into the room.

Inside the cellar, she stared at the dark-red bloodstain on the flagstone floor where the body of Chester Armstrong had lain. She shook her head again.

'I still can't fathom how he ended up down here, Gladstone.' She looked around at the wine racks lining the space. Her brows flinched. 'It seems unlikely Mr Armstrong was here to pilfer the contents of another man's cellar.'

In her mind she heard Clifford's voice. 'It may be unlikely, my lady, but we can't afford to make assumptions.'

Gladstone glanced at her over his shoulder and cocked his leg on a nearby barrel.

'No! This is a crime scene!' She shooed him away.

Now, what would Clifford do, Ellie?

She pulled out her notebook and the pen he had bought her two Christmases before. She then produced a small jar of honey. Clifford's voice came back to her.

'And which of us is going to protest loudest that we aren't superstitious, my lady?'

'Honouring the superstitions of another's country does not necessarily mean you believe in them yourself,' she whispered. 'Although Armstrong was, of course, American, not French.'

Twenty minutes later, she was close to abandoning her search for anything the police had overlooked. Her assistant hadn't been of much use either. In fact, she'd spent most of the time stopping him cocking his leg on various wine cellar paraphernalia. She pursed her lips.

'Not so much as a speck of lint, let alone a clue! Except a champagne cork and a few tiny slithers of glass, I suppose, if you can call that evidence. But it's hardly surprising to find such items in a wine cellar. Particularly in a French wine cellar.' Her brows knitted. 'Whoever dispatched Mr Armstrong did so without leaving a trace, it seems. Except, of course, for the sabre plunged through... ' She swallowed hard. 'Come on! We can't be squeamish if we're going to solve this mess and get Clifford back. Have you found anything, Gladstone?'

She looked around, but the errant bulldog was nowhere to be seen. She sighed and walked between the racks, desperately seeking some indication as to why Armstrong had been in her cellar. And, more importantly, who had killed him. Gladstone appeared from behind the racking at the far end of the cellar and sneezed violently. A fine spray of dust lifted off his coat and wafted back down.

'Bless you!' She walked over to him and patted his head. 'Now, concentrate, will you? I know you're not a bloodhound, but still, do try!' She threw her hand out in exasperation. 'I mean, it's incredible our murderer left no trace since Armstrong was far from a weedy bantam of a man. Didn't he play the part of some warrior hero or other in a film?'

Gladstone sniffed the air and lumbered off behind more racking. She guessed he didn't know or was unwilling to say.

'It doesn't matter, because I've remembered anyway. He played Perseus, the Greek mythological hero who slayed Medusa and rescued his bride to be.' She called after the bull-dog, 'You see, that's what I mean. Armstrong would have been perfectly capable of putting up some sort of fight if someone was trying to finish him off.' She frowned. 'Unless, of course, he was surprised. Or already incapacitated in some way? Mmm. I don't remember Damboise mentioning any other injuries on Armstrong. Then again, I don't suppose he has sent the body off for an autopsy as cause of death seemed horribly clear, given that the sabre was sticking out of his chest as well as his back.'

She sighed. What had she overlooked? Perhaps there was another way into the cellar other than the main door? A quick scout around showed there wasn't. She shook her head. It looked as if she'd have to carry on investigating on her own a while longer. And Clifford would have to stay in jail.

'No!' she said aloud. 'I'm not letting him rot in some French prison any longer than he already has. Somewhere in here there must be... something... useful!'

She stared in disbelief. In front of her, a very dusty Gladstone held something in his slobbering jaws that glinted in the flickering candlelight.

8

The drive down to Garbonne sur Mer police station was uneventful, except for a few more minor scratches on the car that Eleanor was almost sure could be buffed out. Stopping outside, she hurried up the steps with Gladstone lumbering next to her and demanded the police officer on the front desk call Damboise immediately.

'That is not necessary.'

She spun around. 'Inspector Damboise!'

'*Oui,* Mademoiselle Lady Swift. This is an unexpected pleasure.' He turned to the policeman on the desk. '*Deux cafés.*' Without waiting for a reply, he led Eleanor to his office. Once she was seated with Gladstone at her feet, he sat behind his desk and regarded her with amusement. 'How can I help you, *mademoiselle*? I was going to call you later today, but' – he held out his hands– 'here you are.'

Without a word, from her handbag she produced one of the small velvet pouches Mrs Butters had made to keep Eleanor's jewellery from scratching while in her luggage. She untied it and let the item Gladstone had found drop onto the inspector's desk.

He looked at it, and then at her, with confusion.

'What is this?'

She tutted. 'Isn't it obvious? It is the piece of evidence overlooked by your men that Mayor Lessard insisted I find in order to secure the release of my butler.'

Damboise's eyes widened. 'But how—'

'Please, Inspector!' Eleanor eyed him coolly. 'Did you really think I would sit around like a good girl and wait for you to contact me? If so, you did not do your research on me very well.'

He shook his head slowly. '*Non, mademoiselle*, I did not. But I did not expect you to act so quickly either!' He carefully picked up the item by its rim and examined it. 'It is a gilt button. Where did you come by this?'

'Glad— I found it in the cellar this morning.' She shot her bulldog an apologetic look.

Damboise looked up sharply. 'But—'

She held up her hand. 'Did you think locked doors would stop me?'

This time he nodded. 'Yes. But it seems, *mademoiselle*, I underestimated you. But tell me, what significance is this item to Monsieur Armstrong's murder?'

She shrugged. 'I've no idea. The agreement was that I find evidence, not that I knew what it meant.' She looked away. 'If, however, Clifford were here, I'm sure he would have an insight into how it relates to the murder.'

Damboise leaned back in his chair, a smile playing around his lips. 'I must remember my recent lesson and not underestimate you, *mademoiselle*.' He tapped his chin. 'Mmm.'

A knock on the door interrupted him. The policeman appeared with the coffees. After he'd set them down, Damboise spoke to him briefly. The man nodded and left. Damboise turned back to Eleanor.

'Now, my man brings Monsieur Clifford.'

'Finally!'

He held up a hand. 'But, *mademoiselle*, I am only letting him out to ask him about this clue. If he answers well, then I will telephone to Mayor Lessard and ask him for permission to release him long-term so he can help you with the rest of the case. Now, let us drink our coffees.'

She went to argue, but changed her mind. Instead she crossed her fingers under the desk. *Let's hope Clifford comes up trumps, Ellie!*

As she put down her empty coffee cup a few moments later, a knock on the door heralded the return of the policeman with her butler.

'Clifford! Oh, gracious.'

With his rumpled suit tails, early shadow of stubble and creases of worry haunting his exhausted-looking face, he would have passed for a distant cousin to the ever-impeccably attired, distinguished man she had come to know.

'My lady!' He gave his customary bow from the shoulders. 'And Master Gladstone.' The excited bulldog lunged at him, exuberantly trying to lick the hand Clifford ran down his muzzle.

Damboise put paid to the early celebrations by explaining the situation. For a moment, Eleanor thought Clifford might argue as she had been going to, but he held his tongue as well. Instead he gently picked up the button by its rim as Damboise had. Then he half bowed to Eleanor.

'My lady, you are to be commended. Well done.'

She waved away the praise, promising herself she would make her duplicity up to Gladstone, the true finder, the minute she got back to the villa. She also hoped no one would notice the dent his teeth had made in the button.

Clifford produced his pince-nez and scrutinised it. He turned it over and did the same to the reverse. Then he placed it carefully back on the desk and put his pince-nez back in his top pocket.

'It is obviously a button. Made, I think, of tin and then gilded. It is a military button from the uniform of a soldier in the infantry division, indicated by the crossed cannon on the front.' He arched a brow at Damboise. 'But I believe you already know that, Inspector.'

Eleanor shot Damboise a glance.

He shrugged. '*Oui*. Monsieur Clifford is correct. It was a little... test.'

A flush ran up her neck. 'Inspector! I am not interested in playing games!'

He picked up the phone. 'Neither am I, *mademoiselle*. But I have to make sure you – and your butler – are as smart as my reports tell me. Ah!' He covered the mouthpiece. 'Excuse me one moment, I must speak with the mayor.'

After a brief conversation and lots of nodding, he replaced the receiver. Eleanor crossed her fingers as he looked from Clifford to her. Her butler's face was impassive. Finally, Damboise stood up.

'*Mademoiselle*, Mr Clifford is free to go.'

She let out the breath she didn't realise she'd been holding. 'Thank God!'

Damboise nodded. 'I am thankful too. And I am sorry for the upset over the business with your butler, but it is my duty to do as Monsieur Lessard commands.'

She pursed her lips, but then nodded. 'I understand, Inspector.' *Back in England, Hugh has to toe the line with his boss, too, Ellie, or risk losing his job.*

Damboise looked relieved. 'Thank you for your understanding, *mademoiselle*. Now, as we must work together, let it be cordial.' He held out his hand.

With only the briefest of hesitation, she shook it.

He smiled. 'I will find out more about this button you have found and tomorrow, please, we meet.'

'Agreed. I will come here first thing in the morning.'

'Ah, *merci*, but no. I send a car for you.' He showed them out of his office and back to the police station's steps. 'Until tomorrow, Mademoiselle Swift. And Monsieur Clifford.'

Once he'd left them, they walked down to the car. Eleanor went around to the driver's side, only to reach for the door handle, just as Clifford did.

He respectfully let go but didn't move. 'My lady, I am eternally grateful for your actions. However—'

She raised her hand. 'Look here, Clifford, I drove here from the villa just fine, thank you.'

'And the cut to your face? Those bends can be hard to navigate without scraping the walls either side of those narrow roads, can they not?'

She leaned against the driver's door, trying to hide the long scratch in the paintwork. *You can pay for that to be buffed out later, Ellie, along with the others.* 'Whatever. Now, come on. Passenger seat. I shall finish what I started. I mean, how am I ever going to improve if I don't practise?'

'Agreed, my lady. I am merely suggesting that you leave off practising until you return home to the familiarity of the less dangerous lanes of Buckinghamshire which might ensure, ahem—'

'Ensure what?'

'That neither of us prematurely age any more quickly than necessary. Though, if I may repeat my heartfelt gratitude at your coming to rescue me.'

'Don't be daft. I would never have dreamed of leaving you there.' She smiled sweetly. 'After all, we're a team. We look out for each other. And we trust each other implicitly, don't we?'

He eyed her sideways. 'My lady, why do I sense the wily tactics of his lordship's nine-year-old niece who always arrived from her boarding school with a raft of ploys to try to get her way?'

She gasped. 'I'm not trying to get around you with

emotional blackmail! Honestly, Clifford. However, even though I'd like to take you to the villa first to recover and change, we'd better make straight for the next village or our agent will be closed for lunch like the rest of France.'

He arched a brow. 'Might one be so bold as to enquire why a trip to the agent is necessary in such haste?'

'Clifford, who owns Villa Marbaise?'

'I do not know. The agent did not furnish that information.'

'But you got a recommendation for the villa?'

'Forgive my correction, my lady. The recommendation I received was for the agent, not the villa. It came from an acquaintance at my butlers' club whose master had used the man to rent a villa in the vicinity a few years back. May I ask why the sudden interest?'

'Oh, nothing concrete. It's just that Damboise – and Lessard – are holding their cards tightly to their chests. Too tightly, for my liking. And they seemed reluctant to tell me who owns the villa. It could be unimportant, but I think we need to have a word with our agent today. And, as I said, if we stand here discussing any longer, he'll be closed.' She glanced sideways at him. 'So...'

The swish of the wind through Eleanor's hair felt all the more invigorating with the steering wheel back in her hands. Gladstone's ears flapped amusingly in the slipstream. Her smile, however, was soon replaced with a frown. The screaming of the engine was quite grating.

Clifford leaned past Gladstone, who was sat bolt upright between them on the front bench seat. 'I believe the trick might be to listen to what it is telling you, my lady.'

'I'm trying, really,' she shouted back above the noise. 'Though, we'll be lucky to catch the agent chap before he disappears off for lunch if we don't hurry. Have you seen the time?'

'No. I have been watching the road intently, as the driver should be.' He urgently pointed to a handful of fallen rocks.

She swerved gracefully past them.

'Slow down for the corner, my lady. Slower still.' Pressing the tip of one gloved finger to the back of her hand, he guided her around the next bend. 'Feel the car's tyres through the steering wheel as you entice her to follow the sweep of the road. Ah, better! Now, before we both go deaf and the engine disintegrates, perhaps you might change into a more suitable gear?'

With gritted teeth, Eleanor gripped the lever and rammed it forwards. They both flinched as it jerked backwards, as if snapping at her hand. She glanced at Clifford and quickly looked away.

'Not like that then?'

'My lady, the motor vehicle is a highly sensitive and complex machine like a...'

'A lady?'

He nodded. 'Coercion and force should never be applied, no matter how much one might feel the need. A delicate, solicitous touch will always prevail.'

She tried it as the next switchback corner appeared all too suddenly. The gear slid in with the minimum of complaint. Encouraged, she continued with her new, less aggressive driving style. Beside her, she was pleased to see her butler's smart-suited shoulders relax. He caught her looking and nodded encouragingly.

'Bravo, my lady. Ever the quick student.'

'Thank you. Apart from my driving the Rolls occasionally, my only other experience of driving is bouncing through the bush of the South African veldt at the wheel of a safari truck. And I didn't have to worry because there wasn't a road or another vehicle for miles.'

'Unlike now! BRAKE!'

9

Eleanor slammed her foot down and wrenched the wheel to the right. A sporty silver bonnet shot past, inches from them, as they slewed into an unforgiving wall of rock. A horrible crunch of metal was followed by a disconcerting shower of shingle.

'Are you hurt, my lady?'

'No, I'm fine.' She glanced at Gladstone who sat stoically between them as if nothing had happened. 'And you?'

She gasped as Clifford pushed her back in her seat with one arm. With the other, he deftly caught a palm-sized piece of falling rock.

'Sincere apologies, my lady. I am also unscathed, thanks to your swift reactions. However, perhaps a souvenir?' He placed the rock on the dashboard.

'Thank you, Clifford.' She willed her heart to calm. 'But gracious, what about the other car?' They both fumbled for their door handles and leaped out.

The other car had skidded across the road and come to rest a hundred yards further on. Eleanor paled as she saw how close its tail end was to the sheer drop that plummeted to the crashing waves below.

'Oh, gracious! Clifford, how do we check they are alright and apologise in French?'

But her butler merely frowned, eyeballing the seemingly mesmerised driver suspiciously.

The man suddenly spun to the stunning dark-haired woman beside him.

'Hey, Kitten, how's that for a rush!' His arms shot high in the air as if riding one of the new Paris rollercoasters Eleanor had read about. 'Woo-hoo!'

'Just perfect, Floyd, darling,' his glamorous companion purred. Teasing his open-necked red shirt to one side with a perfectly painted fingernail, she planted a kiss on his suntanned skin. 'You always did know how to thrill me. Even before lunch.'

This drew laughter from the two athletic-looking men in the back seat, their arms looped around the diamond-encrusted neck of a curvy young blonde sandwiched between them.

'Well,' Eleanor said, feeling her aid was quite unnecessary. 'I just came to apologise for my part in our mishap. At least one of our cars is still in one piece.'

'Hey!' The woman the driver had called Kitten stood on her seat and leaned over the windscreen, the crossover of her peach trouser suit emphasising her flawless complexion. 'You're one of us!'

'Categorically not,' Clifford muttered under his breath.

Oblivious, the woman pointed at Eleanor and let out a musical laugh. 'Well, almost. English, right?'

'Yes. And you're American then?'

The driver smiled. 'Not half, honey. We're the Fitzwilliams!' He stood up and swung himself lithely over the top of the door, revealing long, tanned legs in navy shorts. He threw his arm out. 'Floyd and Kitty Fitzwilliam. And a car full of other great folk. Good to know you.'

Eleanor shook his hand, appreciating his easy-going

manner. She estimated the couple were only five or so years older than her.

'Sir.' Clifford stepped forward with a firm stare. 'This is Lady Eleanor Swift. The very lady whose vehicle you just ran off the road!'

Floyd leaned in towards Eleanor with a grin. 'Now he is *definitely* English. No one'd be that stiff otherwise.'

Clifford's lips pursed.

'Oh, come on, fella.' He clapped him on the back. 'You're way tall enough to take a good-natured joke on the chin. Consider my sincere apologies laid the full length of this crazy ribbon of racetrack tarmac and the lady's car all fixed up as good as new. Drop it into any workshop and I'll pick up the bill.'

Kitty clicked her fingers. 'Oh, but they can't take the car in today, Floyd darling.'

Eleanor turned to her. 'Why not?'

'Because you'll need it, of course, silly. To drive on out to us. We're having a party tonight.'

The more square-jawed of the two men in the back seat reached over and pushed her playfully between her exposed shoulder blades. 'When *aren't* you having a party!'

'Never, darling,' Kitty cooed. 'What on earth would be the point in being alive otherwise?'

'That's so kind of you, but I am otherwise engaged tonight,' Eleanor said with a glance at Clifford, still not looking himself after his ordeal in a French jail. Tonight she planned on a quiet game of chess with her butler.

'Tomorrow night, then,' Kitty purred.

Floyd slid back over the door into the driving seat and pulled Kitty down before cupping her chin lovingly. 'See you tomorrow.' With a salute to Clifford, he revved the engine. 'You too, Starchy Archie. Ha, just kiddin' friend!'

'Wait!' Eleanor called as they skidded off. 'Where do I find your place?'

Kitty kneeled up backwards on her seat and waved a diamond-bracelet-clad wrist. 'Hotel d'Azur! Anytime!'

As they walked back to their car, Eleanor flapped a hand at the driving seat. 'Do you mind, Clifford? I think that's probably enough practice for today.'

He nodded. 'Not at all, my lady. But please reassure me—'

'That I won't ever get in a car with Floyd? No problem there. One near crash is one too many for me. But I believe we have just met the very Americans whom Lessard and Damboise want me to get to know. The ones who behave so *incroyable*, as he put it. That little preview was enough to confirm that, wouldn't you agree?'

'Most heartily.' Clifford sniffed.

'Floyd did apologise. And, in truth, I was probably partly to blame for our near miss. This car is hard to judge the width of.'

He raised an eyebrow. 'It was not the gentleman's apology, nor the ready offer to pay for the damage I was referring to, my lady. The entire party seemed rather, ahem, animated for this time of the morning, did they not?'

'As in artificially stimulated, you mean? Then, yes, now that I think about it. Well, don't worry, I've never found the need for anything more stimulating than coffee. Speaking of which...'

In the hilltop village, it took all of Eleanor's resolve not to insist Clifford pull over so she could saunter through the pretty stalls of a little market. Myriad different cheeses competed with loaves of crusty bread of every conceivable shape and size. Strings of dried meats hung above blackened pot-bellied cauldrons of slow-boiling boudin sausages. Pyramids of white, yellow and red onions vied for space with olives, green and black, and figs, fresh and dried. Displays of fish, oysters, mussels and lobsters were all eyed greedily by the noisy seagulls squabbling between the bag-laden shoppers. Further on, the food gave way to stalls of cloth, pretty home-made aprons, tablecloths and napkins. Then in the last aisle, an Aladdin's cave of tables was filled with ancient furniture, clothes, clocks, lanterns, crates of housewares, crockery, tankards and glassware.

'We simply must bring the ladies here, Clifford. They would love this.'

'A fine suggestion, my lady.' He nodded as he turned onto a side road. 'Almost there. This is Avenue des Toits Rouges. The agent's office should be about... ah, here.' He pulled up.

A moment later, Eleanor sighed. 'Dash it, Clifford!' She pressed her nose to the glass of the agent's office. 'Closed, just as I feared. Now we'll have to wait until he comes back from lunch.'

'That will be quite the wait.' Clifford pointed to the sign taped to the inside of the glass door. 'And quite the lunch. Even for a Frenchman, dining right through to the end of August will be a remarkable feat.'

She shrugged. 'Oh, I don't know. Sounds heavenly. Perhaps I should marry a Frenchman?'

He gestured across the narrow street to the cream-scalloped awning fluttering above a smattering of café tables on the pavement. 'In the meantime, shall we settle for second prize and partake of a coffee?'

They trooped over. As Eleanor sat down, Gladstone promptly collapsed at her feet and started snoring. She put it down to delayed shock. Or delayed idleness. The coffee when it arrived was one of the most delicious cups of rich roast she'd ever had. She took a slow sip and gave a quiet moan of pleasure. The heavyset, aproned man flapping a linen napkin at the red-and-white tablecloth next to them paused.

'*Bon, mademoiselle?*'

'*Non. Mag-nif-ique!*'

The man nodded and looked between her and Clifford. 'On holiday? American?'

'Yes. And, no, *monsieur*. English. We wish to speak to Monsieur Thibaud, the accommodation agent opposite,' said Eleanor.

'Not possible. Marcel is out.'

She reluctantly put down her cup. 'Is he always closed until September?'

'*Non*.' He shrugged. 'But perhaps his wife want to go shopping.'

'For over a month! Even for me, that would be a stretch. How many things can one woman need?'

The café owner clucked his tongue. 'Like me, Marcel Thibaud has no wife.'

She looked at Clifford for help.

'It is, I believe, a French expression, my lady. Our continental cousins have a... refreshing outlook on commerce. They open their shop, café or' – he indicated the closed agent's office – 'business to suit their lifestyle, not their, ahem, customers.'

The café owner nodded again. '*Naturellement*. How else is a man to live! Tied by chains to the metal tin he keeps his money in. Pah! Never!'

Eleanor shrugged. 'Well, no such chains for Monsieur Thibaud, it seems. Good for him. But perhaps then you might be able to help us?'

'With what? Why you want to speak to Marcel?'

'Because, you see, I rented a villa through him. It's up in the hills there. It's Villa Marbaise. Perhaps you know it?'

Clifford pulled out his wallet to pay.

'*Non*.' The café owner waved the proffered note away. He grabbed the metal rod leaning against the wall and wound the awning back. 'Now, café is closed. My wife wants to go shopping too!'

10

Clifford's measured tone called from somewhere she couldn't fathom as she stepped onto the terrace.

'My lady.'

She spun in a circle. 'Where are you hiding? More to the point, *why* are you hiding?'

His disembodied voice answered, 'If averting one's eyes in the presence of an unsuitably attired lady of the house constitutes such—'

'Clifford, we are on the French Riviera, dash it! I am, in fact, overdressed.' She pulled her robe sash tighter and folded her arms, still unable to spot him. 'You booked me a villa with a swimming pool, remember? How on earth am I supposed to swim covered demurely from head to toe? I'll flounder, suffocated by yards of fabric, and then you'll have to leap in and rescue me. And I'm sure grappling with the lady of the house while her wet bathing suit is clinging to her is against the rules.'

His horrified silence made her smile.

'So, while you reconcile your admirable sense of propriety, I shall change into something to spare your blushes this time, and then be on the terrace.'

A few minutes after she returned, Clifford materialised through the French doors. He nodded appreciatively at her mint-green tea dress with matching lace-capped sleeves. His eyes flicked over her face. 'Despite the generous measures, perhaps last evening's Oloroso sherry was still insufficient to induce sleep, my lady?'

She groaned. 'Even with that port we had as a nightcap afterwards, yes. Thank goodness, though, that you thought to bring both even though we've supposedly booked a perfectly stocked wine cellar. Neither of us could face going down there last night.'

'Indeed. There is only the one deficiency in the cellar that I noted – the lack of a decent red. However, my inventory was rather, ahem, curtailed.'

'By poor old Armstrong,' she said softly. 'I bet you didn't sleep a wink, either. Mind you, it's impossible to tell how you slept. You always look the picture of health. Even after the ordeal you've been through. How is that possible?'

He eyed her like a small child. And one of reduced intellect. 'Because I am a butler, my lady.'

'So? Even you must feel under the weather on occasion. Yet you never show it.' She shook her head in disbelief.

His hand strayed to his neat black tie. 'I know that you intend to meet Inspector Damboise. If I might venture another proposal?'

'Try me.'

'That you telephone Monsieur Lessard, the mayor, and tell him you have changed your mind.'

She gasped. 'What! I can't. He'll have you back in that awful cell on the charge of murdering Armstrong before I've even replaced the handset. Whatever are you thinking?'

'That I cannot countenance you becoming involved in a murder investigation on my behalf.'

'Clifford—'

'My lady. With apologies, my mind is made up. And I am fully prepared for the consequences.'

'Well, I'm not!' She stood up. 'Much as I am overwhelmed by your thoughtfulness, my mind is also made up. I'm going to stick with my agreement with Lessard even if you turn yourself in to try to stop me.' She held up a hand as he went to protest. 'Come on, I've been in all manner of situations before and you've never actually mutinied.'

His lips pursed. 'Mutiny, my lady, is for bounty hunters and pirates.'

'Exactly, Clifford. You're being admirably selfless but an infuriating donkey at the same time. We'll solve this murder and keep you out of jail together. However, you know logic and planning come as easily to me as growing a beard. They are your department. And as well as my flair for the, well, unexpected, we'll both need to solve the mystery of how a famous American film star ended up dead in our wine cellar. And, as you mentioned, your impeccably suited behind is in this too.'

He gave a sharp tut at her mention of anatomy and then hesitated before sighing. 'I agree.' He bowed. 'My sincere, if reluctant, gratitude. Please forgive my previous mulish manner.'

'I'll chalk it up as dutiful insurgence, don't worry.' She frowned. 'That reminds me. I thought the café owner's reaction when we told him we were renting this villa a little odd.'

Clifford nodded. 'I also, my lady. It seems there is another mystery to solve – that of Villa Marbaise. However, Inspector Damboise awaits...'

'Mademoiselle Swift.' Damboise's now familiar dark moustache swung upwards with his smile. 'And Monsieur Clifford, with your handsome dog. Welcome, or *bienvenue* as we say.' Opening the rear car door, he offered Eleanor a hand.

'Inspector.' She looked around. They were in a suburb of

Garbonne sur Mer, the dirt road lined with modest houses of white stone. 'Why has Pierre brought us here?'

Damboise seemed amused by her confusion as he gestured towards the wooden swing gate. 'I learn the lesson at my police station. I sent Pierre to make sure you arrived on time. No cold coffee today! But' – he frowned – 'it took longer than I expected. Pierre?'

The young policeman's eyes slid apprehensively over to Clifford, who was sitting next to him.

Damboise laughed. 'Ah! Monsieur Clifford is the one to tame the racing driver in Pierre. Now, come in, please.'

Eleanor accepted his elbow – cream suited as it was today – and tapped her leg for Gladstone to follow them through the gate. She paused to take in the unexpectedly homely scene of a winding stone path leading through leafy peach and apple trees to the pretty painted shutters of the open front door. *Chickens! Garden swings. What on earth?*

Figuring they could only be there to interview a local suspect, she glanced down at Gladstone, then questioningly at Damboise.

'No problem, *mademoiselle*. Your friend with four legs is welcome. When I sent Pierre, I expected you all.' He looked back out towards the car, but then shrugged.

They stopped to let a line of buff brown hens peck their way in front of them. She was relieved that even though Gladstone eyed them with deep suspicion he did nothing more than warily trot around them.

She followed Damboise into a wide floral-wallpapered hallway where a profusion of shoes of many sizes lay in neat-ish pairs below overflowing coats. She pointed to the heavy oak dresser, the top two rows of which were occupied with hats, each with a different coloured band above the brim. 'You've invited me to... your home?'

'*Naturellement.*' He looked puzzled. 'What is the surprise here?'

'Because... because you're a policeman!' *How can you explain that your beau is a policeman and you don't even know where he lives?*

His face lit up. 'And I am a husband and a papa also. Here, the policeman has lunch with his family.' He inclined his head. 'The English policeman never does the same?'

She sighed. 'Not in my experience.'

He tutted. 'Lunch is the most important meal of the day. Here you must enjoy it with your family if possible.'

In the delicious-smelling kitchen, Damboise slid his arm around the woman stirring a pot on the stove. 'This is my wife.'

'Delighted to meet you, Madame Damboise.' Eleanor held out her hand.

'*Ah, non.* It is Celeste, please.' She stepped across the red-tiled floor, making her auburn curls bounce. Drawing Eleanor into a hug, she kissed her on each cheek. 'Welcome to our home.'

'Thank you, Celeste. Please call me Eleanor.'

Celeste leaned back and looked her over with warm hazel eyes. '*Parfait!* Thank you that you help my Jacques.' Despite her pretty, blue floral-print dress that skimmed her shapely calves and hung from her elegant hips, perfectly softened by mother-hood, there was something capable and strong about her poise.

'Papa! Papa!' The sound of running footsteps heralded the arrival of what Eleanor hazarded was a boy of about nine and a girl who looked a year or two younger. A giggling doll of about three or four followed in their wake, waving sun-kissed arms. Damboise accepted their exuberant hugs with obvious delight, then swung up his youngest to rub noses with her. He put her back down and nodded at Eleanor.

'*Mes enfants, Mademoiselle Lady Swift. Elle est anglaise.*'

The youngest squealed and wrapped her arms around a bemused Gladstone.

'Hullo, *mademoiselle*. How are you?' The two elder children chorused, poking each other in the ribs as they did so.

Eleanor smiled. 'Very well, thank you.'

'You are hungry, *oui*?' Celeste asked.

'Always. But, please, I didn't mean to interrupt your family lunch.'

'Nonsense. For now, you become family.'

Damboise turned to his wife. 'Can we help, *cherie*?'

Celeste shook her head, smiling, and shooed them out into the back garden along with Gladstone and the two older children. The youngest remained glued to her skirt.

In the garden, the boy and girl rushed back to a game of something between boules and cricket with Eleanor's excited bulldog trying to steal the ball. She took the seat Damboise proffered at a long wooden table beneath a curved scrollwork canopy, almost hidden by a thick covering of vibrant orange trumpet vines. The chairs each had what looked like a home-sewn patchwork cushion of different patterned fabric. On the table was a higgledy-piggledy collection of glasses, pretty seagull-print napkins and plates.

Just as well Clifford is waiting outside, Ellie. He'd be itching to put this lot in order. And no tablecloth! He'd never cope with that.

She dug in her handbag and produced her notebook. Damboise waggled a finger at her. 'In France, always the meal before business. Never I try to solve a case on a stomach that is empty.'

'Oh, yes. Fine.'

'Tell me, why does Monsieur Clifford not join us? The invitation is to him, too.'

'Apologies. Perhaps I should have said yesterday. He has respectfully declined.'

Damboise spread his hands. 'Because I arrested him? I did not think he is the man who likes to make the face.' He gave an exaggerated pout.

She laughed. 'I think you mean "sulk". But he is not sulking. Clifford is a butler.'

It was Damboise's turn to look lost.

She tried to explain. 'It simply isn't done, to his mind, to eat with his employer.' She knew. She'd persuaded him to on a couple of occasions and he'd been most uncomfortable.

Damboise shook his head. '*Oh là là!* Never will he dine with his mistress, though he is companion to you much of the day, I think? No matter. My wife will make him some sandwiches. And for Pierre too.'

Celeste appeared and called to the children to wash their hands before setting down a tray with rabbit stew, raised pancakes and roasted vegetables. Damboise broke three freshly baked baguettes into pieces and passed them around.

Swallowing her impatience to get on with discussing the case, Eleanor joined in with gusto. She laughed at the children's attempts at telling jokes in English and caused much hilarity herself over trying to get her tongue around the French phrases they tried to teach her. Gladstone was in seventh heaven as the children tickled his ears and fed him titbits in between.

To Eleanor's surprise, helping Celeste between the courses gave her an unexpected warm glow. As they stepped around each other, passing dishes and refilling glasses with fruit cordial or wine, she felt a peculiar wash of contentment.

Celeste paused by her elbow and whispered, 'To spend all the days as the wife to a good man is the treat of life to me. Maybe to you too, Eleanor?'

Is that what you want, Ellie? Could you really give up your independence? She sighed. *For Hugh? Perhaps.*

Forty minutes later, even she had to admit defeat after her second helping of mouth-watering spiced apple tart. Damboise laughed as she set her spoon in her dish and pushed it away. '*Mademoiselle est complet?* Full, I think you say.'

'Completely *complet*. Thank you. That was delicious.'

'*Eh bien*.' Celeste smiled, setting down one more tray. 'But not too *complet* for cheese and Calvados? It is good to talk business with.' She kissed the top of Damboise's head. Picking up a wicker trug, she left, calling for the children to help her find the chickens' eggs in the front garden. Gladstone trotted alongside the youngest child, his greedy eyes on the ice-cream wafer she clutched.

Damboise poured them both a glass and then raised his.

'*Mademoiselle*. To catching a murderer!'

She nodded solemnly. 'Absolutely.' The Calvados turned out to be delicious brandy infused with hints of apples and pears. She savoured a second sip. 'I only hope I can be of real help.'

He waved his glass. 'This you are already. But we have much to do.' He smoothed his notebook open on the table. 'So, we start with the weapon. A sabre.'

'A Napoleonic sabre, in fact.'

'*Mademoiselle!* I am impressed.'

'Be impressed with Clifford, Inspector. It was he who told me about the finer details of the murder weapon. My butler really is the most incredible fount of knowledge.'

'He is a man who lives to learn, I think.'

She nodded. 'But what's particularly irritating is that he seems able to retain everything as well. Honestly, he leaves me feeling like quite the blunt brick half the time.'

Damboise seemed to wrestle with the image. 'Yet, he finds his mistress interesting company? Me, also. We both teach each other.'

The compliment took her by surprise. 'How refreshing, Inspector. In England the police hardly think it worth taking a woman's statement, believing them naturally feeble-minded and vapid!' She turned to her own notebook. 'Do you use finger-printing here in France?'

He looked at her with admiration. 'You are indeed well informed, *mademoiselle*. Yes. But it is early days, like in your country. Truthfully, we do it to improve the technique, more than to trap the criminal.'

'But did you find any fingerprints on the sabre?'

'*Non*. Not even on the...' He mimed grasping a sword as if pulling it from its sheath. 'What is this part called?'

'The handle. Or, to be more precise, as Clifford delighted in being when he described it to me, "the grip".'

'*Merci*.' Damboise wrote this down in tiny, neat writing next to a remarkable lifelike sketch of the weapon itself.

The question that had been burning since Eleanor had stared down at the lifeless body in her cellar broke to the surface. 'So when was Armstrong killed?'

He looked up at her. 'For the investigation. Or to sleep better you ask this?'

'Both. It was such a tragic scene. I hate to think he had lain there for too long.'

His tone was sombre. 'Murder is always a tragedy. But, *mademoiselle*, we gave the promise to discuss only the truth, so I tell you Monsieur Armstrong was last seen at *midi vingt-trois*.' He thought for a moment. 'Twenty-three minutes past twelve at lunchtime. The security man at Chateau Beautour remembers opening the gate and thinking it strange Monsieur Armstrong leaves before filming is finished.'

'Chateau Beautour? That is where they were filming?'

Damboise nodded. 'And we believe he died between then and midnight of the same day. Which was Thursday.'

'Thursday! But Clifford didn't find him until the afternoon —' The words stuck in her throat.

'Of Monday. Sorry, *mademoiselle*. But it is the truth.' He

peered at her. 'At least, this is what your butler told me over and over at the police station.'

She looked up sharply. 'Inspector. I thought you and Mayor Lessard had acknowledged that Clifford had nothing to do with Armstrong's murder?'

'Again, I say to you that I am happy he is no longer in my jail. But' – he held up his pencil –'with the murders you solved before, you understand one always suspects the one who finds the body, *non?*'

'Initially, at least.' She frowned. 'What about rigor mortis, though? When poor Pierre turned the body over, it wasn't rigid. Stiff.' She shook her shoulders for clarity.

'Ah, but rigor mortis fades always after a few days. People do not think so, but it is so. This you do not see on the other cases you solved?'

'Never. Somehow I've always come across the body a lot sooner than a few days after the person died, it seems.'

I bet Clifford has already worked out Armstrong died a while before he found him, but said nothing to spare you more nightmares.

Damboise nodded. 'I think so, too. Always the mistress come first for him.'

'What! How did you know what I was thinking?'

'Because I am a detective as well as the husband and papa. Some faces I have to study hard to learn their thoughts. But not yours, *mademoiselle.*'

Resolving to make sure it was the last occasion that would be the case, she noted the time of death in her notebook and then tapped the page so hard her nib spayed a trail of ink. Her brows knitted. Then she slapped the table. 'Look here. If Armstrong was killed on Thursday.' She tapped the entry in her notebook again, this time more gently. 'We didn't arrive at Villa Marbaise until Monday!'

Damboise shrugged. 'It is true, *mademoiselle.* But it is also true, *n'est-ce-pas*, that you stayed in a hotel not twenty-five kilo-metres from here from the Wednesday before?'

'Yes. But that was because the rental on the villa didn't start until Monday and I wanted to start my holiday straight away, so we came to the area early.'

He nodded. 'I know. You went out in your rented car every day, including Thursday. The hotel owner is very clear that you left after breakfast and did not return until the afternoon. Ample time to—'

'Yes, yes, alright, Inspector.' *There's no use arguing with him, Ellie. You'll only do more harm than good. He has his orders from the mayor. Let's pick a fight you can win.* She forced herself to concentrate on her notes.

'So that means Armstrong was murdered on the day he disappeared, since he had gone through rigor mortis and out the other side. All alone.' She sighed sadly.

'*Mademoiselle*,' Damboise said softly, 'to be alone after death is not possible.'

'You really think that?'

'I am certain.' He pulled a folded sheet of paper from his inside pocket and waved it. 'But the report of Monsieur Armstrong's body includes only the facts of this world.'

'Indeed. May I have a copy?'

'Of the report!' His eyes shone with amusement. 'I think we do not have the word in French for a lady with the noble title who is content to dirty her hands like this. Oh, Jacques!' He tapped his forehead with his pencil. 'Apologies, that came out impolite. Some days my English is not even the apprentice. What do I mean? Ah, "eccentric", people say of you, *oui*?'

'Rather regularly,' she whispered behind her hand. 'But don't tell Clifford. Poor deluded chap still thinks I might actu-ally make a dignified lady one day.'

Damboise laughed heartily. 'A long time he has to wait for this, *non*?' He poured them each another small measure of

Calvados and cut her a wedge of a delectable-looking soft creamy cheese, placing a sprig of succulent black grapes on top. 'You can take this copy. I have a second one in my office. But our problem, *mademoiselle*,' – he sobered quickly as he waved the report – 'is that everything of which we have certainty ends on this paper. The rest lie heavy on the shoulders of you and me.'

She let out a long breath. 'Or our murderer will walk free.'

11

The pot of coffee Celeste appeared with at that moment distracted Eleanor from her sombre thoughts. And the accompanying miniature chocolate florentines persuaded her she wasn't too full to eat just a little more, despite what her stomach had told her.

But savouring the mixture of sweet tangy fruit, cocoa and salted hazelnuts and almonds, she felt a pang of guilt. Even for a man born with seemingly limitless patience, Clifford had been waiting for ages. Stuck in a hot car with Pierre.

Celeste unwittingly put her mind at rest as she left.

'*Monsieur Clifford aide la vieille madame d'en face avec son vélo. Homme courageux, eh, Jacques?*'

Eleanor cocked her head. 'Clifford's doing what?'

Damboise laughed. 'Your butler, he helps the old woman who live over the street to mend her bicycle. She is very... fierce. *Mademoiselle*, I think later you must rescue Monsieur Clifford again!'

Eleanor shook her head. 'You don't know him like I do. He'll be fine. So, let's start with getting to know Chester Armstrong. Albeit rather too late.'

Damboise returned to his notebook. 'The film he was to be the star of is—'

'Something from the Napoleonic period, perhaps?'

'Ah! Like me, you make the connection with the sabre. *Oui*, it is a film about how Napoleon's heart was forever consumed with Josephine.'

'Well, Hollywood loves a love story.'

Damboise rolled his eyes. 'Maybe. But it is *une catastrophe* I am sure! They make too huge of the drama that he divorced Josephine because he needed a son for the good of the French Empire, I think. A son she could not give him.'

'I didn't realise Americans were actually interested in the history of the French Empire.' She winced. 'Oops! No offence.'

Damboise laughed. 'No offence to me. You think this because you are English. Our countries are neighbours but for a small stretch of sea. Like people in the houses next to each other, they find fault in everything and good in very little for centuries.'

'Well, we're working together. Does that mean we are making history?'

'Yes. When we catch the murderer.'

'I appreciate your optimism.'

'*Non*, it is confidence.' He raised a fist. 'Mademoiselle Lady Swift and Inspecteur Jacques Jean-Baptiste Damboise are the formidable team!'

She smiled. 'We'd never fit all that on a calling card. Now, I take it you've interviewed the film people?'

'My men ask them only the very simple questions. I must tiptoe on the shells of eggs with this. Because, remember, *mademoiselle*, apart from the director, they believe Monsieur Armstrong died of a weak heart.'

She turned back to her notebook. 'Okay. So, what do we know about Armstrong that could have driven someone to kill... Wait a minute. Where are they filming?'

'I say before. At Chateau Beautour along the coast. Twenty kilometres from Garbonne sur Mer.'

'Then how did Armstrong end up dead, miles away, in the cellar of my rented villa?'

'How indeed, *mademoiselle*. The puzzle, *non?*'

She pondered this for a moment. 'And what about the button I found?'

'Ah, yes.' He went over to a side table and returned, dropping the button onto the tabletop.

Eleanor looked at him quizzically.

'It is okay to pick it up, *mademoiselle*. There are no fingerprints.' He laughed. 'Maybe we have Monsieur Gladstone to thank for that?' He waved his hand at her guilty look. 'It is of no matter. It is, as Monsieur Clifford said, a button from the uniform of the infantry. And Napoleon, even though he was head of the army, often wore the uniform of a simple colonel in the infantry.'

She picked up the button. 'So, you think it comes from Armstrong's uniform, as he was playing Napoleon?' She frowned. 'But he wasn't wearing a military uniform when I saw his body.'

Damboise nodded. 'Monsieur Armstrong had taken off the top half of the hat and jacket, yes, but not the trousers. I think to save time. I ask the assistant director and he said sometimes the actors only change their top half of uniform when they have break as too much time and nuisance.'

That would explain his mismatched clothes when we found him in the cellar. She stared at the button. 'So, it would have come from his trousers, I presume?'

He nodded. 'It seems the costume company have more the historical accuracy than the American film company! Well, it may not help catch his murderer, but as you found it, you may keep it.'

'Thanks. I think!' She dropped it in her purse. 'Tell me, did Armstrong tell anyone where he was going?'

'*Oui*. To the Hotel Le Blanc where the film company rent the rooms for the actors. And important, please, to remember again that when you speak to anyone connected to the film, that they believed he died of a heart attack in his car on the way to his hotel. For us it is better. Also the director – a Monsieur Herman Truss – he has asked the film crew to keep quiet about Monsieur Armstrong's death until he arranges a replacement in case the backers stop the film.'

'Mmm. Inspector, doesn't something strike you as particularly odd about the whole affair?'

'Perhaps.' He sipped his coffee, eyeing her over the rim of his cup. 'Like what?'

'The major star of the film disappears in a foreign country and yet the director doesn't report him as missing to the authorities? He was absent for four days!'

'True. But the director tells me Monsieur Armstrong often made a big scene before leaving with much angry shouting and waving of his arms.'

'And he would stay away in a sulk for that long?'

'Overnight is the longest that he stayed away before.'

'So, you mean to tell me that the director didn't go to anyone when Armstrong failed to show up the next day? Or the next?'

'Oh no, he went to see the American couple.'

'Why did he go to see them?'

'Mr Truss knows this couple, it seems. They have nothing to do with the filming and have never been on the film set as far as I know, but he trusts their opinion on this matter as fellow Americans living here.'

'And what did they tell him to do?'

Damboise's moustache shot into a straight line as he pursed his lips. 'To stay as far away from the French police as they can!'

'Marvellous. Well, we'd better speculate on possible motives then. The first one that springs to mind is jealousy or greed. What about the understudy? Perhaps he wanted Armstrong out of the way so he could have the role for himself.'

'This is a good thought but the director told me there is no second... what is the word you just use?'

'Understudy.'

'*Merci*.' Damboise added this to his notes. 'Yes, there is not one because if Monsieur Armstrong or the leading lady are not in the film, the men with the money also throw a tantrum.' His lips twitched into a sardonic smile. 'And take back their money like the spoiled children.'

'Yours are beyond delightful, by the way,' she said genuinely.

'*Merci bien, mademoiselle.* I am the proudest papa. And you, the proudest mama, one day, maybe?'

Her heart stilled at his words. Children? A family of her own? Settling down still felt too daunting to her wildly independent spirit. Marriage looked like someone else's life – someone she didn't recognise. And children? Well, that sounded terrifying. And achingly wonderful, she admitted, her breath catching as the cheerful chatter of childish voices floated out from the back door.

Focus on the investigation. No time for sentiment. Clifford's freedom, and maybe more depends on it.

'Wait though. Does that mean the film is in trouble now that Armstrong is gone?'

'You are quick with the thoughts, *mademoiselle*. *Oui*, it is a big problem, the director told me over and over, but he looks for someone the investors tolerate to take the place of their dead star. A lot of money has already been spent. They do not wish to lose it all.'

'Ugh! I don't envy him that job. Fancy trying to find someone even half as popular as Chester Armstrong at short notice.'

'And one the famous lady star – a Mademoiselle Clara Spark – accepted too.' He reached into the file by his side and showed her a newspaper clipping of a strikingly beautiful woman with coiffured curls. There was no denying that with her sharp cheekbones, perfect nose and the confident poise reflected in her shapely figure, she could be anything less than the darling of the camera.

'Well, she's very attractive. I'm sure I've seen her at the picture house. Isn't she supposed to be a bit of a prima donna, though?'

'I think it is natural. To be the queen of drama cannot stop just because the camera does. When Monsieur Armstrong left in his angry temper, only minutes later she marched off like a black tempest shouting she would not film another scene until he returned.'

'Trying to upstage him, perhaps?'

'Perhaps. One of my men tell me there is a rumour that they are more than just co-stars.'

'Mmm. Did the rest of the cast stay on?'

'*Oui. Et non.*' Damboise flipped a few pages backwards in his notebook. 'Some stayed and filmed, some went. My men are checking the movements of people there at the minute when Monsieur Armstrong left, but it is slow.'

'And you'll share that with me?'

'*Naturellement, mademoiselle.*'

'Alright, what other motives can we think of then?'

'Anger. The American couple upset a lot of people. And Mr Armstrong consorted with them, so I think was, how you say...'

'Tarred with the same brush.'

He shrugged. 'Perhaps.'

Eleanor frowned. 'And this American couple upset people because... of the way they behave?'

'Exactly because of this. Now, we French do not wish all the world is like us.'

He caught her raised eyebrow and held his hands up in surrender.

'Perhaps. But the behaviour of this American couple and those like Armstrong and the film crew who consort with them is too... extreme. All the time, wild parties, treating the local people like they are something unpleasant to step in. And always throwing around money like it means nothing. People here live the hard life. A lot have little. Especially after the war.'

She nodded. 'Everyone deserves respect. But I wonder if the actors particularly realise that is how their behaviour is perceived. Think about it. Hollywood is the height of glamour. Film stars are draped in jewels and courted by foreign royalty. Always in the news. It's probably hard for that not to affect your behaviour. But even if Armstrong did anger someone enough for them to kill him, I still can't fathom how he ended up in my wine cellar. Something is telling me that the director is the key here.'

Damboise thumped the table. 'Precisely! It is a pleasure our thoughts walk together.'

She hid another smile. 'Did the director have any theories as to a motive?'

Damboise's lips turned down doubtfully. 'He told me he thought it must be thieves who grabbed Monsieur Armstrong when he marched away in a temper.'

She caught the look in his eyes. 'But you believe he's holding something back from you, don't you?'

'*Oui*. He is careful, I think, not to tell me about...' He frowned. 'How do you say in English?' Gritting his teeth, he mimed pulling a rope back and forth between his hands.

'Tension?'

He nodded.

She gave him a short round of applause. 'Film-worthy acting yourself, Inspector.'

'*Merci. Oui*, he told me nothing of the tension there is between the actors, but I think it is there.'

'Hmm, so there's infighting between the actors and the director is hiding it?' She half closed her eyes and then opened them wide. 'Ah! Mayor Lessard said this is the first film to be made here and that the Americans have only just started coming. So how would Armstrong know anyone other than the people connected with the filming?' She looked thoughtful for a moment. 'So, do you think the murderer was someone on the film set?'

'It is the early days, but I think this must be so. The director told me yes, that Monsieur Armstrong has never been to France before. I must check with the American authorities on the truth of this.' He held up his pencil. 'So, here is your next puzzle. The director said maybe Armstrong's death was not related to the filming. Perhaps it was thieves looking for a fat wallet and it all went wrong. What do you say of this?'

She ran her eyes over the report. 'But this says Armstrong's wallet was still on him when his body was removed. And still with enough dollars to suggest no one took any of his money. So, maybe someone had been following him and was waiting for just such a moment. But not to steal a few dollars. To kidnap him and hold him for ransom for a serious amount of money, perhaps?'

Damboise shrugged. '*C'est possible*. But normally always he left with the other actors. Kidnap is a complicated crime. It needs much thinking ahead, much planning of every detail. It is too easy to fail because someone makes one move you do not expect.'

'Mm. Like chess. And it still doesn't explain why they would risk taking him all that distance out to my villa. There must be others closer that are empty too, given it is out of season.' She shook her head. 'I think it's still the most likely scenario that the murderer is connected with the filming in some way or other.'

Damboise nodded. 'And it is possible there are two people who may know the answer to this riddle. The American man and his wife who came here some months ago, after living in Paris. The ones who advised the director not to go to the police! Their name is Fitzwilliam.'

'Aha!'

'They also brought some musicians and artists, some of them well known in France and beyond. And always they have wild parties. But this couple, like the film people, Monsieur Lessard will not tolerate to become upset. He believes they have the influence to draw more rich Americans to this area.'

'Why? Are they particularly rich?'

He threw out his hands. 'They rent the Hotel d'Azur for the whole summer! The entire hotel! *Mon Dieu!* I cannot afford to spend one night with my wife in this hotel! But we know little of this couple. The American authorities tell me only that he made his money in banks and the clever trade of shares.'

'Legitimate dealings?'

'There are rumours that he fixed share prices. But suddenly, he stopped all dealing with the stock market. And then he came with his wife first to Paris and then here.'

'Interesting.' Her mind flew back to her near car crash yesterday and the glamorous Kitty in the crossover top. 'And his wife, what does she do?'

'She is an amateur painter and set herself up like a patron to art. Always she invites artists to stay and to their parties.'

'Do you suspect the Fitzwilliams of having anything to do with Armstrong's murder?'

Damboise shrugged. 'Perhaps. But they were not at the filming when Monsieur Armstrong leave. Never they go to the set, I think. But they have plenty of money to pay someone to do anything dirty they wish. It is not so hard to find men for that kind of work in this region. Especially since the war. There are many soldiers with nothing but the empty thanks of their country to survive on.'

'And, Inspector, as the only other Americans here, and wealthy, influential ones at that, they could have been pretty certain that the actors and director would be happy to know them. Or did our director set his film here because the Fitzwilliams are here? Something else he could be keeping from you, perhaps. Not recently befriended maybe, but old friends?'

Damboise nodded. 'This I wish for you to find out, *mademoiselle*. So, we must fix a plan. You must talk with the director, Monsieur Truss. Also with Mademoiselle Spark. And also with any other actors that were close to Monsieur Armstrong. But to do this without arousing the suspicion, first you must become the acquaintance of these Fitzwilliams.'

She waved a hand. 'That's no problem. I'm going to their party tonight.'

Damboise eyed her in disbelief. 'Again, *mademoiselle*, I must remember I underestimate you at my peril!'

12

'No, Master Gladstone! Not after your disgraceful behaviour this afternoon.' Clifford fixed the bulldog with a stern look.

Gladstone shuffled forward and laid his head on Clifford's impeccably shiny shoes.

'And playing the poor beleaguered beast will not work either.' He snapped his pocket watch closed, then lowered his voice, not quite enough for Eleanor's sharp hearing to miss. 'At least not for another five minutes.'

Sitting on the edge of her villa's swimming pool, swishing her feet back and forth in the delectably warm water, Eleanor looked up from under her wide-brimmed sun hat. Clifford was eyeing her sideways with the same admonishing look he'd given her bulldog.

'What?' she protested. 'I can't be in your bad books as well, can I?'

'No, my lady, you cannot. But only since I did not pack them on account of mistakenly imagining that a titled lady holidaying on the French Riviera would naturally maintain at least the rudiments of decorum.'

'Clifford, I had no choice but to help retrieve the numerous shoes Gladstone had spent the luncheon secretly burying around the Damboises' garden! I could hardly sit back and let poor Celeste unearth them all while the inspector chased after Mr Naughty for the last of his slippers. Luckily, they all thought it was hilarious.'

'My lady, you were kneeling on a mound of earth, wielding a seaside spade, while flinging soil over your shoulders.'

She held up a finger. 'True, but with a giggly four-year-old in my lap.'

His tone softened. 'With a delightfully giggly four-year-old assisting you, yes.'

'And anyway, Clifford,'– she rose and padded over to him, leaving a trail of wet footprints on the warm tiles – 'you were rather indecorously engaged yourself. If you're going to make up to the older female neighbours of the hosts I'm dining with, you might want to be a little more discreet. I mean, really, in her front garden of all places!' She laughed. 'Even allowing for the French custom of kissing someone on both cheeks, she seemed somewhat over grateful that you had fixed her bicycle.'

He shuddered. 'Intrusively so. And I stand corrected on what constitutes a lady not maintaining even the rudiments of decorum.'

Still chuckling, she returned to the pool, dangling her feet in the glistening water again. Leaning back on her hands, she drank in the setting, concluding it was simply too divine. The area was secluded from the rest of the garden by a series of scrollwork arches twined with lush vines. Between two lemon trees in giant urns, six deep-cushioned cane loungers were dotted temptingly around.

Clifford departed and returned with a silver tray bearing a deliciously light fruit cocktail. As he passed it to her, she sighed.

'Thank you. It really is too heavenly here to spoil it all with talk of murder, but I need your infallible logic and meticulously ordered brain. My thoughts are a jumble after talking with Damboise. Dash it, Clifford! I've been aching for us all just to come and enjoy a carefree holiday. Now, instead of being up to my neck in this soothing water kissed to the perfect temperature by this glorious sunshine, I'm up to my neck in another case.' She shrugged. 'And feeling guilty that I didn't tell Hugh when he telephoned. I must ring him later.' She glanced at the pool and then at Clifford. 'Perhaps...?'

He cleared his throat. 'My lady, I finally, ahem, concede that what constitutes propriety must change a little with the advanced times we are living in. I will take notes while you swim.' He turned his back to her.

'Thank you, Clifford. You're a sport!' She threw her hat onto the tiles and slipped her silk dress over her head, leaving her in her sleeveless woollen one-piece bathing suit. Horizontally striped in mint and holly, the matching over panel covering the shorts section ended mid-thigh. Stepping down the semicircular mosaic-tiled steps, she savoured the feel of the warm water against her legs and the sun's caresses against her arms. 'I'm in,' she called.

Clifford turned back and sat at the table. Producing her notebook he waited, pen poised. 'So, my lady, would it suit for me to write an ordered summary of the conclusions you drew with Inspector Damboise?'

'Perfectly.' She pushed herself off into the pool and swam lazily to the other end.

Clifford read out his notes while he wrote. 'Mr Chester Armstrong. Murdered with a Napoleonic sabre. Body discovered... Monday fifth of August at thirteen minutes to five.' He looked up. 'Last seen?'

'It's noted there somewhere.'

He scanned some of her scribbles. 'Ah! Twenty-three

minutes past twelve. On the previous Thursday by a security guard at the film set.'

'At Chateau Beautour apparently.' She reached the end of the pool and started back. 'I'm told it's about twenty kilometres from here.'

'Indeed, my lady. So, I deduce the first question is, how did Mr Armstrong come to die such a distance from where he was last seen?'

'Exactly! And why here? In this villa?'

'And the inspector's conclusions, my lady?'

'Huh! You mean those he chose to tell me? I still think he's holding back. Actually, though, he seemed quite genuine about not having any idea yet why Armstrong was found in our villa.'

Clifford noted this down. 'So, on to the question of why someone would want Mr Armstrong dead.'

'Well, Damboise thinks it might be one of the other actors – apparently they don't get on quite as well as the director would have it.'

'So possibly professional jealousy or a personal feud, perhaps?'

'Perhaps. As Armstrong was supposed to be on set all day, it seems unlikely someone recognised him leaving the chateau in a huff and decided to kidnap him on the spot.'

'Agreed. Kidnapping has too many potential pitfalls to attempt on the spur of the moment.' His brow furrowed slightly. 'So Mr Armstrong left unusually early and failed to return. Hmm.'

'Yes.' She started on another lazy lap. 'But the suspicious thing is, even given such a lengthy absence, compared to those of his previous fits of theatrical pique, the director did not report him as missing.'

'I do not find that suspicious, my lady.'

She paused mid lap and trod water. 'Why?'

'For two reasons. Were the financial backers to have learned of Mr Armstrong's absence, they might very well have added to the director's already considerable stress of finding himself without a star. But more so, because of the reputation of the French police abroad.'

She swam to the middle step and sat, swishing the water round her in an arc with her arm. 'Lessard mentioned that, actually. What reputation?'

'One of being rather... vigorous in their treatment of those from other nations when it comes to matters of the law.'

'Well, I can't say I'd be the first to ask for their help either after the way you were hauled away and locked up so readily. Although, having spoken more to him now, I believe Inspector Damboise is of a milder, more open mindset.'

'Indeed, my lady. Unfortunately, he is also duty-bound to do Mayor Lessard's bidding.'

'I know, more's the pity. Anyway, what strikes you next?'

He stared at the notes. 'Mr Armstrong's role, perhaps? The murder weapon was a Napoleonic sabre, and he was playing the part of Napoleon Bonaparte, I believe.'

'Y-e-s. So you think there might be a connection?'

'Possibly. Possibly not.' He thought for a moment. 'Nothing concrete comes to mind, so perhaps we can return to that idea later.' He wrote a new heading. 'Next we come to known enemies of Mr Armstrong.'

Eleanor pushed off from the step and continued her interrupted length of the pool. 'None. According to the director again. Certainly not here. It was apparently Armstrong's first ever trip to France. Damboise is checking. Also, there was no jealous understudy waiting in the wings to grab the part should Armstrong mysteriously die, since none was employed. Interestingly, the leading lady is as much a diva as Armstrong apparently was. Though that doesn't automatically give her a reason to want to kill him, as far as I can work out.'

'The lady herself was on set the entire time?'

'Not once Armstrong had left. She also stormed off. Rumour says she and Armstrong had been—'

'Ahem, well acquainted off the film set, as it were?'

'Yes. So our best suspects – if you can call them that at this early stage – are the director and the leading lady.'

'Mr Herman Truss and Miss Clara Spark?'

'That's them. And any other actor close to Armstrong who might have fallen out with him, given the infighting Damboise reckons was going on. Oh, and possibly the Fitzwilliams themselves. So, that's who I'll be concentrating on finding and getting to know at the party tonight.'

She climbed out of the pool and took the two fluffy cotton towels he handed her, his eyes averted.

'However, Clifford.' She wrapped one towel around her. 'If Miss Spark and Armstrong were an item, that still doesn't give her a reason for murder.' She shook her hair before wrapping it in the other towel.

Clifford cleared his throat again, this time less gently. 'Ahem, did I mention that this villa's pool has the very latest treatment system using chlorine? Good for swimming but not so for suit jackets?'

'Ah, sorry!' She tilted her head. 'Did you say chlorine?'

'Indeed, my lady. It operates as a powerful oxidising agent, combining with oxygen to attack harmful bacteria. Chlorine production for such usage is ingeniously created by passing an electric current through a simple saltwater solution. Essentially, like the brine Mrs Trotman employs to create your favourite gammon steaks, in fact.'

'How marvellous. Then I must be thoroughly pickled after that wonderful swim. Is the pool the only modern wonder of this villa then?'

'Actually, no, my lady. Once you are more suitably attired, I believe the ladies are itching to give you a tour of some of the other wonders they have discovered, if you would be so gracious?'

She threw her head back, basking in the warmth of the golden sun. 'To be honest, I think we've covered all we know at this point, until we attend the Fitzwilliams' party and hopefully learn more, so that sounds like just the distraction I need. Lead on!'

13

Having changed into wide-legged sage silk trousers and matching mid-sleeved blouse, Eleanor rejoined Clifford.

'Ahem. Apologies for bringing up the subject, my lady, but you mentioned earlier contacting a certain gentleman this afternoon?'

She blanched. 'Hugh? I don't think so. I mean, how can I? I specifically took his advice to go and rest away from murder and mayhem and... well!'

'That may be, my lady, but it is not your fault the two pursue you as relentlessly as Orestes was pursued by the Furies. Although, of course, there were three of them.'

'Of course,' Eleanor said drily, rolling her eyes, as if she knew exactly who or what he was talking about. 'Either way, after I've spoken to the ladies, I'll decide whether or not to confess to Hugh that our holiday has taken a macabre turn.' *And that when he rang, you were in jail, Clifford!*

Outside the kitchen, the cook and housekeeper's excited voices drifted out to them.

'Ooh, Trotters, must be all this hot sun. Fancy that!'

'I did, Butters. But 'twasn't the sun! More his big dark eyes and strong arms. Never imagined 'twould be so much fun having them foreign tradesmen call while we're here!'

Raucous giggling followed. Clifford pushed the door open. The two women jumped, red-faced, as he fixed them with a stern look.

'Ladies?'

'Oh, my stars!' Mrs Butters muttered as they bobbed a curt-sey. 'M'lady. Mr Clifford.'

On top of a footstool, Polly swung around, trying to curtsey while precariously holding several serving dishes. Clif-ford quickly stepped over a sprawled Gladstone panting on the floor and took them from her with a quiet shake of his head.

Eleanor pretended she hadn't overheard her staff's saucy conversation. 'Good afternoon, ladies. I just wanted to see how you're settling in?'

Mrs Trotman wiped her floury hands on her apron. 'Finer than this endless sunshine itself, thank you, m'lady. 'Tis like a palace down here and no mistake.' She gestured around the kitchen.

The walls were tiled in cream, rising to an arched brick ceil-ing. Five enormous carved dressers filled with every conceivable type of chinaware stood between one of the many oak or marble-topped preparation tables. A massive cooking range presided over the central wall, its gleaming cowled hood a work of art in itself. And above her cook's head, a pan rack held shiny copper saucepans of every size and shape.

'Trotters doesn't know herself,' Mrs Butters said before chuckling. 'Mind, none of us do. It's all so new.'

Lizzie flapped the duster poking from her apron pocket. 'Aye, it was beyond kind of you to bring me. And Polly, m'lady.'

Mrs Butters beamed. 'Said for all of us, Lizzie, my girl. Just think, the likes of us at the French seaside!' She and Mrs Trotman bumped hips.

Clifford stiffened. 'Which is for walking along, not disgracing yourselves in. Again!'

Eleanor couldn't help laughing at the memory of Mrs Trotman, Mrs Butters and Polly on the beach in Brighton, squealing in home-made bathing suits as they ran the gauntlet of the freezing waves. It had been last March and they'd believed she and a horrified Clifford hadn't seen them.

Mrs Trotman pulled an innocent face. 'You know us ladies, Mr Clifford. We only packed our best behaviour.'

He closed his eyes momentarily. 'Somehow I sincerely doubt that!'

Eleanor gratefully accepted a cup of tea from her housekeeper. 'Anyway, ladies, what's all this I hear about wonderful modern inventions abounding in our holiday home?'

Mrs Butters shook her head. 'Where to start, m'lady.'

'Not with the washing machine.' Mrs Trotman nudged her friend. 'Seeing as you're terrified of it, Butters. It won't eat you, you know.'

'It's just so different to our Wepwawet back home. Never seen so many dials and knobs. I don't want to break it.'

Eleanor smiled. 'I'd forgotten you all named our washing machine after, who was it again, Clifford?'

'The Egyptian God of, ahem, water, my lady.'

Eleanor knew Wepwawet was no such thing, but loved the fact that he didn't want to disillusion the ladies, especially Polly.

Lizzie held out a hand to help the young maid down from the stool.

'Go on, Polly,' Eleanor said. 'You show me these domestic innovations and Clifford can suggest names, and we will vote on them. And if we really like one of these modern wonders, when we get back, we might just buy one for Henley Hall. How's that?'

The young girl bit the edge of her apron. 'Yes, please, your ladyship.'

'First item then, Polly?'

'The cold cupboard,' she whispered in awe.

Mrs Trotman sniffed. 'We're not wanting one of them at the Hall. Never gets hot enough to need a thing like that more than a week or two each year. Manage just fine with the cellar, we do.'

Mrs Butters poked her in the ribs. 'Come on, Trotters. That cold cupboard 'tis like magic.'

Mrs Butters led Eleanor over to a tall white enamel-fronted cabinet on sturdy legs and opened the door with a flourish. A breath of delightfully chilled air stroked her cheeks. She looked at the crisp, cool food inside. 'I say, how wonderful. I've heard of these refrigerators, but never seen one. Now, it needs a name. Since we are in France, Clifford, what do you suggest?'

'Romeo!' Mrs Trotman slapped her hand over her mouth. 'Sorry, m'lady.'

Clifford tutted. 'Romeo is not a French name. I suggest Raoul, Roland or Rigobert instead.'

All hands shot up at the last one.

Eleanor laughed. 'Rigobert the Refrigerator it is!'

Clifford groaned and shook his head.

It took close to an hour and several pots of tea for Eleanor to be given the full tour of the villa's 'newfangleds', as the ladies referred to them. The electric blender amazed her, and she insisted on several demonstrations with various fruits and vegetables. After rigorous testing and tasting – Gladstone was the only one unimpressed with the results – they dubbed it 'Blandine'. Although with Polly's tongue-tied pronunciation, that quickly became 'Blendine the Blender'. Clifford dispelled Mrs Butters' fear of using the washing machine with a thorough explanation of the controls and the suggestion they christen it 'Weraphina'. That he had avoided Eleanor's questioning gaze confirmed to her it was a name he had made up, but the ladies loved it.

Once they'd moved Gladstone to a safe distance, they put the vacuum cleaner through its paces before declaring it a worthy equal to Victor, their vacuum cleaner back home. They unanimously named it 'Valerie' in case the two should ever get together. And after Eleanor had watched in amazement as the electric kettle boiled for the fifth time, puffing out clouds of steam, the ladies named it 'Guillaume'. Despite Clifford's protestations that the rules were it had to alliterate, the ladies decided it was too heroic a name to let go of.

'After all, Mr Clifford, we all love a cuppa. Even you.'

'Perhaps, Mrs Trotman. Now, we have taken up enough of her ladyship's time. Mrs Butters, is the rosemary and vinegar preparation ready?'

''Tis, Mr Clifford. Trotters and I made it earlier in Blendine.' They all laughed.

'And don't forget the rum,' Polly blurted out, then clamped her hand over her mouth. 'So sorry,' she whispered, shuffling closer to Lizzie.

'That'd be my fault, Mr Clifford.' Lizzie stepped forward. 'Back in Scotland, my nana always added a dram so's to make everything shiny.'

'Then, I am sure your grandmother's addition will work wonders, Lizzie.' He took the glass jar of amber liquid with fine green specks Mrs Butters had retrieved from one dresser and held it out to a bemused Eleanor.

She stared at it. 'Erm... am I supposed to drink this?'

'Definitely not, my lady. It is a cleansing and softening tonic for your hair to counteract the effects of the pool's chlorine.'

'Clifford! Gracious, that was particularly thoughtful.'

He adjusted the cuffs of his jacket. 'My lady, even if you are attending the Fitzwilliams' party purely with the intention of aiding Inspector Damboise's investigation, there is no reason why standards should be lowered. Polly will be up shortly to, er, assist you.'

Eleanor left the kitchen and climbed the stairs, stopping on the landing and calling to Clifford below.

'And don't worry. I'm not taking Gladstone and I doubt I'll come across any giggling four-year-olds to build mud pies with.'

'More's the pity,' she heard him mutter as he turned back to the kitchen.

14

Eleanor stopped fiddling with the emerald organza overlay of her silk dress and let out a low whistle as Clifford drove slowly along the Hotel d'Azur's impressive drive. A regimental line of umbrella pines towered sixty feet above their heads while a forest of cypress, mimosa and giant succulents proliferated in lush abundance.

As they neared the palatial expanse of ivory stone that was the hotel itself, the sounds of jazz music filtered in through the open windows of the car. They rolled slowly on past a large raised oval terrace, with an ornate glass roof supported by fluted pillars. It had been set with a series of linen-covered tables, cane chairs and potted hibiscus trees, each slender stem ending in a perfectly sculpted sphere of magenta blooms. Eleanor caught Clifford scrutinising the neatness of the presentation before nodding approvingly to himself.

'Yes, Clifford. It's all very pretty, but somehow a bit more English respectability than American flamboyance, wouldn't you say?'

'Ahem.' He held up a gloved hand to obscure her view. 'Not entirely, my lady.'

'I'm sure my delicate sensibilities will cope with whatever it is.' She nudged his hand out of the way. 'Oh, well, so it's going to be that sort of evening then!' A half-suited man finished his slow waltz across the drive with a giggling woman riding high on his shoulders, the hem of her silver silk dress riding up her thighs. He spun round and leaned into Eleanor's side of the car.

'Say, new faces. Howdy doo dee, folks.' He pointed a wobbly finger at Clifford. 'You need to get this waggon parked up, buddy. Party started hours ago!'

His companion giggled again. 'Right after breakfast, so you'd better drink up quick too.' With a hearty slap on the car's roof, they continued off on their waltz, only to upend headfirst into a thicket of green.

Eleanor peeped at Clifford. 'Well, we'd best get inside then. Ready?'

He turned slowly to stare at her. 'Not in a thousand years, my lady.'

The sweeping curve of the driveway's end was flanked by a set of wide steps that ran the full length of the hotel's setback central edifice. Imposing wings had been added to either side, each spacious enough to accommodate Napoleon and his army had he ever stopped by. But it was the hotel grounds that really caught her attention. Or rather, the party in progress in them. She'd expected a much smaller soirée than the swathes of men and women she was staring at. Groups, large and small, filled the immaculate green expanse, laughing, shouting, singing and drinking in equal measure. Around half of the men were dressed in relaxed evening wear and half the women in barely there dresses. The rest sported elaborate costumes. Plumed feathers, gold-braided pirate hats and jackets, fur-trimmed crimson capes and Chinese brocaded outfits abounded. On the lawns, velvet-clad cats danced with ermine-trimmed judges and tiara-adorned queens cavorted with harlequin jesters. She blinked at the sight of a scantily togaed Caesar arm-wrestling a shambolic Shakespeare, both holding champagne bottles with their other hand. In one corner, away from the general chaos, was a distinct all-male group, their silk scarves and multi-coloured embroidered jackets forming a mesmerising kaleidoscope.

Inside, the grey-suited Frenchman on the reception desk looked Eleanor over with a thin smile followed by a sniff. Clifford fixed the man with a disapproving look.

'Are you the manager?' Eleanor asked.

'I am,' he said wearily.

A group of instrument-wielding musicians tumbled out of the heavy oak door to his right. He watched them stumble through into the gardens with a deep frown.

'But perhaps do not ask for how long.'

A harried-looking waiter slid up to the desk and hovered. The manager turned to him questioningly, and, at the waiter's shrug, groaned.

'In fact, definitely do not ask this.'

Eleanor hid a smile. 'The Fitzwilliams, if you might be so kind.'

The man winced. 'The Fitzwilliams? They are' – he threw his hands out – 'who knows where, *madame!*'

'Hey, is it?' a hearty male voice called. 'It's gotta be, right?'

Feeling a hand on her shoulder, Eleanor spun around to find a flushed-faced chap with a tablecloth draped across his shoulders staring at her. The blonde-bobbed woman beside him glared at her with a look that could have shattered the glass chandelier above their heads.

'I don't think we've met, actually,' Eleanor said.

The man laughed and reached for her hand, which he planted a kiss on the back of. She could feel her butler's palpable disapproval. The man, however, seemed unfazed.

'Course we haven't, ma'am. But this party just got even better.' Grabbing his partner's arm, he moved off, whispering to her, 'Don't be huffy, sweetie, that was Gloria Swanson! No sane fella's gonna turn down that opportunity, I can tell ya.'

Eleanor groaned quietly. She had an uncanny resemblance to the famous red-headed American actress of the moment, something that had proved useful in a previous investigation. And, she mused, might prove useful again. Or not!

Just then, two familiar voices cut across the reception area.

'Why'd I want dessert when I've got you, Kitten?'

'Oh, you know how I love a permanently hungry man.' The couple entered the lobby, Floyd stroking Kitty's cheek. 'Hey! See, honey, I knew she'd come. It's Eleanor, right?' He grinned and lifted Clifford's arm to slap palms with him. 'And Starchie Archie.'

Eleanor smiled at them both. 'Hi! And, actually, his name is Clifford.'

'Sure, honey, but that's not as funny.' Floyd turned back to Clifford. 'It's a party, anything goes and everything's just in fun. Right, friend?'

'If you say so, Mr Fitzwilliam.'

Floyd laughed. 'I hope you know how hilarious you are. I so gotta show you to a bunch of folks.'

'It's a splendid party.' Eleanor felt she ought to rescue her butler before Floyd unwittingly went too far. Even Clifford had his breaking point, and she'd seen first-hand just how effectively, but politely, he could render a man unconscious.

'Which is why,' Kitty said, taking Eleanor by the shoulders, 'you should be out there dazzling everyone with those flaming-red curls and mesmerising pussycat-green eyes of yours. And that darling figure in that dress! Titian sure missed a muse with you.' She held up a thumb and scrutinised Eleanor's face, then clapped her hands. 'Floyd, I just have to paint her. What d'you say?'

Eleanor wasn't certain if she should be taken aback or

pleased by the sharp way that Floyd ran his eyes over her before breaking into a grin.

'Absolutely!' He pulled Kitty to his side and kissed her forehead. 'Cute, gorgeous and brilliant. Tell me, just how did I snare you, Kitten?' He waved at a flustered-looking waiter bearing a large tray of empty glasses. 'Hey, shiny buttons, furnish these great folks with some of the best liquor, won't you?' He pointed at Clifford. 'And make his a stiff one. It's gotta be his kinda thing.'

Clifford cleared his throat. 'Thank you, Mr Fitzwilliam, but I am here purely in the capacity of chauffeuring Lady Swift. Perhaps, however, while her ladyship enjoys the festivities, I might assist the hotel staff in serving your numerous guests?'

Floyd looked bemused. 'Weird, but sure, whatever stokes your motor, fella.' He slipped his hand into Kitty's and led her away, calling over his shoulder. 'Catch you later, Eleanor.'

The manager stared after them, shaking his head. He then flounced into his office, indicating for Clifford to follow him.

Eleanor hid a smile. 'Well, I've already made contact with two people who are on my list to see tonight. Let's hope I can track down the director and Miss Spark. Wish me luck, Clifford.'

'Good luck,' Clifford said in a low voice. 'I'll see what I can find out from the staff. And, my lady, be careful.'

She rolled her eyes. 'You mean behave!'

Left alone, she stared out through the glass doors at the garden, wondering how exactly to find the people she wanted to talk to. Consoling herself that she had travelled solo across the world by thinking on her feet, she took a quick peep into the room the musicians had spilled out from. What had once been an elegant hotel sitting room now resembled a bachelor pad. Tangles of shirts and trousers hung over the arms and cushions of the blue velvet settees, which had been unceremoniously shoved aside to create an impromptu rehearsal space. Empty glasses littered the tables and floor, overnight bags sprawled on every piece of furniture. The only order was in the neat row of instrument cases along one wall.

A scraping noise in the furthest corner pulled her up short. Tiptoeing forward, she realised one of the velvet settees piled high with bags was obscuring the narrow oak door of a telephone booth set in the wall.

'Yeah, I think they've gone. Come on, I'm dying out here.' A distinctly American male twang hissed. 'You owe me one. A big one. Pull some strings. Pull a ship's worth, I don't care. Just help bail me outta this.' She held her breath at the long silence that followed, fearing she would be discovered eavesdropping, but then the nasal tone cut in again. 'No! Sure it wasn't my plan for it to end like this. But now it has, you gotta help get me out of this mess or some dirty little secrets of your own might find their way out of the woodwork!'

She peeked into the booth, but at the crash of the handset on its cradle she grabbed the sides of her dress and sprinted silently from the room. In the lobby she accosted Clifford, who was dressed like a waiter in a long, white apron.

'Keep an eye on the man about to appear behind me,' she whispered, pretending to take her time choosing between the cocktails he carried on a tray. 'From the description on the notes Damboise gave me, I'm pretty sure it's Truss, the director.'

Clifford nodded imperceptibly and followed the man out to the garden. She stayed where she was, listening to their conversation.

'Drink, sir?'

'Heck, I'll have two. And keep 'em comin', would ya.'

Before she could hear any more, her arms were seized and swept around the neck of an admittedly not unattractive chap in a black smoking jacket. He whizzed her off to the end of the terrace in a series of fast-paced steps that had a few hallmarks of the tango, but more of tipsy improvisation. He jerked them to a stop in full view of a large group on the stretch of lawn below.

'What'ya drinking, babe?' he cooed.

Angry at having lost her quarry, she fixed him with a firm look and waved her empty glass. 'Nothing now, thank you. It's all down your back. Except for the trickle running down my arm, that is.'

'Oh, heck, sorry.' Suddenly seeming far more sober, he released her with a sheepish shrug. 'That was so dumb of me. I'll go get you another.'

'It's fine, really.' She recognised him now as the flushed-faced man in reception who had mistaken her for Gloria Swanson. 'What's your name?'

'Tuttle. Walter Tuttle.'

She scanned his face, noting his eyes kept darting to the elegantly curved beauty below, whose blonde tresses were piled up in a theatrical crown of coiffured curls and pearls. *Clara Spark. And it seems you're not the only one looking for her.*

'A piece of advice, Mr Tuttle. Just go and talk to her instead of trying to make her jealous by grabbing any unsuspecting female that happens to come to hand.'

His face fell. 'I wasn't... really, I—'

She folded her arms. 'And you didn't really think I was Gloria Swanson, did you?'

He looked abashed. 'Well, no. I mean, you do look a lot like her, but I've seen the real thing, you know, on set.'

She nodded to Clara Spark. 'Is Gloria as beautiful as her then?'

But her unexpected dance partner had vanished. She frowned and turned to find Clara Spark had gone too. She groaned. It was going to be a long night.

15

The next hour was a blur of random conversations, names and energetic dances as she tried to track down the Fitzwilliams, the director, Herman Truss, or the leading lady, Clara Spark. Unsuccessful on all counts, she eventually found herself engaged in increasingly elaborate excuses as to why she couldn't join the swaying pirate in front of her in a late-evening dip in the hotel's fountain. As the pirate finally admitted defeat and dived in alone, Clifford appeared with a tray of canapés.

'Bravo, my lady. An artfully defensive parry with your verbal cutlass.'

'Actually, I was quite tempted,' she said impishly. 'But, any news? Other than that the chef here is a sublime whizz?' She popped another delectable gougère ball into her mouth, savouring the creamy nutty cheese and the salty choux pastry.

'Perhaps most pertinently,' – he paused to press a tall glass of water into the hand of a surprised, green-looking chap stumbling past – 'Mr Truss, the director, who you asked me to observe, is currently on a one-way odyssey to oblivion in the small boules court.'

'Well, I'm going to grab him before he disappears! He's our

main suspect at the centre of it all. So let's find out exactly what he knows about his ex-star meeting his unfortunate end!'

'Oh, gracious, sorry!' Eleanor tumbled into the rectangle of the boules court, her landing broken by the soft sand that formed the playing surface. A muscular hand helped her up. She'd only glanced at the director's face as he'd passed before, so had missed how well built, if relatively short, he was. He was dressed in tan trousers that flared down from the knee and a blue sleeveless wool jerkin over crumpled shirtsleeves.

'You need anything medical after that tumble, lady?' He slurred his words slightly.

She laughed. 'Does the hotel have anything for a bruised ego, do you suppose?'

He snorted with amusement, but his expression quickly fell back into a troubled frown. 'Can't say that's likely.'

She sat down on the lion's claw stone bench. 'Did I miss the highlight of the party, do you know? I heard some of the actors were going to show off their dance routine.'

'Huh.' He sunk down on the other end of the bench. 'Would have been a thin show without my leading man. So whatever you missed, you didn't miss much.'

'Wait! You're the director? Well, what a treat.' She grabbed his hand and shook it, which seemed to surprise him. 'With every moving picture I've seen, it's struck me at the end that the director really should come and take a bow to the camera. I have no idea how you juggle so many scenes, costumes and storylines into such a... such a seamless and entrancing feast for our eyes and emotions.'

He nodded slowly. 'Why, thank you, ma'am.' His face darkened. 'But I gotta tell ya, all that's the easy part. It's the goddamn actors that make this job hard!' He leaned backwards. 'They're... what can I say?'

'Sensitive.'

He snorted again. 'Something like that, only not repeatable in the vicinity of a lady.'

'I was sorry to hear about Armstrong.'

He jumped. 'You heard, huh?'

Tread carefully! He obviously still believes no one else knows Armstrong was murdered.

She nodded. 'Don't worry, I won't mention it to anyone outside the film crew. So unfortunate to have been blighted with poor health, especially when on camera he looked so robust.'

His shoulders relaxed again. 'Oh, yeah, and he made a great Napoleon. He had that king-of-the-world attitude nailed down tighter than a ranch roof. A real emperor. On, and off, camera,' he muttered.

That must have ruffled some feathers on set, Ellie!

'Didn't that make him hard to work with?'

'What!' He looked away. 'No, it's a... technique some actors use to, err, you know, stay in character.'

'Of course it is. Maybe causes a bit of friction, though? With the other actors?'

'No, lady. My actors are like... like family. I make sure everyone gets along just fine.'

His insistence that there was no discord among the actors despite the evidence to the contrary jarred, but she let it slide for the moment.

'So are there lots of giant battle scenes for you to choreograph?'

'Oh no, we're only filming a few fight scenes. My movie is an honest-to-goodness, wrench-at-your-heartstrings love story. A box-office smash!' He mimed a curtain opening. 'It's gonna be wall-to-wall wet hankies for the ladies. Empty husks, they'll go a'weeping on home.'

'But Napoleon divorced his beloved Josephine, didn't he?'

'Not in my picture, he doesn't!' He took a swig from the bottle he was still holding.

Eleanor didn't know what it was, but it looked lethal. She considered how to find out if there was any connection between the movie and the Fitzwilliams without being too obvious.

'Why did you come all the way out here to film, though? Couldn't you have done it in a studio back in America?'

He shook his head. 'Wouldn't have been the same. No authenticity. Chose this area on account of it being out of season. No crowds. And with the dollar so strong, it's cheap to hire a chateau or two to film in. And cheap to get locals as extras for the fight scenes.'

'But you didn't know anyone here, did you? Didn't that make it really hard when you first arrived?' She tutted. 'But, of course, you probably knew the Fitzwilliams from back in the States.'

He shook his head. 'Nope. Met them here. And, yep, it was tough, but the local mayor has been really helpful.'

'But losing your main star must have been an enormous blow. Have you lost every chance of the film being made with Mr Armstrong having... passed away?'

He took another swig from his bottle and eyed her sideways. *Dash it, Ellie, maybe that wasn't very subtle!*

'Thought so.' He scrutinised her face. 'Yeah, I think I could.' She stiffened. 'Could what?'

'Could conjure up the perfect little walk-on part for you. Ain't no harm in having Gloria Swanson's double in my movie. That's what you were angling for, wasn't it, lady? Come see me at the set tomorrow. Now, 'scuse me, I need to find a bathroom.'

As he stumbled off across the lawn, she noticed a sandy-haired young man a few yards behind her. He was dressed not dissimilarly to the director, although being a good deal taller and leaner, his balloon-legged trousers were considerably more flattering. The man gestured after Truss.

'How is he? I mean, how far gone is he?'

Eleanor grimaced. 'Right now, he could still walk a reasonably straight line, but not for long, I don't think.' She took in the sandy-haired man's pale face and haunted expression. 'A friend of yours?'

'No. My boss. Unfortunately. I'm Daniel Brockman, the assistant director. Call me Daniel, won't you?'

The assistant director? He's not on your list, but he may know a lot about Truss and the other actors.

She smiled. 'You seem rather... young for such a position?'

He shrugged. 'Herman's always championing "new talent", as he calls it. He lives for moving pictures. Lives and breathes 'em. He's a swell guy and brilliant at directing, but when things go belly up, the old man loses it. And, boy, have things gone wrong!'

'Now that Armstrong is... no longer in the picture, you mean?'

'Yeah. What's really crazy though is that Herman never wanted him to play the lead. Spent days cussing.'

Eleanor's ears pricked up. 'Really? Why was that?'

He scratched his arm thoughtfully. 'He said Mr Armstrong was so much trouble before and would waste hours of precious filming time throwing his tantrums, disrupting the schedules like he always does.'

'So this wasn't the first time Mr Truss had worked with Armstrong, then?'

'Heck no.' He frowned, staring after the director.

She stayed silent, hoping his thoughts would continue spilling out. They did.

'I thought Herman was taking it bad that he'd gotten no choice but to work with Mr Armstrong again. But, it's the backers, ya see. Whatever the money men say—'

'Goes?'

'Right. But this is worse than I've ever seen with him before.

Maybe that row he had with Mr Armstrong just before... well, you know, is haunting him real bad.'

Her ears pricked up again, but before she could speak he grimaced.

'I think I've probably shot my mouth off enough.' He sighed and nodded in the direction Truss had disappeared in. 'And I thought I'd only have to keep the actors from getting too out of it to film tomorrow.'

She winced in sympathy. 'I think it's tomorrow now.'

'Sure, it is. And a bunch of them are still dancing on the roof.'

'Figuratively?'

'Nope. Literally dancing on the ballroom roof.' He held out a hand. 'I'd love to stay, but I'd better track down Herman and make sure he's at least halfway sober by the time he hits the film set.' As he walked away, he called over his shoulder. 'Has anyone told you that you're the spitting image of—'

'Yes. They have. Repeatedly,' she called back. She gritted her teeth in frustration. *It's no good, you'll have to risk it. Who knows when you'll get the chance again?* 'Daniel?'

He stopped and half turned. 'Yeah?'

'What was Truss' row with Armstrong about?'

He started walking away again. For a moment, she thought he wasn't going to answer.

Then, without pausing, he called over his shoulder, 'I don't know, but he swore one way or another it would be the last time he ever worked with Armstrong.'

She stared after his receding back. 'Well, Daniel,' she muttered. 'It seems Truss got his wish!'

When she returned to the main action of the party, even Eleanor had to admit things had escalated. Clifford caught her eye from the terrace and gave an imperceptible shake of his head in disapproval of the antics on display. In truth, she thought the general merriment quite infectious. The impromptu hare-brained races on the hotel's selection of guest bicycles from the entrance steps down through the steep gardens particularly appealed to her. Even the near-hysterical group trying to swim in formation in the shallow fountain pool looked delightfully cool in what was turning out to be a very humid night. Her pirate admirer stood up in the water and beckoned her in. Tempted, she caught Clifford's horrified face out of the corner of her eye and sadly declined again. *I suppose he's right. Your dress would be practically see-through if wet.* She fanned herself instead, wondering if the heat accounted for so many of the other party-goers lying at sporadic intervals around the grass, but she doubted it.

Staring upwards, she saw that Daniel Brockman had been correct. On the roof of the ballroom a swathe of the actors were waltzing, turkey-trotting and engaging in activities Clifford would be most disapproving of. She, however, was more concerned that they would soon have another death on their hands if the actors danced any closer to the edge.

Even the previously earnest group of men in vibrant silk jackets and scarves now seemed dangerously animated. Kitty Fitzwilliam lay across their table, waving a champagne flute in each hand, while Floyd was deep in an intense conversation with an olive-skinned young man who he had pulled aside. She shook her head. There was no chance of grilling either of the Fitzwilliams about any connection they might have with Armstrong with everyone around.

A wave of sympathy for the hotel staff flooded through her as another harassed-looking waiter passed her with a tray of drinks. In front of her, the musicians were still playing, albeit with a rather unsteady rhythm section. Her gaze honed in on the crown of coiffured blonde curls and strings of pearls twirling slowly between the drummer and the double bassist.

Ah! Miss Spark! And she appears to have a thing for a man who can wield an instrument.

She danced her way round to that side of the haphazard circle, scooping up the two drinks that Clifford indicated as he passed with a tray.

'Whooo, hot work all this partying.'

Clara Spark gave her a head-to-toe once over, then reached for the glass she offered.

'Only if you're out of practice, honey.' Her big blue eyes blinked as slowly as her southern drawl inched out her words. 'And didn't no one ever tell ya, it's rude to stare?' She laughed. 'Don't fret, doll, I'm used to it. Mind,' – she ran her perfect, crimson nails through Eleanor's fiery curls – 'you probably get a lot of looks yourself. If not for the right reason.' That laugh came again, this time accompanied by a pointed running of her hand over her curvy hips, then a finger gesturing down Eleanor's lack of them.

Bite your tongue, Ellie. Give her the benefit of the doubt. Maybe it's the drink talking.

She shrugged. 'I guess it takes all sorts.'

Clara laughed cruelly. 'Folks say it takes all sorts, but huh, folks only watch movies, they don't star in them. I do.' She winked at the drummer and took a long sip of her drink.

Eleanor reminded herself again she was doing this for Clifford's sake. If she didn't have anything useful to report to Damboise, Lessard would have her butler back in jail for sure. She smiled sweetly. 'It must be exciting. And exhausting. Constantly receiving so much attention, I mean.'

Clara smirked. 'Well, it's a burden. But if my public need me, what's a gal to do?'

'Quite.' Eleanor switched tack. 'Isn't it going to be awfully hard now, though?'

'Now what, doll?'

'Well, now that you'll be playing Josephine to a different Napoleon.'

Clara's whole body crumpled like a popped balloon.

Eleanor reached out. 'Oh, gracious, I'm sorry. I didn't mean to be insensitive.'

'It's alright. Well, it will be in time, I s'pose.' Clara dabbed her fingers along each eyelid as she sniffed. 'We were electric on set together.'

'And maybe off set too?'

Clara seemed to quickly recover some of her sparkle. 'Well, as I said, what's a girl to do?'

Eleanor took that as a yes. Clara took another sip of her drink. 'But the truth is, sweetie, Chester's charisma on set never ran dry, but off set, that was a different matter.'

'Really?' Eleanor frowned. 'Why was that?'

Clara shrugged. 'You'd need to have known him... Intimately.' She looked Eleanor over again. 'And, let's face it, that was never going to happen in your case, sweetie.' She let her glass drop to the ground and walked past her quickly.

Resisting the urge to swipe the leading lady's feet from under her, Eleanor gritted her teeth again. *So the leading lady's relationship with Armstrong wasn't all roses off set? Had Armstrong rubbed anyone else up the wrong way?*

'Miss Spark!'

The woman stopped but didn't turn around.

'Who else did Armstrong's charms wear thin on off set?'

Clara's sardonic laughter hit her ears. 'If you really want to know, sugar, ask the director!'

16

Eleanor awoke and stared blankly around the luxurious ivory-and-gold-appointed bedroom, recognising nothing. Except her... shoes? Her bleary vision tuned in to them, hanging on the ears of a rather over-ornate lampstand on the bedside cabinet.

'Who imagined a growling lion's head would be just the thing to wake up to?' she muttered, gingerly swinging out her legs from under the purple silk bed sheet, her skull pounding and her stomach rolling.

It wasn't an excess of alcohol to blame. She'd kept her wits about her and had travelled too much to be caught out by something being slipped into her drink. Clifford had also discreetly supplied her all night with a series of suitably dangerous-looking, but deceptively weak, cocktails. It was simply that she never functioned at even half capacity without a restful night's sleep. Peering at the elegant, dark-blue porcelain clock on the inlaid rosewood writing table, she flopped back on the bed with a groan.

'What is that? Less than four hours?'

'Less than three, actually, my lady,' Clifford's measured tone called from the other side of the door.

Padding over, she wrenched it open to find only an empty corridor except for, on the walnut display bureau opposite, her chic emerald silk dress with crossover bodice and delicately flattering side frill, which gave her the illusion of having at least a modicum of curves. Next to it was a steaming cup of tea. She leaned against the doorframe and took a much-needed gulp.

'GAH!' She hung her tongue out to relieve the burning sensation.

'Ha!' a voice croaked. 'Wild night, hey, sugar?' The man clearly spoke from experience as his hair stuck out at all angles and his near-colourless eyes stared out from bone-china-saucer sockets. His entire attire was the smallest pair of shorts she'd ever seen. He ambled on, calling over his shoulder, 'Breakfast's almost out if you're planning on eating.'

Far from the quiet groans she expected on entering the breakfast room, she was greeted with peals of raucous laughter. The faces round the table, however, told a different story. Despite the near-universal suntanned arms and legs, pallid complexions prevailed, everyone leaning heavily on their elbows, eating with forks exclusively. Only the Fitzwilliams, from where the laughter had emanated, seemed in perfect form. She rolled her eyes. She hadn't been able to find them all night and now here they were! She briefly considered engaging them in conversation, but the thought of trying to come up with any sort of intelligent questions before she'd drowned herself in coffee was impossible to imagine.

'Hey! Eleanor, honey.' Floyd waved from his seat in the middle of the table. 'Haul on over and tell us how an English lady with a fluted title knows how to party that hard.' He chuckled as he ran his lips over Kitty's exposed shoulder. 'Surprising, huh, Kitten?'

Unlike many of the others, Kitty was almost over-dressed in

her sleeveless soft-blue playsuit that was nipped at the waist with a white belt and ended mid-thigh as figure-hugging shorts. She waved Eleanor into the seat opposite them. 'Oh, I don't know, Floyd, darling.' She held her hands up as if imagining Eleanor's face in a frame. Her eyes narrowed. 'I want to meet the man who can immortalise the iron determination behind those pussycat-green eyes on canvas.' She held Eleanor's gaze for a moment longer than was comfortable.

'Well,' Eleanor said, looking around for a waiter, 'until these eyes have had the chance to be swimming in strong coffee, he'd have a job finding anything in them.' She sensed Clifford having appeared behind her. 'Ah, salvation!'

'Starchie Archie's here too!' Floyd hurrahed. 'How did you sleep, fella? Standing upright to keep those amazing suit tails from getting creased, I reckon?'

Clifford gave a half bow. 'Suffice to say, Mr Fitzwilliam, I slept sufficiently well. Thank you for inquiring.'

The whole table laughed.

'See, what'd I tell ya? He's hilarious. I love this fella.'

Clifford filled Eleanor's coffee cup first, then continued along the other guests, averting his eyes from the low-cut bathing suits most of the women were wearing. Clara Spark dramatically waved him away, demanding he bring her a glass of fresh juice instead. Eleanor sighed. She'd finally found the Fitzwilliams and the leading lady, but couldn't really ask them anything worthwhile with the others there. She'd just have to bide her time. She looked around for the director, but he was nowhere to be seen.

As befitted the elaborate display of silver serving platters and domed hot dishes, breakfast was a substantial affair – much to Eleanor's delight as her stomach was growling most inelegantly. Over at the food table she filled her plate with a selection of savoury pancakes, toast, thick-cut ham medallions and what appeared to be grated potato sautéed with fine herbs. As

Clifford materialised beside her to collect another pot of coffee, she caught his lips quirking at the unladylike amount she had taken. She ignored it and flapped a discreet hand at him.

'Orange or apricot juice, my lady?'

'Neither. But thank you for my dress and the tea.' She lowered her voice. 'Where did you sleep?'

He lowered his voice too. 'In the staff quarters. Once I had established which room you had finally... fallen into.'

She peeped over her shoulder. The table seemed occupied with an animated discussion over which beach they would descend upon the minute everyone had eaten. 'I didn't "fall" anywhere, as you well know,' she hissed. 'What I did do, though, was stumble in on room after room of people up to all manner of things that would drain all the starch from your impeccable shirt collar and curl your suit tails at the same time. None of the staff could tell me which room was free. It's preposterous!'

'The staff's thoughts also. Universally so, my lady.'

'But hang on, they're all French? No disrespect intended, but the nation has something of a reputation for being as far from prudish as one can get!'

He took a glass bowl and artfully arranged a selection of sliced fruits. 'True. However, it is not the, ahem, multiple indiscretions that have upset the staff. To the French, there is an elegant way to do everything, including such... bohemian behaviour. And' – he looked down his nose – 'last night I saw nothing remotely elegant.'

She tutted. 'They're only having fun. What is it about this lot that rankles you so much?'

'Let us say, would that I am never the man who would travel appreciating only the contents of my own suitcase.'

'Fair point. They aren't being very respectful of the local customs or ways of behaving, but there's no malice intended.' She peeped up at him impishly. 'Well, let's hope I'm immune to their terrible influence.'

'Indeed. Since you will be safe on the beach among such a crowd, with your permission I will remain here to continue sounding out the staff. Sincere apologies, however, for being remiss in not bringing your swimming attire.'

'Tsk, tsk. Now I'll just have to upstage our American cousins in disgraceful behaviour and swim in my under—'

He stuck his fingers in his ears. Once he was certain she'd stopped speaking, he took them out, picked up the fruit bowl and pressed it into her hands. 'I'll find you something suitable immediately.' He hurried away, leaving her smiling.

Whoever had won the vote on which beach they should invade had chosen well. The secluded cove was doubly private, since it was owned by the hotel. It was edged by pale-grey limestone cliffs, dotted with miniature pines and fleshy succulents sprouting at haphazard angles. But it was the sea that mesmerised Eleanor. She swore she could see every known shade of turquoise through to jade in its waters. The beach itself was already almost too hot for bare feet, but the fine caramel sand felt too good between Eleanor's toes to resist. Clifford had, for the first time she could remember, turned up blank, having failed to find her any swimwear. Although Eleanor suspected he'd found plenty, just none he thought were modest enough. However, she soon forgot that the green ruched swimsuit Kitty had lent her was more revealing than she would normally be comfortable in as she joined the throng watching the antics of a group offshore. Antics that would surely end in disaster.

Recognising the man in striped shorts a way off, she waved him over. 'Morning, Mr Tuttle. What on earth are Floyd and that other chap doing strapping those oversized skis to their feet? And why are they each holding a rope tied to a motorboat?'

He laughed. 'It's called "waterskiing". And, please, call me Walter.'

She smiled. 'And I'm Eleanor.' She gestured back to the waterskiers. 'Who thought that up?'

'Apparently some pals of Floyd's invented it last summer up in Minnesota. It's the latest riot.'

'Once you get the hang of it, I guess.' She laughed, pointing at Floyd's partner, who was flailing wildly behind his towboat, his legs stuck out sideways. Floyd, however, appeared enviably competent and shot off in an impressive arc, even briefly waving to his cheering audience.

She desperately wanted to give it a go, but reminded herself that she wasn't there for beach and water games, but to catch a killer. *And to keep Clifford from the noose. Or maybe the guillotine!* She shook her head. Surely they didn't use the guillotine any more? She briefly considered asking Clifford, and then thought perhaps not!

She frowned and decided it was time to cast her net wider and find out whatever she could from any of the actors or film crew. 'I thought you were all supposed to be filming today?'

Tuttle laughed. 'Should be. But Daniel – he's the assistant director – said before breakfast that today's scenes were being rescheduled. Don't know what Herman's thinking, but I sure am happy for a break and a day on the beach.'

'Who do you play, by the way?'

'I'm Napoleon's right-hand man.'

'Really?' She tried to tread carefully, even though she was excited at having found another actor who was obviously close to Armstrong on set, and maybe off.

'What's it been like? Filming the moving picture here, I mean?'

He waved a hand at one of the picnic rugs that had been spread out. 'Do you mind? After last night's... dancing, the legs aren't too dandy.' He waited for her to get comfortable before joining her. 'So, filming this movie's been interesting, let's put it that way,' he said sarcastically. Another of the actors flopped down beside him, a shorter, leaner, darker-skinned version of his friend.

'What's interesting?' said the friend.

'Working on this movie.'

'Interesting be darned! Herman's out of his depth on this one, for sure. I mean, what did he expect, bringing us to Europe to shoot? Those French extras are hopeless as well!'

'I know, but it's more than that,' said Walter. 'Herman's been almost as impossible as Chester was.'

'And they say girls are moody.' Eleanor rolled her eyes.

Walter laughed. 'Take my word for it, only actors, especially the leads, really understand what moody is.'

'But doesn't that mean you're forever tiptoeing around the leads, whatever moving picture you're working on?'

The two actors shared a look and shrugged in unison.

'You get used to it,' Tuttle said, an edge of bitterness in his tone.

'But surely the stars of this picture can't have been tiptoeing around each other? Clara Spark and Chester Armstrong, I mean. No one can shoot a love story if the leads are arguing off set, can they?'

Tuttle jumped up, his face flushed. 'Like I said, it's been interesting.'

'Nope.' His friend joined him. 'It's been hell. Ain't ever been so much love lost as between those two stars. On, or off set!'

She watched them stroll away, wondering just how deep the animosity between Clara Spark and Armstrong went. *Perhaps murderously deep?*

17

Apparently neither high-stakes waterskiing – it had resulted in one broken leg – drinking games or sunbathing appealed to the small group of earnest men mooching in her direction. Hands in the pockets of their flannel trousers, they sported colourful patterned scarves over artistically blouson-sleeved shirts, vivid jackets hanging over one shoulder.

Ah, the group who kept away from the main partying last night, Ellie. Maybe they're local actors? They don't look American.

One of the group sported a shirt of soft lilac heather and a matching scarf that Eleanor coveted, even though both had obviously seen better days. She was struck by the man's unusually fine, almost feminine features.

Of course, he was the olive-skinned young man Floyd had been talking to last night just before you buttonholed Miss Spark.

The man crouched to stare at a long tapering shell on the sand, while the others walked on by. Eleanor was intrigued. She had already collected a small pile of shells she couldn't resist, plus one long smooth pebble in the exact grey of the suit Hugh almost invariably wore. But on the whole, men were usually unmoved by the ready trinkets the sea threw up daily. She watched him trace each intricate line of the shell's closely packed corrugations that ran from base to tip. The swirls alternated from nutmeg to ochre, each ringed with fine threads of amber.

'*Magnifique!*' he breathed, turning it in his hand.

'It is indeed,' Eleanor said.

He looked up. '*Mademoiselle*, imagine if an artist can paint this to so much perfection, it makes even the man with no soul for beauty stop and look! What a world we live in then!' His strong French accent and intense black eyes added passion to his words.

'You're a painter, I take it?' She groaned inwardly. *Where have all the actors and film crew gone?*

'Of course he is,' an amused Italian voice said.

They both looked up to see an older man from the group. 'For my new little friend Augustine here, canvas is his only bed, paint his only meal.' He ruffled his companion's hair. 'So, always he is hungry.'

'It isn't always easy to follow your passions.' She gestured hopefully over to the others who had paused to light cigarettes. 'None of you are with the film people, then?'

'No,' the new arrival said. 'Kitty brings us together here. She is the uncommon American lady who love art but also to forever party.' He rolled his eyes. 'How she parties! I meet her when she live in Paris with Floyd. She come to an exhibition I give.' He shrugged. 'She send me letter saying to come to here for the summer and bring any artist I know. The others, she send the same.' He pointed round the group. 'They come from many country in Europe because she know many famous artist and many rich people who like to fill the walls with paintings.' He leaned over and lifted Augustine's head. 'But we need to paint what the people want to buy, *si*, little one?'

'Pah!' Augustine pushed his hand away and leaped up like a

cat. 'Painting is to capture beauty. No one pays more for my work than if I am a dog, because they do not see it with their soul, only their wallet!' He marched away to rejoin the group.

Apparently it isn't only actors who know how to be moody, Ellie!

As she was trying to think of her next move, her attention was caught by Floyd hailing a long straggle of rather dishevelled individuals hauling instrument cases down the steep steps towards the sand.

'What is it folks say about musicians?' He laughed. 'Can't live with 'em—'

'Can't party without 'em!' the second-to-last of the line hollered back, waving his drumsticks.

This drew a raucous cheer from the whole beach.

Fun though it was chatting to artists and musicians, she really needed to get closer to the film crew. She looked around for Clara Spark but failed to spot her anywhere among the myriad risqué bathing suits and close-to-indecent shorts now gathering around the champagne hampers. The musicians also apparently needed to take on liquids of the alcoholic variety before they could play a note. Kitty had joined Floyd in happily handing out bottle after bottle, chatting with everyone as if they were the oldest of friends. Three men and one woman stood slightly off to one side, all poring over something. *Perhaps they are from the film crew.* And, indeed, Brockman appeared and waved at her. Her eyes lit up. Just the person she needed. She strolled over.

'Morning, Daniel. I don't think we had a chance to chat yesterday evening.' She grimaced. 'But forgive me if we did, it was quite a night.'

He laughed. 'I know what you mean. And no, we didn't.'

She indicated the group of four people. 'Who are they? Actors?'

Brockman looked in their direction. 'No. The three men are

a writer, playwright and biographer. They're helping us with the script and the details of Napoleon's life. The woman's a poet. Like most of the creative types around, excluding the actors, I think she's here for the introductions Kitty can give her to Europe's "literati" as she calls them.'

'Gracious! The Fitzwilliams really are the most incredibly magnetic couple I've ever met. I'm sure there's a great tale there, somewhere.'

He nodded. 'Their "tale" as you put it, seems to start in Paris. That's where everyone here knows Kitty and Floyd from, I think.'

Eleanor looked across at the large number of people now dancing on the sand. There had to be close to fifty and that was far from the whole of the party revellers from last night.

'The Fitzwilliams' days in Paris must have been exhaustingly busy. They seem to have attracted every creative type in Europe and beyond!'

He tapped his nose. 'Perhaps it is easier when you are rich.' He blushed. 'But that's probably not very charitable of me as I'm at one of their parties, drinking their liquor.'

Eleanor smiled. 'I think they'd forgive you. But I wonder how they became so rich in the first place?'

'Sharp investments. And a silver tongue from what I've heard. Although not from Floyd himself. He seems to keep how he earned his money close to his chest.' He shrugged. 'But then again, it's his business, no one else's.'

Unless he's a suspect in a murder case!

He gestured over at Floyd, who was twirling Kitty romantically, centre stage on the sand, to the delight of the musicians but the quite evident frustration of the girls in the chorus line.

'Our host is as far from the giddy playboy he pretends to be as I am from Hollywood right now. Least he was when he was making all his money.' He shrugged. 'Stands to reason. You can be sure there's no clown who can throw money around like confetti.'

She nodded. *He's right. No matter how easy-going Floyd appears, he must have something of the predatory beast about him to make that sort of money. Especially somewhere as wild and unregulated as America.*

She looked in Floyd's direction. He had the whole crowd linking arms and dancing the Parisian can-can to the increasingly fast beat the band was belting out.

'Say, someone shoot back to the hotel and organise another hamper of champagne!' he yelled. 'And who's for lobster?'

Two hours later, the afternoon sun was scorching hot, yet the dancing hadn't diminished in popularity or speed, unlike the champagne, which was disappearing like it was going out of fashion. Finally some of the musicians waved the flag of surrender and placed down their instruments.

Tuttle was among the twelve or so who then made a run for the sea to cool off. Grabbing her hand on the way past, he grinned. 'No point wearing that bathing suit all day and not giving it a taste of the Mediterranean.'

Her infallible fount of all knowledge, Clifford, had informed her that no matter how hot the weather, the sea in the Riviera was always relatively cool due to the mistral, a cold, north-westerly wind that blew into the sea. She had to admit that the clear azure water felt like a much-needed cooling salve to her skin, which she now realised was going to scream all night with sunburn. No doubt Clifford would have something medicinally spiteful to hand to make sure she learned her lesson.

Some of the young men started a water fight by flinging armfuls of seawater over each other. Given that she was a strong swimmer and extremely nimble, she delighted in joining in whilst avoiding the worst of the attacks. But as she dived under the waves to escape a double onslaught, she cracked heads with someone unseen. She retired back to the beach, nursing the bruise.

A few minutes later, a group of giggling girls straggled by. From the snippets of conversation Eleanor caught, they were obviously dancers from the film company. Even though it seemed doubtful they would have been close to such a famous star as Armstrong, she rose and nonchalantly followed them. After all, sitting there on the sand on her own nursing her throbbing head wasn't moving her investigation forward.

The dancers were all in their early twenties with enviably long, shapely legs and figures and, from their remarks, burning aspirations to make Hollywood sit up and notice them. But none of their conversation gave Eleanor any further insight into who might have wanted Armstrong out of the way. Discouraged, she turned to try another part of the beach when a throwaway comment between two of the women made her pause.

'Why d'ya suppose Herman waited so long to bring one of his pictures out here, Ruthie?'

'No idea.' Her friend giggled. 'But who cares when we get to see those long, sun-kissed legs of Floyd's in his darling little shorts for an extra day today! And up close, since he's finished showing off on his waterskis.'

Her friend stopped and placed her hands on her hips. 'Huh! So looks like you ain't missing the almighty Mr Chester Armstrong knocking on your door at all times of the night, girl!'

18

'Thank you, Mrs Butters.' Clifford exchanged a silver chafing dish of damp face flannels and several spent compresses for the fresh set she had brought. 'Please inform Rigobert the Refrigerator he is in for a long night.'

Mrs Butters threw a sympathetic smile to Eleanor who was sitting stiffly on the chaise longue. 'So pleased as we've got him to help take the heat out of your sunburn, m'lady. 'Tis easy to be caught out. 'Specially with your colouring.'

'The cold cupboard is indeed a blessing, Mrs Butters.' She held up her late uncle's pocket watch and threw her butler a look. He nodded.

'Mrs Butters, please inform the other ladies that her ladyship has been gracious enough to grant you the rest of the evening to yourselves. Please enjoy the gardens or the lower terrace. And,' he pretended to whisper, 'a nip of something unnecessarily warming.'

Eleanor's housekeeper clapped her hands. 'Thank you, m'lady, Mr Clifford! Too kind. 'Tis the most beautiful view any of us have ever seen. If Polly's eyes get any wider, I think they'll fall out and roll down the hill into the sea.'

After she'd left, Clifford lifted the lid of the chafing dish and passed Eleanor a chilled flannel with a pair of silver tongs. She reached out for it and winced as her sunburnt skin brushed against the chaise longue. She tutted at his disapproving look.

'What was I supposed to do? I'm meant to be blending in with the Fitzwilliams' party-goers, so no one suspects I'm investigating this wretched murder. And, today, that involved spending hours fooling about on the beach. I didn't know you needed to lather yourself in coconut oil or whatever it was in that little tin you'd secreted in my dress pocket. No one sunbathes in England!'

Clifford's expression softened. 'Entirely understandable, my lady. And it looks very painful.' He placed a glass of amber sherry and a tiered stand of delectable finger savouries on the side table.

'And they look divine. Now, we've a murderer to help Damboise apprehend, so, let's hurry up and catch him. Then we can all really let our hair down for the remaining weeks of this supposed holiday.'

He shuddered. 'Why am I suddenly not encouraged to solve this case?'

She thought of throwing a flannel at him, but wasn't sure he'd see the funny side of it. Instead, she leaned back on the chaise longue, enjoying the much-needed cooling effect of the flannels now draped along her arms and neckline. Gladstone, who had been relegated to lying on the floor next to her, lifted his head hopefully. She patted him, but shook her head.

'Sorry, old chum, but I don't think your bony elbows and sharp claws are what I need right now.'

The bulldog sighed and laid his head back down.

'So, Clifford, under your heading of "Suspects..."' She looked at him beseechingly. 'I can't really take notes like this.'

'Indeed, my lady. One moment.' He produced her notebook and pen and sat at the table.

She turned back to the view to clear her mind. 'Right, I think Damboise was correct about our first three suspects: Clara Spark, the leading lady; Truss, the director; and, in the centre of everything, it appears, the Fitzwilliams. Let's start with the director, for no particular reason, if that doesn't upset your sense of order too much?'

Clifford hesitated, but then nodded and wrote: *Suspect: Herman Truss (director)*. He raised a finger. 'I am afraid I did not learn much of use concerning Mr Truss from the staff at the Hotel d'Azur, my lady.'

'Don't worry, I learned a lot. For starters, I overheard Truss on the telephone asking for help to get him out of a sticky situation, if you remember. And if the help wasn't forthcoming, he'd reveal the other chap's "dirty little secrets".'

'That sounds like a desperate man.'

'Exactly. And, as you remarked, he was bent on drowning his troubles in unhealthy amounts of alcohol and other substances at the party last night. He is certainly being eaten up by something.'

'Guilt?'

'I couldn't tell. I'd love to know who he was talking to. Anyway, to be fair to Truss, he's in the hideous position of having a raft of investors to keep happy but no leading man for his film.' She thought back to her meeting out by the boules court. 'Although there's more to that. His assistant, Brockman, told me Truss had never wanted Armstrong in the film in the first place because he was too hard to work with and too disruptive. In fact, he told me Truss swore that this would be the last time he worked with Armstrong.'

'Well, he got his wish, my lady,' he said, unknowingly echoing her words.

'Yes. But how?'

'By murder, perchance? We certainly seem to have hit upon a motive for Mr Truss, although Mr Armstrong's death has resulted in the potential collapse of his picture. Perhaps he thought it worth the risk, though?'

'Perhaps.' She waited until he had finished his notes. 'Now, on to our second possible suspects. The Fitzwilliams.'

'Who were not on the film set the day Mr Armstrong left in a temper.'

'True. But they are definitely the sort who can pay handsomely to get hold of a sabre and a couple of thugs. Or a professional hired killer, as Damboise suggested.' Her brows knitted. 'And Brockman pointed out that you don't get as rich as Floyd by being a fool. If he's bright enough to make as much money as he seems to have at such a young age, then I'm sure he's bright enough to have worked out how to kill Armstrong and potentially, at least, get away with it.'

Clifford nodded. 'An astute observation. I also gleaned some information about the Fitzwilliams from the staff.'

'Excellent.'

'They arrived at Hotel d'Azur on the third of June. They were the only occupants for six to eight days.'

'Rattling around that enormous hotel on their own! What on earth did they do all day?'

'They spent a great deal of time on the telephone and haring about in their rented vehicle, apparently.' His lips pursed. 'Much to our vehicle's cost later on.'

'Which Floyd offered to have repaired. So, moving on?'

Clifford slapped his hand. Gladstone's ears twitched, but his eyes stayed closed. 'Reprimand noted. Anyway, it seems no one at the hotel knows exactly where they went, although there is an old fort on the peninsula and the manager thought he saw their vehicle coming back down the track that leads to the fort one evening. But he couldn't be certain, given the light was fading. On an unrelated, but interesting, side note, Napoleon was imprisoned in that very fort during the French Revolution.'

'Fascinating, Clifford, but shall we save the history lessons for later?'

'As you wish, my lady.' He cleared his throat. 'From the tenth or twelfth – the staff could not quite remember – the first of the artists and musicians arrived. The difficulty for the staff was that no one knew who was coming or when. It appears Mrs Fitzwilliam's invitations were very much of the open-house variety. Many of the staff threatened to leave given the, ahem, general behaviour of the guests. However, it being out of season – most hotels here close on May first – there are very few positions available, so the manager was able to sway them into staying. And,' – he held his hands up in surrender – 'as you graciously acknowledged, the Americans are particularly generous and frequent with tips. Their money has been welcomed, if not the people themselves.'

Eleanor risked moving to savour a long sip of her sherry. 'That is heavenly.' She raised her voice slightly to be heard over Gladstone's increasingly loud snoring. 'So, when did the film mob descend on the town, then?'

'Around two to three weeks later. Helpfully, the manager thawed out once he and I had found sufficient common ground, and he felt able to bend the rules of breaking guest confidences.'

'Ooh, I'm intrigued. What was the common ground? Let me guess. You two held a "who-can-give-the-best-disapproving-sniff" contest?'

He gave her a withering look. 'No, my lady. He is a mutual fan of Voltaire. Once that was established, it was easy to extract a few pertinent details.'

'Such as?'

'That the Fitzwilliams were particularly friendly with Mr Armstrong. To the point that he came alone to visit them on two separate occasions.'

'That's very interesting. But as the leading light of the film, as it were, wouldn't it be quite natural for Floyd and Kitty to do everything to get to know him? It's obvious they see themselves as the king and queen of notable society.'

'Agreed, there may be no more to it than that. Perhaps the only other really pertinent bit of gossip at this juncture is that Mr and Mrs Fitzwilliam also reportedly courted the friendship of Miss Spark. Likely, again, as you said, to widen their circle. However, the manager and several of the staff, too, told me that even though it was believed that Mr Armstrong and Miss Spark were, ahem, more than just colleagues, they had to be kept apart when at the hotel or anything throwable or breakable would, indeed, be thrown and broken.'

She sat up. 'Ah! I basically heard the same from Tuttle and his friend about them acting like that on set. So maybe this is a good juncture to move onto our second suspect, Clara Spark. I mean, we need to find out more about the Fitzwilliams' relationship with Armstrong, but we haven't unearthed any motive for them wanting him dead yet.'

'Agreed.' He made a note against the Fitzwilliams – *no known motive* – and then wrote: *Suspect: Miss Clara Spark*. He looked up. 'And your first impression of meeting the lady in person?'

Eleanor thought for a moment. 'Miss Spark believes she is irresistibly beautiful – which, admittedly, she is.' She sighed, feeling as far from glamorous as she ever could. *Not surprising. At the moment you look and feel like a boiled lobster!* 'In truth, her face and divine figure would light up any stage or screen.'

Clifford continued writing. 'I believe the same is often said of Miss Gloria Swanson.'

'Thank you, Clifford. Anyway, Miss Spark is certainly one of the most determined and ambitious creatures I've ever met. And a complete madam.'

He gave her a pointed look. 'Perhaps "determined", "ambitious" and "a madam" qualify her more as a leading lady than a murderess?'

'Perhaps. Perhaps not.' She flapped a hand at him. 'But I know one thing. I'm not convinced I could ever tell if she was lying or not.'

'That aside, might I enquire what she said to you about Mr Armstrong?'

'Well, that's the point. She made a very barbed comment about...' She thought hard. 'Oh, yes, about his charm wearing thin very quickly, which points again to her having a stormy relationship with him off screen.'

Clifford topped up their sherries, shaking his head at the excited squeals from the ladies rising from the lower-level garden.

'Oh no, please don't close the window,' Eleanor said. 'It's so good to hear them having fun. They deserve a break. They really work so hard all year. Like you.' She took her glass. 'So, to play fair, be warned I shall think of a suitable treat for you before we leave here once this murder business is out of the way.'

He sighed. 'If you must, my lady.'

She scanned his face. 'There's more, isn't there? I can tell. Maybe I'm finally learning to read *your* face? The manager told you something else after you'd swapped enough of your favourite Voltaire quotes.'

'Actually, after having swapped tasting notes on sufficient quantities of wine from around the region, yes.'

She laughed. 'Excellent devious tactics on your part, Clifford. You definitely missed your vocation in something terribly underhand and likely illegal.'

'Thank you, my lady. I'll assume that was intended as a compliment. More flannels?'

'No, thank you. These have worked wonders.' She peeled the last from her arms and dropped them into the chafing dish he held out. He placed it on the sideboard and returned to the table.

'Continuing our discussion, the hotel manager confided that, again, even though it was rumoured they were—'

'Lovers?'

'Ahem, yes. The manager heard Miss Spark telling Mr Armstrong that...' He passed her the notebook and tapped the open page.

She read aloud. '"One day you'll go too far and someone will finally teach you the lesson you think you're too darn important to learn!"' She frowned. 'Interesting. And an extra titbit that might tie in with this came from one of the dancers when I was on the beach today. She hinted that Armstrong had been carrying on with her friend. And maybe she wasn't the only one?'

Clifford looked up from writing. 'If Mr Armstrong was "playing the field" to use a parlance from horse racing and having... ahem, intimate liaisons with other women on the set at the same time as—'

'He was professing his love for Miss Spark.'

'Then we may, indeed, have found a compelling reason for—'

'Murder!'

19

Chateau Beautour rose from its steep grassy headland like a monolithic fortress. Dominated by seven castellated towers, its forbiddingly fortified entrance was awash with activity. Eleanor frowned as Clifford slowed the car to avoid the raft of people milling about in front of them.

'It's not quite what I was expecting, Clifford. I mean, it's an amazing setting, very atmospheric and romantic. There's even a Romeo and Juliet balcony. But Napoleon and Josephine? Am I missing something?'

He swept his gaze over the men carrying crates, boards and, oddly, fake horses into the chateau. 'I can only assume, my lady, that we are about to witness the conjuring trick that is Holly-wood. In reality, nothing is as it appears in the finished spectacle we are spellbound by for less than a shilling.'

'Then let's go see more.'

At the entrance, however, the colossus of a security guard blocked their way. 'Neither of you got a filming pass, ma'am,' he said, folding arms that were straining the seams of his dark-blue shirt. 'So you ain't allowed in.'

She waved a hand airily. 'Actually, you're correct. We haven't a pass since we've only just arrived, you see.'

The guard stared at her from under hooded eyelids. 'Nope, I don't see.'

Clifford stepped forward. 'Is Mr Truss, the director, on the other side of this impressively vaulted barbican, my good man?'

The guard nodded. 'Course he is. Filming starts soon.'

Eleanor gasped. 'Oh, gracious, then I shall be late on set!'

He leaned down and glared at her. 'Nice try, ma'am. But if I had a dime for every time a dame's tried that trick on me, I'd live in a castle, not guard one! Want to be in the picture, huh?'

'Actually, no,' she muttered.

Clifford threw her a look.

'I mean, yes. I do. Mr Truss invited me personally.'

'It's alright, Sam,' a breathless voice called out behind her.

She turned to see Brockman struggling under the weight of what appeared to be armfuls of bound paper. Clifford relieved him of the top half of the teetering pile.

'Oh, thanks.' He rolled his eyes at the security guard. 'Boss asked this lady to come and audition. I heard him myself.'

'Well alright, I s'pose, Mr Brockman, as you're the assistant director.' He lumbered aside reluctantly. 'But they still ain't got a pass,' he muttered as they walked under the arch.

Eleanor hurried after the assistant director. 'You've got good security.'

He nodded and threw out a frustrated arm. 'No! Not over there, flags and cannons! You should be on the upper lawned area. The spoils from the battle, inside the Grand Hall! People, please!' He turned back to her. 'Sorry. It's quite the operation to keep everything on track. Especially shooting abroad. But, yes, security has to be absolutely tight. We get as many idiots trying to steal a souvenir from the set as begging for a star's autograph. Or worse, sneak into shot.'

'Well, you can be sure no one's getting past *him*.'

'Sam's a good fella. Been with Herman for years. Now, I should get you folks to somewhere a heck less—' He groaned. 'Cameras! Where are you going?'

Six men lugging heavy-looking equipment all stopped.

One struggling with a tripod as tall as he was yelled back, 'Tower three for the Napoleon in bed with a fever scene.'

'No! Didn't you get the latest schedule? It's Josephine reading the love letter in the forest first. How can we shoot the fever scene when the new Napoleon isn't arriving until later today?'

Eleanor's brain whirled. She was sure Damboise had said that there was no understudy for Armstrong? And, anyway, how had Armstrong's replacement got from America to France so quickly? The only way was by ship and the fastest crossing still took around two weeks...

Behind Brockman's back, Eleanor shared a look with Clifford. 'New Napoleon?' she mouthed.

He discreetly mimed treading softly.

'Oh, so no charging in like a rhinoceros then?' she whispered louder than intended.

Brockman spun around, wide-eyed. 'Did Napoleon have a run in with a rhinoceros? 'Cos we've only got horses.'

'Rest assured, Mr Brockman,' Clifford managed with a remarkably straight face. 'When in Africa, the venerated Emperor of France was more at loggerheads with the Northern Egyptians than the wildlife.'

'Darn. That woulda made a heck of a scene. Still, I doubt if anyone other than you educated folks know the real version, so I might just suggest it to Herman. I'm sure we can rustle up a couple of rhinoceroses from a French circus or zoo nearby.' He checked the watch hanging upside down on his breast pocket. 'Say, we'll be shooting for real soon so how about I set you up to see the forest scene from the wings? It's going to be a while before Herman's free to audition you.' Without waiting for an answer, he hurried on ahead.

'An actual audition?' Eleanor stared at Clifford. 'He can't be serious?'

'Hmm, perhaps. But—'

She followed his gaze to one of the lower battlements where a female figure all in white was marching back and forth, arms gesturing angrily. As the woman turned, Eleanor could see it was the film's leading lady, Clara Spark. She had the director pinned to the stone wall, repeatedly poking him in the chest.

'But perhaps not.' Clifford eyed Eleanor mischievously. 'Perhaps Mr Truss spotted something of the leading lady in you?'

Before Eleanor could think of a suitable reply, Brockman returned and directed them to a nook in the wall where they could watch the filming. Leaning back into the cool stone recess created by the two towering four-foot-thick pillars, she gently batted off Clifford's explanation of the architectural benefits of such clasping buttresses.

'An enchanted forest slap in the middle of the main court-yard?' she breathed. 'I must be seeing things.' She stared at the verdant proliferation of Scots pines and giant heathers all sprouting out of sandy soil, slabs of grey rock covered in velveteen moss dotted amongst them.

'I believe, my lady,' Clifford said, 'it is our first glimpse of the magic of film.'

'It's no magic.' Brockman sidestepped three men struggling to wheel another enormous potted pine tree onto the set. 'More like hours of setting up, chasing the prop makers and then discovering at the eleventh hour that they can't read simple dimensions. Miss Spark would have needed a ladder to scramble onto what they started making for that central outcrop where all the action happens!'

'Is that what she is so upset about?' Eleanor said.

'Nope. I got it all fixed before she knew. But, oh no, don't say. Is she?' He glanced around nervously.

Eleanor nodded.

'Poor Herman.' Brockman lowered his voice. 'Between you and me, I really thought he'd buck up when Mr Armstrong was, you know, off the picture. But he's been totally... oh, here they are.' He hurried forward. 'All set to go, Miss Spark.'

Eleanor watched the leading lady take up her position, or 'mark' as Clifford told her it was called. There she would be in shot for the camera.

'Quiet on set,' Brockman called. 'Act two, Scene Seven, Take One.'

Eleanor's breath caught as the clapperboard fell and the actress instantly transformed from a furious diva to a dream-struck lover. As the beautiful Josephine in swathes of ivory silk and lace, Clara Spark was every inch the love-smitten young woman; the one dreading the news the unopened letter she was holding with trembling fingers might contain. One of the film crew held up a board reading *if you be injured in battle, my dearest, I will ride like the wind across the ocean to be your nurse, your medicine.* Clara clutched the paper to her chest with a sob.

'A remarkable transformation, Clifford,' Eleanor whispered.

'Quite, my lady. A ready set of masks up the lady's sleeves, whether or not in costume, perhaps?'

'Cut!'

Eleanor jumped as Truss yelled through a loudhailer.

He slid from his collapsible canvas chair. 'Clara, honey. Real tears, too. What a star!'

'Like that's a surprise!' she snapped and stalked off set, the train of her dress billowing behind her across the dirt floor.

'Good job that scene's in the can,' Brockman muttered as he hurried over to Truss.

'No need for another take,' Clifford translated at Eleanor's confused look.

Brockman came back over and shrugged at Eleanor apologetically. 'Herman's got his work cut out for a good while I think.'

'Maybe I could get out of your hair and wait in one of the, erm—' She glanced at Clifford for help.

'Rehearsal spaces?'

Brockman nodded. 'Great idea. You can watch how the extras get their cues, in case it all works out for you on this picture. This way.'

He led them through a maze of stone passageways, cluttered with painted backdrops, rails of costumes and, peculiarly, several front halves of the fake horses they'd seen earlier. She paused to peer inside an ornate gilded carriage that had been mounted on a giant version of a rocking horse mechanism.

'For the climactic chase scene.' Brockman beckoned her to squeeze past it.

'Ah! Who's chasing who?'

'Napoleon's on his charger trying to save his broken-hearted Josephine from driving her carriage off the cliff after her jealous admirer lied and told her Napoleon had been killed in battle. Naturally, Napoleon stops the carriage just as it's about to plunge into the sea and she ends up wrapped in his arms. You know how all that true love stuff goes.'

Eleanor closed her eyes as her heart clenched, her thoughts filled with the image of her handsome but ever awkward and ever busy beau. 'No, I don't,' she murmured.

'Perhaps not yet, my lady,' Clifford said softly behind her. 'But soon.'

The rehearsal spaces were a great deal more functional than she had imagined. The bare-walled room had nothing more than one long table at which two tired-looking men sat surrounded by a mess of scripts and a scattering of hard wooden chairs. An equally tired plate of lemon and lime slices was the only colour in the otherwise drab surroundings. She turned to Clifford.

'It's a far cry from the Little Buckford Amateur Dramatics rehearsals I misguidedly attended.'

'It's not much of a replacement cocktail but, erm, sorry all the same,' a voice said behind her.

She spun around as Clifford melted away. Standing in front of her was a man in his thirties, dressed in a striking scarlet-edged navy jacket over a white waistcoat and matching trousers. *One of Napoleon's generals, perhaps?* In his hand, he held out a glass of water with a twisted lime slice balanced on the rim.

'It's not much, but it's all there is.'

'Ah! Of course, Mr Tuttle. I mean, Walter.' She took the drink, then realised she hadn't asked him about the leading lady who he obviously had a thing for.

'What did Miss Spark say the other night by the way?'

He stopped and hesitated. 'What d'ya think? Nothing, of course.'

'That must be hard since you must be in scenes with her. I mean, you're one of the main actors, obviously.'

He nodded. 'Thanks for noticing. Not that most people do.' His jaw pulsed. 'But they will.' His voice dropped. 'I'll show them! He didn't have anything I don't.'

'Chester Armstrong, you mean?'

He looked at her in surprise. 'Yeah.' His eyes lit up. 'And now I just gotta prove I'm every inch as good.'

'So, this is your big chance? You could step into Armstrong's shoes?'

He scowled. 'See, that's what I keep telling the director. Why have me playing Napoleon's second in command now Armstrong's... gone, when I could play the lead? And I wouldn't waste everyone's time. But no! He goes and gets Rudolph blasted Perry when I could have aced it!'

It seems, Ellie, Mr Tuttle may be the actor you're looking for who knows both Armstrong and Clara Spark. What luck!

'Was Armstrong a little... prickly sometimes, then?'

'Sometimes? Nope. Always! Man was a pain in the seat of everybody's pants. He couldn't act a tailor's dummy with any conviction either. Only got the top roles because he looked good on camera. I can't deny him that, but that was all he had.'

'And... a way with the ladies, perhaps?'

He stiffened. 'If acting like a heartless cur to them qualifies, then yeah!'

She chose her next words carefully. 'Including a certain leading lady?'

He clenched his fists, his face suffused red. 'Armstrong treated her like dirt, and for some reason she took it all. Right up until the wretched cad dumped her! Clara's a saint. She was way too good for him.' He shook his head. 'Anyway, I've got about as much chance with her as I have the director giving me a shot at Armstrong's lead.'

'Mr Tuttle. Makeup!' a voice called from the doorway.

Eleanor watched him go, a frown on her face. *So, Tuttle is definitely carrying a torch for Clara Spark, who Armstrong wronged, according to him. And he coveted Armstrong's leading role.* She nodded to herself. Despite what Tuttle had just said, he had a much better chance of winning Clara's hand and landing the lead role with Armstrong dead. *Which means, Mr Walter Tuttle, you may just have become a leading suspect in this murder investigation!*

20

Eleanor ran her hand distractedly over the red-and-white-checked tablecloth as the sounds of an accordion started up nearby. Sitting in a cane chair under the shade of a floral parasol, the hum of chatter around her felt somehow comforting but, being in French, displacing at the same time. Gladstone sat under the table, alert for any titbits that might come his way. That nobody was eating didn't seem to concern him. He was always optimistic.

With a jump, Eleanor tuned into Damboise, leaning on his pale-green jacketed elbows, staring at her, his black moustache quivering.

'Are you alright, *mademoiselle?*'

A small sigh escaped her. 'My thoughts are rather confused, being filled with all the places I've been in the last few days and all the people I've met.' She picked up the handwritten menu card. 'However, since I remember that we need to eat before we discuss business, shall we choose quickly and then you can tell me how the children and Celeste are?'

'My sister and her children are very well, *mademoiselle.*'

She looked up to see a head of thick nut-brown curls

framing a suntanned face. She glanced at Damboise and then back at the newcomer.

'Ah! You're brothers-in-law?'

The newcomer nodded, setting a green bottle, two glasses half filled with ice, and a jug of water on the table. 'And this is my restaurant. Welcome. *Mademoiselle* is hungry?'

Damboise laughed. '*Toujours*, Christian, *toujours!*' He smiled at Eleanor. 'Or "always", as you say.'

Having ordered them both 'specials', Damboise poured them each a drink that was as green as the bottle.

'That looks positively lethal,' Eleanor said.

Damboise shook his head as he let the ice settle before adding a precise amount of water. The liquid turned a cloudy white. 'On the contrary, it is my favourite apéritif.' He pointed to the label.

'Pernod,' she read aloud.

'We do not say the "d", *mademoiselle*.' He raised his glass. '*Santé*. Or good health.'

She took a sip. 'Ah! It tastes like liquorice. It's delicious.'

The restaurant's special turned out to be equally delicious: mussels with white wine, garlic and parsley, served in a lidded casserole dish, accompanied by a basket of toasted olive baguette. The whole meal was wonderful. As was the chilled, crisp wine that accompanied it. Copying Damboise, she mopped the last of the savoury sauce from the bottom of her dish with more toast. She dropped the last few pieces into the mouth of her patiently waiting bulldog, while Damboise settled back in his chair and pulled out his notebook. Once the plates were cleared and coffee ordered, he tapped the open page with his pencil.

'So, to business, *mademoiselle*.'

She nodded. 'You first.'

He shrugged. '*Ça va*. Okay. I start my report with talk of the sabre. We know already there were no fingerprints on the one that killed Mr Armstrong and still I do not find out where it came from.'

'Wait though. The film company are shooting Napoleon's love story, aren't they?'

He rolled his eyes.

'Actually, Inspector, I think you'll be surprised. Assuming it ever gets finished, that is.'

'You wake up the curiosity in me, but tell more of that later, *oui*?'

'Of course. What I was going to say is that as the film is about Napoleon, isn't it likely they have, or had, sabres as props?'

'Yes. Many. And this I check already. The props came from the same company in Marseille that supplied the uniforms. They delivered two crates of sabres as well as other things. But the director told me the Napoleon expert they sent down, a Monsieur Poudray, told him nobody bothered to count the number of sabres in each crate.'

'But surely they would have been kept locked away somewhere?'

'No more than anything else. The guard on the gate of the chateau stops anyone coming in who should not be there.'

'Hmm.' Eleanor nodded. 'And I've experienced first-hand how fiendish he is about that. At least the one I met was. I have a question, then. Do you believe a woman could run a man through with a sabre?'

He thought about this for a moment. '*Oui*. Yes, if it was sharp enough. And the clothing of the man was not too thick.'

'Armstrong was only wearing a thin shirt when we...' She fought off the image of his body on the cellar floor, pierced through.

'And a jacket for summer, *oui*, and this was not buttoned. But if a lady did this, she would have to have the...' He clenched his fists and curled his arms.

'Strength? Vigour? Determination?'

'All of these.'

'Then we definitely need to talk about Miss Clara Spark, because—'

Damboise held up a finger. 'But she is not the first name on your page, *mademoiselle*. To go along in order is good, I think.'

She shook her head. 'You and Clifford should work together.'

'And where is your loyal butler today?'

'Oh, just running some errands.' She omitted he was probably also somehow close by keeping a watchful eye on her at the same time.

Damboise gave her a disbelieving look. 'The first names on your page then, *mademoiselle*?'

'Floyd and Kitty Fitzwilliam. But I've hardly spoken to them. Even though I've spent a considerable time at the hotel they've rented and mingled with their guests, they've proved elusive.'

'Deliberately?'

She frowned. 'I don't think so. And I can't say I suspect them of anything concrete at the moment. They seem entirely caught up in partying. They definitely knew Armstrong quite well, though, but I haven't found out if they met him here or in America first. It can't have been Paris, as you told me this was his first trip to this country. All I know at the moment is that the Fitzwilliams are high on my list to ask a great deal more questions of.'

'*Bon*. Then I concentrate on other names. Now,' he said, nodding at her notebook, 'we come to Mademoiselle Spark. I checked with the staff at the Hotel Le Blanc that the film company booked for the actors. The maid remembered that she saw Mademoiselle Spark's car in the car park of the hotel at half past two in the afternoon on the day Monsieur Armstrong disappeared.'

'And was it there before then?'

He pulled a face. 'Nobody looked. But also nobody saw Mademoiselle Spark at the front desk. Maybe because the lady has a key to the doors on the terrace at the back.'

'Isn't that odd?'

'*Non*. Monsieur Armstrong, he has the same. It is normal, I am told, for the big stars to have a way to get in without seeing a crowd or the men from the newspaper.'

'Fair enough. But you said her car was seen at two thirty and Armstrong left the film lot just before twelve thirty. Mmm. So, she could just about have had enough time to follow Armstrong to my villa, kill him, and return to her hotel.' She wrinkled her nose. 'She would have been in a bit of a mess, though, surely? You can't run a man through with a sabre without getting some of the poor chap's vital fluids all over you, can you?' She shuddered.

He shrugged. 'If you are an expert with such a weapon, perhaps. But this is a good point.' He made a note. 'And for this and other things I will return to the Hotel Le Blanc to learn the chittle-chattle from the staff.'

She hid a smile at his expression. 'I agree it's worthwhile to see if anyone overheard anything between Armstrong and Clara Spark.'

'Yes. Maybe even at night when they shared the bed, perhaps?'

Eleanor's wine spluttered up her nose.

Damboise offered her a napkin. '*Excusez-moi, mademoiselle*. I think in France we are more open to talk of these things.' He looked over his shoulder. 'And Monsieur Clifford is not here to tell me off for speaking thus to his mistress.'

'Just as well,' she muttered. 'Anyway, I was told, despite them apparently having a relationship, that there was no love lost between them. So I reckon it must have been a very stormy one. I heard a rumour that Armstrong threw Clara over in a very ungentlemanly fashion. And that he might have been courting at least one of the dancers while still with her.'

Damboise looked at her quizzically and mimed hurling someone over his shoulder.

She laughed. 'No. To "throw someone over" means to end a relationship.'

'Ah, *merci*! So Mademoiselle Spark had reason to wish Monsieur Armstrong ill, it seems.' He made another note. 'Next you have...' – he peered at her notebook – 'Monsieur Truss?'

'Yes. Herman Truss. The director.'

Damboise nodded as he topped up their wine. Eleanor shook her head, smiling.

'A word of friendly advice, Inspector. Never come to England with the intention of working as a policeman. I think it might be a horrible surprise. Definitely no wine on duty and no hour for lunch.'

He frowned. 'Then how do the English inspectors live a life that is worth getting out of bed for?'

She thought of Hugh, with his two pieces of toast and morsel of cheese that usually made up his lunch when he was lucky enough to snatch even ten minutes. 'I've genuinely no idea. Now, back to Mr Truss. What have you learned about his alibi?'

'Well, if you remember he said he stayed for about an hour after Monsieur Armstrong left so angry from the film set? Then he went out looking for his star actor. He went first to the hotel but no Monsieur Armstrong. Then he gave up looking and returned to Chateau Beautour at fifteen minutes before four o'clock. I checked this alibi and the security guard at the chateau confirmed the last part.'

'But Truss would still have had time to follow Chester to my villa, kill him and get back to the film set.'

'*Absolument!* More time than Miss Spark. Time enough to change his clothes if they had blood on. And take a bath.'

'And I was told by Brockman, the assistant director, that Truss never wanted Armstrong in his picture. Truss swore one way or the other this would be the last time he worked with him.'

'So Monsieur Truss has also, perhaps, reason to wish Monsieur Armstrong ill.'

She nodded. 'Absolutely. Moving on, I've got a new name. Walter Tuttle. I haven't had a chance to add him to my list of suspects since I only spoke to him properly just before I came to meet you.'

'Ah! This name I have also. One moment, please.' Damboise licked the blunt end of his pencil and used it to turn his note-book pages. 'Here it is. He is one I questioned, too.'

'Did you single him out specially? I mean, did something make you suspicious about him?'

'*Non*. I talk to as many people as I can on the film set without waking up their suspicions. Monsieur Tuttle was merely one of them.'

'And what did he say?'

'He told me, when Monsieur Armstrong left, the scenes he is in were cancelled. So he took the car and drove around.'

She took a sip of her coffee that had arrived a few moments before. It was smooth and creamy. And hot. As she blew on it, her brow furrowed.

'You know, I would have thought only the lead actors would get their own car?'

Damboise took a large sip of his coffee. *The roof of his mouth must be made of asbestos, Ellie.*

'You are right. Only the lead actors have their own car. There is one car for the other actors, but they must share. But it seems Monsieur Tuttle took it this day without asking. The assistant director was not happy.' Damboise clucked his tongue. 'But I still have to learn if Monsieur Tuttle's story that he stopped for coffee in a café is true.'

'What café?'

'He told me he does not remember. So my men are asking at them all in the area, but there are many.'

She nodded. 'Good idea, because I believe he is hopelessly in love with Clara Spark and hated Armstrong for, as he saw it, treating her appallingly. And he was jealous of Armstrong's success.'

'Then, along with Mademoiselle Spark and Monsieur Truss, he is indeed someone with a wish to do Monsieur Armstrong ill.'

'Exactly! So, we have motives for three of those on our list – Clara Spark, Truss and Tuttle. The Fitzwilliams we must investigate further.'

He glanced over at her notebook. 'I think that is all the names, *non*?'

She shook her head. 'There's another new name for you. Rudolph Perry.'

Damboise took a piece of blue from the cheeseboard that had come with the coffee. 'This name I do not have.'

'You wouldn't. He only arrived yesterday, apparently. He's Armstrong's replacement.'

'But if he just arrived in France, he cannot be the man guilty of the murder?'

'No. But he still might be the *reason* Armstrong was murdered.'

'*Bravo, mademoiselle*, there is that possibility.'

'And I think you need to check how he arrived in France. He seemed to get here awfully quickly.'

He nodded and made a note. 'You have been good help today with the information you tell me.' He eyed her sideways. 'But maybe not so much with what you do not tell me?'

'Likewise, Inspector. But why would I keep anything from you? I'm only spending what was supposed to be a relaxing holiday embroiled in your murder investigation so my butler stays out of your jail. Remember?' She arched an eyebrow.

'I do.'

'Well then.' She folded her napkin and offered her hand. 'Thank you for my delightful lunch and the chance to meet Christian. If you will excuse me, I'm expected on a yacht, hopefully to meet this Rudolph Perry and some of the names on our list, all too shortly.'

And I need time to work out exactly what game you and Mayor Lessard are playing, Inspector Damboise!

21

It had seemed like a justifiable white lie when Eleanor told Damboise she was due on the Fitzwilliams' yacht shortly, because her intuition had urged her to cut the conversation short. But now, she really was expected.

'And expected seventeen minutes ago.' Clifford tutted as he slowed the car to a stop at the tropically landscaped entrance to the marina. He nodded in thanks as a wiry man darted out of his white-painted hut to haul up the barrier.

Eleanor ran a hand over her wide-legged emerald silk trousers, which matched her beaded capped-sleeve blouse. 'I confess, I might have taken longer than intended choosing a suitable outfit.' They passed under the barrier and drove along the waterfront. 'Honestly, though, it took me ages since all my previous times afloat were largely on sailboats, not luxury yachts. And it was spent in comfortable togs you could haul ropes in or hang over the side wearing.' She glanced at his impeccable black suit. 'Hmm, "scruffy-wear", I believe you would have called it. That's assuming, of course, you could pronounce that whilst sniffing disapprovingly.'

'I doubt it, my lady.' He stopped the car and gestured through the windscreen. 'She is an exceptionally fine craft.'

'Gracious! She must be a hundred and sixty footer,' Eleanor breathed.

Resplendent in ivory paint with a forest of polished handrails, mid and aft masts, the two upper decks of the yacht were strung with blue and white lights, darkness already having begun to fall. The first deck was a long, enclosed run of sumptuously appointed wood, velvet and brass, the second a partially covered seating area for at least forty. A warm yellow glow shone out of each of the portholes of the below decks.

At the top of the central gangway, Eleanor reflected that she didn't seem to be half as late for the boat's departure as she was for the partying. The whole scene was one of shimmering outfits, swaying lights and swinging music. She also wasn't the last to arrive, as her sharp hearing quickly discovered.

'You know how these actor types love to make an entrance, Kitten.' Floyd's unmistakable voice floated up through an elongated hatch that gave access to a swirling wood staircase. 'So we can't chug off just yet. Besides, what's the hurry? We can all party swell enough tied up in this boat park.'

Eleanor dropped to her haunches, tipping the contents of her handbag onto the floor in case she was discovered. She could see the back of Kitty's dark-haired head bobbing as she spoke. Her tone was surprisingly sharp.

'It's called a marina, Floyd. And we're not actually here to party, remember!'

Eleanor ducked her head. This was no time to be caught eavesdropping.

'Come on, Kitten,' Floyd pleaded. 'The plan's going just great. But because of the hiccup with Armstrong, we gotta play along a little more. I—' He raised his voice. 'Hey, look, honey, there's the king and queen of partying.'

'Darlings!' Kitty called out brightly. 'It would have been a waste of champagne if you hadn't made it.'

Eleanor held her breath until their voices faded, absorbed by the hubbub of syncopated jazz and raucous laughter. Scrabbling for her scattered things, she rammed them back into her handbag and hurried up the staircase to the next deck. Hearing Armstrong's death described as a mere 'hiccup' was disturbing.

As she worked out her next move, a series of smart waiters in white jackets approached the guests, each bearing a tray of drinks. She took a champagne flute, shaking her head at the other offerings.

A quick scan of the luxurious cream leather seating identified a raft of familiar faces from the film set, including the dancing girls from the beach. Their daringly short sequined skirts showed off their long, toned legs to maximum effect, if the admiring glances of the male guests were anything to go by.

At the furthest end, she spotted several of the artists she'd also met before. And sitting further along with two other actors she'd seen on the set was Walter Tuttle. From their blank faces, his companions had either already over-indulged or Tuttle had buttonholed them and bored them witless with his complaining. She turned her head to hear him better.

'Well, here we go. Another round of being overlooked the minute our illustrious director's preferred choice of leading man hits the set tomorrow. Trust Herman to get him scurrying over at the drop of his sun visor!'

Her ears pricked up. *Preferred choice? So Truss had really wanted this Rudolph Perry as the lead man all along, not Armstrong?*

Someone bumped into her.

'Oh, heck, sorry.'

'No harm done, Daniel.' She took in the assistant director's flushed face and anxious look. 'You're doing a remarkable job of a most unenviable task.' She indicated the actors partying around them. 'I'd be hopeless at keeping this lot in any sort of order.'

He grimaced. 'And you'd call this any kind of order?'

'Well, they're still all conscious... for the moment.' She grabbed a champagne flute from a passing waiter and held it out to him. 'How's your boss?'

His cheeks flushed. 'Herman's up one minute.' He raised his hand above his head. 'I mean way up here. And not because he's had any extra artificial help, like this lot.'

'Perhaps when he secured Mr Perry to take over as Napoleon, for example?'

'Right. You should have heard him whooping and hollering. And then only two hours later' – he dropped his hand – 'he's dragging himself round like his boots are made of concrete.'

'But he hasn't told you why?'

He shook his head. 'Even when I started out as a movie-set runner for him five years back, he took something of a shine to me and shared about lots of things. But he's been real cagey about whatever's eating him this time.' He checked his watch. 'Sorry, I better go find him. With Mr Perry being so late, Herman's probably had a sackload of kittens already.'

'See you later, Daniel.' Eleanor smiled as she waved him off. Alone, she resolved to grab the Fitzwilliams before the new leading man joined the party, concluding she'd never get a look in after that.

'Pretty, but I liked the bathing suit more,' a jovial voice said in her ear.

She spun around to see the pirate – no longer dressed as such – from the Fitzwilliams' party who'd tried to entice her to a late-night swim in the fountain. She pretended to look him over.

'And I preferred the pirate costume.'

He bowed. 'For you, I would wear it every day and sail the high seas forever a'plundering and a'thieving to shower you with stolen goodies.'

She laughed. 'You know, that's a tempting offer.'

'Good! Now, come listen to me blowing my trombone with the band downstairs fit to blast this boat right outta the water.' He held out his hand and led her over to the stairs.

They joined the other musicians on the lower deck, Eleanor wincing at the volume and furious tempo being belted out. She spotted Clara Spark leaning against the boat's polished handrail. The woman threw her an icy glare.

What on earth is her problem? She can have any man on this yacht she wants. She can't be huffy that a mere trombonist is keen on you, surely?

Before Eleanor could approach her, Floyd stepped into her vision.

'Hey, Eleanor, honey.' He raised his voice over the noise of the band. 'How's the party working out for ya?'

'Great.' She tilted her head over at her musician companion who had now joined his band. 'I've scored an unshakable admirer already.'

'Lucky you. He's a great guy.'

'This is a beautiful yacht. Is it yours or rented?'

'Well, you might say it's a bit of both.'

'Ah!' Eleanor nodded sagely. 'A new business venture? More fun than stuffy board meetings and forever scrutinising share prices, I bet. Banking must seem quite the straightjacket for a man who loves to throw a great party night after night. Have you moved out of the financial world altogether into something else?'

Floyd stared at her for a second. 'Everyone alive has financial interests, Eleanor. You can't spend if you ain't earning!'

Kitty slid under his arm to lean against his chest as Clara Spark walked away. He kissed her forehead.

'France is just the best place, Eleanor darling,' Kitty purred. 'Art, fashion, music. I mean, it's like being nestled in the cradle of culture, don't you find?'

Eleanor tried hard to hide her double disappointment at her conversation with Floyd being cut short and losing her quarry in Clara Spark. This was happening too often.

'Honestly, I don't know. I've only really been here as a nurse during the war. But I'm eager to learn more.'

Floyd tipped up Kitty's face. 'Say, Kitten, this lady's getting more interesting by the minute. Nurse, adventurer *and* party girl.' He laughed. 'She's a crazy cat.'

Eleanor hesitated. 'Speaking of parties, is that how you knew Chester Armstrong?'

Kitty nodded. 'He came to one of our hoedowns back in the US and then sort of became a regular.'

'Oh, so an old friend from the States? I thought you'd only just met out here. It must have been a funny coincidence to bump into him again. I love coincidences.'

'He wasn't an old friend, exactly.' Kitty sounded guarded. 'Just someone we knew from our parties back home, like I said.'

'Yeah, all the great folk came to them.' Floyd raised his drink. 'They were legendary!'

'I can imagine. So how did you find out he was here filming?' Eleanor said.

He frowned. 'What? Oh, we were driving on out past that chateau whatever-it's-called. Saw the cameras being lugged inside and asked the hulk of a security guard what was going on.'

Kitty nodded. 'And we told him to tell the director that the entire crew simply had to come to our next party. Which they did.'

'And Chester Armstrong just happened to be among them?'

'That's right, honey. Who doesn't love an unexpected reunion, right?' Floyd scooped three tumblers filled with triple measures of amber liquid from the hovering waiter's tray. 'We'd better get back to guest duties now Rudolph's arrived, Kitty.

Captain's probably going to raise anchor and sail us all off into the deep blue.'

Eleanor put a hand on each of their arms. 'Well, friend or not, I still want to offer you both my condolences for Chester Armstrong having passed away.' She watched their reactions closely. 'It's particularly hard when it's someone close in age, don't you think?'

'Life isn't forever,' Kitty said distractedly. 'Excuse us, won't you? We have to welcome our newest guest.'

Without a backward glance, they left, swallowed up in the stream of people now coming up from the bottom deck.

'Your rouge, *mademoiselle*.'

'Excuse me?' Eleanor turned around.

The French artist from the beach who had been entranced by the tapering shell on the sand was holding out her compact case.

'Oh, thank you. I must have missed it when I dropped my bag.' *I didn't notice him around when I was eavesdropping on Floyd and Kitty.* 'How are you enjoying the party... erm, I'm so sorry, I've forgotten your name?'

'It is Augustine. And I am not enjoying the party. I came here only to further my art, not to drink and dance away my problems with my supposed new friends.'

She watched him go. 'I think selling paintings, like everything else, might just have a lot to do with getting to know new friends,' she murmured.

Eleanor worked her way through the heaving mass of people now partying as if tomorrow had indeed been cancelled, before giving up in frustration. Rudolph Perry, the much-awaited new star of the film, was definitely on board somewhere. Everyone was talking about him and the fact that they'd just met him, but evidently, he was precisely wherever she wasn't. She leaned on the starboard handrail and took in the view. The yacht had sailed out of the harbour, the twinkling lights of Nice receding, and was making its stately progress along the coast. Ahead, in the moonlight, she could make out the looming foothills of the Maritime Alps and what had to be the beginnings of Monte Carlo's own twinkling lights.

Half an hour later, she groaned as she recognised the telltale feel of a boat slowing down and turning to motor into dock.

There goes your last chance to talk to Armstrong's replacement!

Then to her surprise, Kitty appeared, minus Floyd, but with a rakishly good-looking dark-haired man clamped to her arm instead. There was no disputing charisma was his middle name, the elite of suit makers his tailor. And, surely, Michelangelo must have been his sculptor, given those defined cheekbones.

'Rudolph, darling. This delicious creature is Lady Eleanor Swift.' She ran a finger down his form-fitting black velvet jacket. 'And Eleanor dear, this sublime work of art is Mr Rudolph Perry. I think you'll find each other quite fascinating.' She gave Eleanor a knowing smile and sauntered away.

Seemingly amused by his introduction, Perry's grey-green eyes, framed by dark lashes, sparkled as he took Eleanor's hand. His American twang was softer, more rounded than she'd heard before. 'How do you do, Miss Eleanor.' He ran his hand along his chiselled jaw. 'More to the point, how well do you play?'

She laughed. 'Well, that depends. What did you have in mind? Chess? Elephant polo? I should warn you, I've no patience for tennis and I decimated one golf course trying to master the game.'

With a deep chuckle, he looped her arm through his. 'None of those, although I'd love to see you on an elephant! We're going to play the casino tables. Watch out Monte Carlo,' he called to the approaching town. 'Rudolph's got Lady Luck on his arm and we're coming in hot!'

22

As the Fitzwilliams' yacht docked in Monte Carlo, it didn't surprise Eleanor to find her butler waiting on the quay with the car. What did surprise her was the selection of her favourite evening gowns laid out on the back seat.

She arranged to meet Perry later at the casino and slid into the car. 'Clifford, you total wizard. How did you know I'd need these?'

'Information courtesy of the harbour master, my lady. He informed me that the Fitzwilliams and their guests always gamble at the famous Monte Carlo Casino when they dock here.'

'Once you'd loosened his tongue with a bottle of something, no doubt.'

'Tsk! Not at all.' He turned right onto the main road. 'It took two bottles.'

'So you kindly detoured via Villa Marbaise to make sure I had everything?'

'Indeed. You also have a hotel room booked opposite the casino and an overnight case packed by Mrs Butters.'

'Thank you,' she said with heartfelt appreciation. Turning

in her seat, she surveyed the selection of gowns and laughed. 'But now I've got more dashed wardrobe choices to make!'

Perry whistled appreciatively as she appeared an hour later beside his elbow at the mosaic-tiled bar of the casino. 'Well, will you look at you? Lady Luck head to toe in red silk. Stand back, these tables are going to crumble!'

Keen though she was to question the indisputably attractive actor about how well he knew Armstrong and Truss, she had to admit the casino itself was even more eye-catching than his film-star looks.

The building's cream stone exterior rose as elegantly as an Italian Renaissance palace married to a French belle époque chateau. Inside it was a symphony of polished glass, marble columns, gold relief, and oil paintings. The ceiling itself was more akin to a baroque palace than a gambling house, she thought. Dominating most of the rooms were the baize-topped gaming tables, surrounded by men in black evening jackets and women in shimmering gowns, bedecked with glittering jewellery.

Perry called her attention back by taking her arm in his.

'This way.' He teased the beaded fringing of her red velvet handbag. 'I sure hope you got your magic wand in this tiny purse here. What is it? Collapsible?'

Eleanor laughed. Perry was proving to be entertaining company. And as he couldn't have actually murdered Armstrong – as he wasn't even in the country at the time – she felt herself relaxing. 'I think you're mixing up luck and witch-craft, Mr Perry.'

'No problem there.' He scanned the room. 'I'll take both. But, please, let's go with Rudolph.'

'So, what's your preferred game?' she asked as he led her past each of the twelve artfully arranged baize-topped tables.

'Roulette. You have a greater chance of winning as you can place bets in different ways. And I like winning!'

She laughed awkwardly. Something about the intense look in his eyes when he said this unsettled her. However, not wanting to admit that she had no idea what roulette comprised except a revolving wheel, chance and something to do with red and black, she simply nodded. He led her into a side room, which was an oasis of azure-blue velvet and gold upholstery, and gilt chandeliers. She slid into the seat the white-jacketed attendant held out for her and crossed her fingers under the table. Not so much in the hope she'd bring Perry good luck, more that, as a total novice, she didn't commit some faux pas.

However, forty minutes later, her companion was fit to burst his fine-tailored shirt buttons as he whooped at the tottering pile of gaming chips he had amassed. The croupier halted proceedings and called for a new ball. Perry turned to Eleanor with his eyes shining.

'Thank you, Lady Luck!'

Again, the fanatical look in his eyes put her on edge. She shook her head. 'I'm not certain I've played any hand in your good fortune.'

'You sure have.' His wide-eyed look diminished. 'But say, sorry, where are my manners? Please, do take a break. But dinner later, if you could bear to? I'd like to say thank you.'

She agreed to meet him at the bar in an hour and stood up to leave.

'Catch you later,' he called. 'Wish me luck.' He turned back to the table.

Ducking into the ladies' powder room, she stared at her reflection in the gold-framed mirror, then reached into her bag for her compact. But her hand closed around an unexpected bundle of French banknotes, meticulously aligned with the director general's signature on the right and bound with a soft leather clasp. Tucked under the binding was a folded card. She smiled at Clifford's meticulous copperplate handwriting as she unfolded the note.

'Almost all life depends on probabilities.' ~ Voltaire

Below, he had added each of what she assumed were the five main games of the casino, the basics of how to play and the odds. Tapping the last entry, she spoke to her reflection. 'Hmm, that looks like our kind of fun!'

She bought some gaming chips and sat down at the quietest horseshoe-shaped table in the furthest salon. The dealer nodded to her.

'*Trente et Quarante*. Thirty and forty or "red and black", as *mademoiselle* may know it, is in play. Closest to thirty, wins.'

She nodded back, blew on her fingers and placed her first chip.

Half an hour later Perry rejoined her, the look on his face telling its own tale.

'Oh, gracious, Rudolph! You finished early? Lady Luck's aura didn't work as well as you hoped in the end?'

He shrugged, but his jaw pulsed. 'I should have kept her by my side.' He rubbed his hands over his cheeks. 'Hey, life's a game, right? And tonight, the tables gave me a sharp reminder we don't always win.' His tone darkened. 'No matter how much we think we've fixed the odds.'

His last comment gave her an unsettled feeling. She'd seen when people became addicted to gambling and he was displaying all the signs. Keen not to show her discomfort, she held her hands up with a wince. 'Then I owe you an apology. Because whatever luck or otherwise I might have somehow attracted tonight, I seem to have taken it with me when I left you.' She gestured to the modest pile of chips she'd amassed.

He grinned. 'Good for you. Long as one of us won. Now, what say we eat?'

. . .

The opulent dining room had the most exquisitely frescoed Renaissance ceiling Eleanor had ever seen. She stopped staring upwards to admire each table's sparkling teardrop chandelier and centrepiece of pink and crimson roses surrounded by artful swirls of petals. Each place was set with an array of shimmering gold-rimmed champagne flutes and wine glasses. She slid into the ivory silk-upholstered chair the waiter held for her, her stomach rumbling loudly at the first three items alone on the gold-lettered menu.

Perry chuckled. 'I don't know what I expected, but can I say without offending you, you are the epitome of the unexpected?'

She smiled. 'You can.'

He raised his glass. 'To being who we really are.'

Intrigued, she sipped her champagne. 'Is it hard to remember who you are, Rudolph? Being a famous actor, I mean, you must always be playing a part? If that isn't prying?'

He slammed his glass down with such force it made her jump. 'I'm fed up to the back teeth with people prying! Newspapers, well-wishers, agents!' He cleared his throat. 'I'm sorry. Look, I don't mind you asking. That feels like a genuine question. So, yes, it gets hellish hard to remember.' His brows knitted, then smoothed as an immaculately uniformed waiter appeared. He looked at Eleanor. 'May I?'

'Oh, with pleasure. I've reached the point of ruling out nothing and thinking I'll devour two of everything.'

She watched with quiet interest as Perry grilled the waiter on a few of the options before giving their order in more than passable French.

When they were alone again, she tilted her head, trying to sound as nonchalant as possible. 'I didn't realise you were a regular to this country, Rudolph?'

He blinked. 'Say what?'

'I didn't realise you'd been to France before.'

'Heck, no. This is my first ever trip here. But, well, you know how it is. Fancy restaurants springing up everywhere back home in the US. Delonidas, for example. Oh, you should see the French food they conjure up. Pure ambrosia with a ripe cherry on top. It's kind of the done thing to master the lingo to order.' He shrugged. 'It's part of the fun.'

'Well, how handy for me. Thank you.' She decided it was time to jump in. Or tiptoe in, as Clifford had insisted on reminding her she needed to. 'Are you ready for your new role, then? Suddenly being called to play Napoleon out of the blue would have thrown some actors, I would have thought. Even experienced ones of your calibre.'

He scanned her face intently, but then relaxed again. 'Hollywood is ruthless, I can assure you. There's no sympathy for the guy who can't make the grade at the drop of a hat. Be that a cowboy's Stetson, an emperor's turban or that flattened cow-horn affair Napoleon had a thing for.'

Eleanor laughed. 'It's called a bicorne, in case it's helpful.'

'No. But thanks all the same.' He frowned. 'A titled lady who's a history buff in her spare time?'

'No, just a girl who was privileged enough to inherit a title and a wonderful butler who devours historical details like I do sausages.'

'*Bon appétit.*' The waiter placed her plate of grilled lobster in front of her with a bemused look.

She tucked in. 'So, have you had to drop another picture to be in this one?'

Perry waved his hand casually. 'Oh, just some rescheduling, that's all.'

'But what about the first film's schedule? I've seen how difficult even one film can be to timetable.'

'You have, huh?' He hesitated, taking a mouthful of his

lobster. 'Alright, in truth, I'd promised myself a break. But, hey, I couldn't leave old Herman in a bind.'

'So you've worked with him before? That's got to make it easier to slide in late in the filming then?'

'What? Yes, yes, Herman's a brilliant director. Makes it easier for sure.' He seemed to anticipate her next question. 'That's how I could take up the role so quickly. Herman already knew I could step into the part, having worked with me before, and I...' He hesitated. 'I was already in Europe.'

'Really?' *This is news!*

'Yeah. When... when I decided I needed a break from filming, I thought, why not take it in Europe? Get away from all those prying eyes.'

'Ah! I see. So when Mr Truss called you, you were...'

'In Switzerland.'

She recognised it was time for a new tack. 'My lobster's fabulous. I don't know if Napoleon had a penchant for it,' – she waved a claw – 'but here's to your success in delighting audiences in his flattened cow-horn hat.'

He laughed and clinked her claw with his glass.

'Goodness, though, Rudolph, I've just thought. How is Truss going to fit in getting your costumes in time? Won't they have to be made to measure?'

He shook his head. 'Chester Armstrong and me aren't... *weren't* so dissimilar. With a bit of nip and tuck, his'll fit me fine.'

'You sound very confident. You must have known him well.' She observed his reaction. 'Rudolph, I'm sorry, I should have offered my condolences.'

'What? No. But, thanks. Sure, we ended up in a couple of pictures together. With Chester always being the bigger name, of course.' He took a glug of his wine. 'Which was fine, you know. He was a reasonable-enough guy to play second fiddle to.'

Snapping his fingers at the waiter, he held Eleanor's stare. 'Now, that's way too much about me. Your turn.'

An hour later, Perry escorted her down the casino steps and handed her over to her waiting butler.

'Goodnight, Lady Luck. Thank you for an evening that, unpredictably, was as engaging outside of the gaming tables as at them. Goodnight and I hope to see you again.'

'At one of the Fitzwilliams' parties?'

'Maybe.'

She flopped into the car and waited for Clifford to come round and slide into the driver's seat.

'Thank you for furnishing me with the perfect casino kit, Clifford. As well as waiting so patiently. It must be gone midnight.'

'It is, in fact, five and ten past two in the morning, my lady. But,' he continued, holding up a gloved finger as she went to apologise, 'breakfast in your hotel will not be served for four hours hence. So, let's go work up an appetite!'

Like the rest of the village, Avenue des Toits Rouges was deep in slumber, disinterested in two shadowy figures around the back of the letting and sales agency. Eleanor watched as Clifford worked his picklocks on the door of the office. A moment later, he put his gloved finger to his lips and pushed it open. They both grimaced.

'Oh, the smell!' she whispered. 'He should have left a window open a crack if he intended to be away until September. Or at least asked someone to come in and air the place. He must have forgotten to wash his lunch dishes.'

Clifford shook his head. 'My lady, I suggest you wait—'

'No. We need to search his office together to be in and out quickly. We've both seen too much of Damboise's wretched police station to get arrested for breaking and entering now. Even if it is on his behalf.'

But Clifford's frown only deepened as he stepped over the threshold and clicked on his slim pocket torch. 'My lady, if I could insist, something doesn't feel— Out! NOW!'

She jumped as he grabbed her by the shoulders and spun her round. 'What is it?'

'Regrettably, my lady,' he said as he propelled her back outside and checked the door had locked behind them before hurrying her to the car, 'I fear we are both about to take another visit to Inspector Damboise's "wretched police station!"'

23

Eleanor glanced at the clock on the bare whitewashed wall of the police station's interview room. Half past five. She groaned.

'This is a disaster!' She tugged on Clifford's jacket sleeve as he passed her, pacing the room. 'Why did you insist we couldn't simply run away and pretend we hadn't found poor Monsieur… Whatever his name is?'

'Monsieur Thibaud.'

'Him. By waking the café owner and asking where the nearest telephone was and then calling Damboise, we've merely fuelled speculation about you being involved in all this… hideousness.' She slumped back in her chair.

'My lady, neither of us would have slept or been proud of our actions if we had not done so. As I know you know in your heart.' He lowered his voice. 'And, neither would we have deceived the inspector when he found out Monsieur Thibaud had been killed! He would instantly have come knocking on the front door of your villa at Mayor Lessard's instruction.'

'You mean I wouldn't have fooled him.' She raised her hand. 'No, don't refute it. You are impossible to read, even for a man as experienced as Damboise. But my face is hopeless.' She peered at him in concern. 'Especially when something matters so much. And, sorry, Clifford. I didn't mean to be testy. Of course we had to do the right thing.'

He waved away the apology. 'Might I suggest we profit from the inspector's temporary absence by working through what you found out yesterday?'

She sat up straighter. 'You're right again. The only answer to this mess is to find Armstrong's killer. Okay, give me a moment to marshal my thoughts.' She thought hard. 'So, first off, Floyd and Kitty Fitzwilliam. On the yacht I overheard Floyd say Armstrong's death was just a "hiccup" in their plans and they needed to "play along a little longer". Rather callous, don't you think?'

'And interesting.' Clifford's brow furrowed. 'My lady, have you noted a change in either of the Fitzwilliams' behaviours at each of the festivities you have attended, as the, ahem, accompanying substances have proliferated?'

'No, but you've put your finger on it. They appeared to join in with all of that, just as hard as their guests did the first night I was at one of their parties. Yet in the morning at the hotel—'

'They were entirely unaffected, unlike all the other guests?'

'Yes! You saw that too?'

'I did, my lady.'

'But what does all that tell us?'

'That, as you told me one of their guests had noted, Mr Fitzwilliam is not the clown he purports to be.' He tapped his chin. 'They are using their parties partially as a front, I feel.' He paced the room again. 'Which means they are up to something. And as they surround themselves with artists, it would be logical to assume that is something to do with that – film making, painting, music and so on. And that "something" also involved Mr Armstrong. But that doesn't mean they necessarily murdered him.'

'You're right. Once we get out of here, we need to dig

deeper into the Fitzwilliams and whatever plan of theirs Armstrong's death caused to "hiccup". I imagine we don't have much time before Damboise arrives, so moving on. Rudolph Perry?'

At his nod, she gathered her thoughts.

'Well, he told me Chester had been "reasonable enough" to work with. But he did seem to be trying a little too hard to convince me he hadn't minded playing second billing to him. He was also rather nonchalant about taking over as Napoleon.'

'However, he is a seasoned actor, my lady. And a notably successful one, as you pointed out. What of his activities prior to arriving in France, though? Did he have to reschedule his workload, for example?'

'That's what he wanted me to believe at first. But then he confessed he'd promised himself a break. And it seems he took it in Europe.'

Clifford raised an eyebrow. 'Which would explain—'

'How he was able to step into the vacant role so quickly.' She wrinkled her nose. 'Given how desperate he was to throw himself at the mercy of roulette, though, I'd say he's struggling with something.'

'Hmm. An enforced break, rather than a chosen one, perchance?'

'That's my feeling. Dash it! I'm even more confused about any connection between Perry and Armstrong's death now. Even if there is one, he can't have murdered Armstrong. Although, he could have murdered our poor villa agent, Marcel Thibaud, if he had been murdered, which he wasn't.'

Clifford's silence made her shiver. 'Look, Clifford. Stop protecting me from whatever it is you know. There's no time. Damboise will be here any minute.'

He shook his head. 'If only I had never suggested you come here. My abject apologies.'

Rising to step around into his eyeline, she said gently, 'I'm the one who jumped at the suggestion. We're in this together. So, please?'

'My lady.' He swallowed hard. 'Monsieur Thibaud did not die of natural causes, as you supposed. He was murdered by being run through with a... a Napoleonic sabre.'

Her mouth fell open. 'Oh, gracious! Exactly like Chester Armstrong!' She stared at him, her hand flying to her chest. 'It's the villa, isn't it? That has to be the key somehow.'

'My conclusion also.'

She clutched at straws. 'Is there a chance Armstrong was murdered elsewhere, though, and taken to the villa, do you suppose?'

'A slim one. However, if you recall, Inspector Damboise made it clear he believes the opposite.' He set off on another round of pacing the room. 'But perhaps that explains Monsieur Thibaud's murder? He might have gone to the villa at just the wrong moment and seen something that then got him killed to ensure his silence.'

'True. But why, then, didn't he just go straight to the police with what he'd seen?'

Clifford's hand strayed to his neck. 'Perhaps he didn't have time before he was killed? Or he was reluctant to do so? Perhaps the American visitors and ourselves are not the only ones who do not wish to be involved with the French authorities?'

She nodded fervently. 'I can understand that! But chin up, Clifford. Look, now we know the unfortunate odour at the office wasn't off food, perhaps Thibaud had been murdered long before Armstrong? In which case, at least Perry couldn't have murdered him either.' She frowned. 'I mean, Thibaud's body could have been there for ages.'

'Possibly. Possibly not. Unfortunately, Monsieur Thibaud's office does not benefit from the naturally cooling effect of being hewn out of rock, as your wine cellar does. So, dead matter... deteriorates more quickly, as it were.'

She wrinkled her nose. 'Enough said. We'll have to wait for Damboise's findings.' She sighed. 'At least it now seems likely the same person who murdered Armstrong murdered Thibaud. I cannot imagine there are two madmen loose in this area running people through with sabres! Ah! The murderer had access to a supply of sabres. Therefore, it *has* to be someone on the film set!'

'I think so too, *mademoiselle*,' Damboise said gravely from the door.

'Inspector!' Eleanor strode to him. 'Why haven't you told me the truth about the villa I've rented? I believe you know something you've deliberately kept from me.'

'*Mademoiselle*, please.' His moustache quivered. 'I have a job to do.'

'And I have a wonderful butler and' – her heart faltered – 'a good friend to save.' She lowered her voice. 'But don't tell Clifford I called him that to you. He'll be horrified.'

'Of course, *mademoiselle*. But this wonderful butler of whom you speak? It is he who has found yet another body.' He stepped into the room and eyed Clifford dispassionately. 'And it is he who make the arrangements that you rent this very villa you now realise is a connection to the two dead men.'

Eleanor waved a hand at Clifford as he went to step forward.

'Inspector, despite what you say, I know you do not have a shred of belief he is in any way responsible.'

Damboise cocked an eye at her. 'I do not see how you make this statement with so much confidence, *mademoiselle*.'

'Yes, you do. Because you've made one fatal mistake in our dealings together.'

He shrugged. 'It is late in the early morning for puzzles. Please, save my curiosity and tell me.'

'You invited me into your home and introduced me to your adoring family.'

Damboise frowned in confusion.

She nodded. 'The man who lives in that delightfully loving home, the husband and papa, he knows exactly the difference between right and wrong. He unquestionably understands love and loyalty.' She held his gaze. 'And he knows doing any more of Mayor Lessard's bidding in this matter goes against every grain of his morality.'

Damboise opened his mouth, but then closed it without a word. He stood, eyeing her thoughtfully. Finally he sighed and dropped his gaze.

'One moment.' The door shut behind him.

Clifford stepped to Eleanor's side. They waited in silence.

Five or so minutes later, Damboise returned. 'Monsieur le maire is not skipping over the moon that I woke him at this hour, but I spoke with him and he allows that I explain everything to you.' For the first time since he'd appeared in the doorway, he smiled. 'So, to a proper French breakfast we go.' Gesturing to Clifford, he held his hands up in apologetic surrender. 'All together, my friend.'

24

Eleanor leaped at Damboise's suggestion they walk to wherever breakfast awaited, even though she was still in her red silk gown and satin heels, and exhausted after no sleep. She needed air to clear her head almost as much as her grumbling stomach needed food. But, mostly, she needed time to work out how to force Damboise to finally tell them everything. He'd telephoned Lessard, but that didn't mean he was going to come clean.

The sun's first rays had only just pierced the horizon as they walked down the police station's steps. The air was sharp, a faint band of indigo-lilac barely hinting at the searing golden glow and fierce August Riviera heat to follow.

Clifford slid off his wide grey scarf and handed it to her. 'Unconventional and inappropriate, but it will ward off the chill, my lady. Regrettably, my jacket would swamp you.'

Wrapping the scarf gratefully round her shoulders, she tied it like an opera shawl and followed Damboise across the deserted street and left onto a smaller road.

A few early risers stumbled out of narrow doors or wandered past with vacant eyes, rubbing their cheeks and yawning. The muffled rumble of a handcart on cobbles a few

streets away reminded her of the time she and Clifford had
pushed a similar cart desperately quietly down a backstreet. It
had been late evening in Little Buckford, the village where
Henley Hall resided. On the cart had been the man trying to
kidnap her, who Clifford had rendered unconscious moments
before. It had been almost a year and a half ago. A seminal
moment, it had persuaded her that her late uncle's butler was
not a killer, but the most loyal retainer and friend one could
ever want.

As Damboise turned one corner ahead of them, Eleanor
stopped abruptly, causing Clifford to run into her.

'Now,' she whispered, 'we need a plan before we
arrive at this breakfast place. How are we going to get
Damboise to tell us everything he knows about this investigation?'

'More emotional extortions on your part? The last one just
now in his office was masterful.'

'Thanks. But he's too quick for that to work again.'

'*Merci, mademoiselle*,' Damboise's disembodied voice
floated back from round the side of the building.

She shared an abashed look with Clifford. 'Dash it!' She
caught up with Damboise. 'Enough games, Inspector. It's
time to—'

He held up a hand, then smacked his lips. 'Smell the coffee?
Believe me, it is as good as the one your young maid gave to my
suit when I first come to your villa.'

In a small rear courtyard neatly stacked with boxes and crates,
Damboise gave a rat-a-tat knock on the blue-painted door. A
second later, it was thrown open and a head of tousled nut-
brown curls bobbed out.

'Christian!' Eleanor stared round her, then at Damboise. 'I
thought we were miles from your brother-in-law's restaurant.'

'*Mais, non. Bienvenue, mes amis.*' Christian smiled and clapped the inspector on the shoulders. '*Ça va, beau frère?*'

'*Oui, merci.*' Gesturing to Eleanor, Damboise added. 'But Christian, we speak in English only to make *mademoiselle* know she and I are the team. Not the enemies.'

Christian swept them all through the gleaming and tidy kitchen and out into a cosy corner at the front of the restaurant proper. 'Breakfast is for the special guests only, so for the English lady I bring...' He grinned at Eleanor. 'Lots!'

With Eleanor seated, Damboise took the place opposite her. He looked up at Clifford, standing his ever-respectful distance away. 'Monsieur Clifford, is this not important enough that you can allow yourself to at least sit with your mistress?'

Damboise glanced at Eleanor, who nodded.

'As you wish, my lady.'

Taking the end seat at the table, he perched rigidly on the edge, which drew a look of wonder from Damboise.

He leaned across and whispered to Eleanor, 'Is he always like this?'

'Always. After all,' – she smiled at her butler as she quoted the phrase he had admonished her with so many times – 'if we didn't have rules, where would we be?' She usually parried back with 'France!' and this clearly struck an amused chord with Clifford now as he looked away and busied himself adjusting the edge of the red-and-white-checked tablecloth.

'Ah, rules!' Damboise examined the point of his pencil. 'I break mine and talk of crime over breakfast. But I see rules were not what the mistress and her butler thought of when they stole into Marcel Thibaud's office in the middle of the night. And they think not of the law either! Perhaps it is fine in England, but here in France... *oh là là!*'

Eleanor fixed him with a scathing look. 'You hardly gave us any other choice since you have deliberately withheld pertinent information regarding Villa Marbaise. Armstrong was murdered there. And now the letting agent for the villa, Monsieur Thibaud, is also dead. Run through with a sabre in the precise same manner! Besides, if we hadn't broken in and discovered poor Thibaud had been murdered, you wouldn't be sitting here now about to finally be honest with us, would you?'

Damboise held up his pocket watch. 'No, *mademoiselle*. I would be asleep in my bed.'

'As would I! And as would Clifford, who waited for me until stupid o'clock this morning while I did your work for you. Not to mention that poor Monsieur Thibaud's body would still be undiscovered for who knows how long? So, enough games, jokes and stalling.'

Damboise looked back at her impassively.

She steeled her gaze. 'Inspector, you should know I was born with exceptionally little patience. And the little I was given had all but run out by the age of—'

'Nine, Inspector.' Clifford looked at Damboise. 'And it was really a very rare beast before that.'

Damboise sighed and held his hands up in surrender. 'Alright, *mademoiselle* and Monsieur Clifford. I agree that you have worked hard to help me. I will talk freely with you.'

They paused as Christian appeared bearing a tray. On it was orange juice, delectable smelling coffee, freshly baked croissants, a still-warm baguette, cheese, jam and a single scrambled egg in a small bowl, which he placed in front of Eleanor.

'Is good? Like English breakfast, yes?'

'It's perfect, Christian. Thank you.'

With the three of them alone again, Clifford automatically set to serving coffee, slicing the baguette and loading up a plate for Eleanor. Damboise watched him intently until he sat back in his seat once he had finished.

'*Mademoiselle*, the villa your butler arranged to rent for you is the house of a rich Frenchman of exceptional business.'

She frowned. 'I expected nothing less. It's exquisitely

furnished and equipped with every modern domestic invention. And with one of the best views I've ever seen. So, why the mystery?'

Taking a sip of his coffee, Damboise eyed her over the rim of his cup. 'This man, he perhaps makes his money in a manner that is not...' – he tapped his forehead – '*légitime*. How to say...'

'Legal?' Clifford said.

'Ah, *merci. Oui*. You hear of the mafia in Sicily? Well, it is to our dishonour, we have similar here also. But they are men of France.'

'And you're saying the man who owns my villa is one of them?' Eleanor asked incredulously. She looked at Clifford.

'Really, my lady, I had no idea when I—'

She waved his apology away. 'Don't be daft. You couldn't possibly have known. But that explains the reaction of the café owner opposite the agent's office.'

Damboise paused in spreading jam on a slice of croissant. 'All the people here know to stay away from Villa Marbaise, *mademoiselle*. And never to have dealing with this man. He is very rich. And powerful. He has many villas throughout France, perhaps Europe. Yours is just one of them.'

'And Monsieur Thibaud?'

'He came to my ears in the six months recently. Before, he was of no interest. But since the villa was bought, he looks after it and since then he has been on our list to watch.'

The news made her bristle. 'Which is how you knew I had rented the villa. And why you went to great lengths to find out all about me.'

'But failed to warn her ladyship she might be in danger,' Clifford growled.

'*Non!*' Damboise looked genuinely troubled. 'I had no suspicion that a murder would happen at the villa. How could Monsieur le maire or me know of this? Monsieur Armstrong had no business to be there that we can find out. Not then. And still not now.'

She rapped the table. 'Wait a minute! Then you found out about my having solved a few wretched murders and thought, what? That I might be useful to you?'

Clifford shook his head. 'But for her ladyship being present, I would demand you step outside, sir!'

Damboise looked confused for a moment, but then seemed to register what the expression meant. He looked at Eleanor. 'So now I have the telling off from your butler?'

'Yes. And with good cause, I think.'

He held up his hands. '*Mademoiselle*, look at it from the view of a police inspector. A foreign lady moved into the villa of a known criminal. Is it not expected that I would investigate that lady? And that I might have suspicions that maybe that lady is also, perhaps, not *légitime*? So, I do not tell her everything until I believe she is not connected with the crime world.' He shrugged in apology.

Eleanor pursed her lips. 'Well... I suppose I see your point, Inspector. But, tell us, why would this man let his villa if he is not "*légitime*" and, as you said, rich anyway? Because that makes no sense to me.'

Damboise nodded. 'And it doesn't to him either. So he does not. He wants nobody in his affairs. Monsieur Thibaud rented it out secretly and pocketed the money, I think.'

Eleanor gasped. 'I hate to criticise the poor chap as he's no longer with us but that sounds incredibly—'

'Stupid?' He nodded. 'Monsieur Thibaud is – *was* – more greedy than he was intelligent.'

She caught Clifford's eye. 'What is it?' She took another croissant, having devoured the first with her scrambled egg.

'The gentleman who I received the recommendation from is a most upright person, my lady. He is butler to Lord Danbury.

He would never have dealt with anyone engaged in unlawful activities.'

Damboise raised a finger. 'Ah! But the man who owns your villa is always too clever and powerful, unfortunately, for us to prosecute him. And Marcel Thibaud has committed no crimes, so to your friend, Mr Clifford, it seemed all is as it should be. But this still is not the answer to the riddle.'

'The riddle of who killed Monsieur Thibaud? And why?'

'*Exactement, mademoiselle!* I will send the body to have the autopsy and we will find out when precisely he died. And then we will learn who saw him last and when.'

'Will *we*?' Eleanor asked firmly.

'Yes, *mademoiselle. We* will. On my honour, I will tell you everything. From the' – he waved an apologetic hand over their breakfasts – 'condition of the body, though I believe the report will say he died the same day as Monsieur Armstrong.' He caught Clifford nodding and held up his hands. 'Never before have I thanked anyone for breaking the laws of my country, but it is good that you found Marcel Thibaud this morning, so, *merci*.' He cocked his head. 'However, Monsieur Clifford, my curiosity is hungry. How is it you know so easily to open the lock of such a door because—'

Eleanor put down her empty coffee cup sharply. 'Not now, Inspector. Let's move on. While you focus on the events around Monsieur Thibaud's murder, Clifford and I will work through the strongest suspects for Armstrong's again.'

Damboise nodded. 'It is good, but I have one more piece of news I think you are not going to like.'

'Go on.' Eleanor noted Clifford had stiffened.

'The sabre that killed Monsieur Thibaud had no fingerprints.'

'Same as the one that killed Armstrong.'

'Yes, *mademoiselle*. But I wished to be certain that all the sabres on the film set could do no more damage.' He shrugged.

'If it is from there the killer took his weapons, as we all believe, though we cannot be certain. But Monsieur le maire, he does not permit me to put them under lock and key at the police station.'

'Because it will interfere with the filming and upset the Americans?'

'*Oui, mademoiselle*. I demanded to the director, Monsieur Truss, that he must himself lock them up and count every sabre out. And count every one back in. Mr Truss agreed that his security will do so but he told me what I already know, that he do not know how many were in the crates to begin with.' Damboise spread his hands. 'It is the best I can offer.'

'It's alright,' Eleanor said, 'with Mayor Lessard on your back, we do understand your position isn't easy either.' She tried to ignore the sense of icy trepidation that was stopping her breakfast settle. 'All we can do then is hope that the two sabres that have been used to kill so far are the only ones missing.'

But what if they're not? What if the killer has another? And if so, whose name is on it?

25

Eleanor grabbed a few hours' sleep in the shade of a lawned area ringed with beds of oleander, late-flowering lavender, cascading hibiscus, giant succulents and soft-needled pines. When Clifford finally roused her gently, it was with a pot of strong coffee and the news from his call to Hotel d'Azur that the planned festivities began around midday and were a themed event.

She flopped back on her lounger with a wail. 'A costume party! Knowing how over the top that lot go, I won't recognise any one of our suspects. They'll all be wearing masks or a tagel, er...'

'Tagelmust, my lady? A turban and veil combined in one as worn by the Tuareg of—'

'Yes, that!'

'Possibly. The theme, however, is "The Arts". And, if you will forgive our collective presumption, the ladies set to work on your behalf while you were resting, given the time restraint.' His eyes twinkled mischievously.

. . .

An hour and a half later, despite the excellent buffet lunch and the relentless good-time spirit of the Fitzwilliams and their many guests, she was finding the charms of Hotel d'Azur rapidly waning. She'd also never felt so ridiculous in her life. Her staff had dressed her up in swathes of ivory satin and silk, with a flowing moss green voile cloak and a tiara of plaited olive sprigs. Clifford's assurances that she encapsulated the epitome of Botticelli's *Athena*, goddess of wisdom, failed to make her feel any less self-conscious.

She scanned the other guests, consoling herself that many of them looked equally ridiculous. A raft of scantily clad muses of the great masters proliferated among the women's costumes. Conversely, the men had opted for heroes – or villains – of book, play and film. A sea of King Lears, Hamlets and Scarlet Pimpernels partied among Buster Keatons and Harold Lloyds with a singular Oscar Wilde draped in women's furs.

Eleanor stopped studying the creative efforts on show and willed herself to concentrate. Her target once again was the capricious Clara Spark. The Fitzwilliams had vanished, so she had refocused on the leading lady. Even if she wasn't the killer, she might have some idea who it was. *You need to dig deeper, Ellie!*

The problem was Clara had, inadvertently or not, thwarted Eleanor's attempts to engage her in conversation. For the last hour she'd been dancing with a series of actors and musicians, leaving Eleanor with no chance to waylay her.

Now, however, she saw her opening. Standing on one of the scrollwork garden tables, Floyd had reappeared and was holding everyone's attention, especially the girls of the film's dance line. Mostly, she thought, on account of the shortness of his crimson Julius Caesar tunic, which rode up repeatedly, revealing his long, tanned legs. Kitty sat at his feet, every inch the perfect Cleopatra, laughing along at his many quips.

'Say, folks,' Floyd called out. 'What happened? Lobsters got your legs? Because someone said this was a party, right?'

'YEAH!' the garden bellowed back.

'Well then, someone give the band a barrel of drinking juice and fire them up right here beside me, because we've two days of dancing to do.'

'Woo hoo! Perfect, Floyd darling,' Kitty cheered.

Before Clara Spark could escape, Eleanor stepped in front of her. 'Hi, Clara, it's nice to see you again.' She didn't wait for a reply. 'Now the director's found a replacement for Armstrong, you can get back to filming properly. That must be a relief. But I don't envy you.' She let out a long whistle. 'Hats off to you though.'

Clara's flawless brow creased in confusion. 'I don't follow. Why not? Everyone envies me.' She flicked a perfect curl over her shoulder.

'Precisely!' Eleanor said emphatically. As the band burst into life, she started dancing on the spot, clapping along and pretending to be absorbed in their antics.

'Say, doll.' Clara pulled on her arm and pinned her with a bottomless blue-eyed stare. 'What do you mean then, that you don't envy me?'

'Huh? Oh, because you've got the weight of the whole film on your shoulders now, haven't you? With Armstrong sadly no longer with us and Perry replacing him.' She grimaced. 'He's a delightful chap, but it's mostly your name that all the picture-house goers will forever remember with the Napoleon love story. I'm sure of that.'

'And what the jumping crickets is wrong with that?'

'Only that if Perry doesn't cut the mustard as Napoleon, won't the film be slated?'

She shrugged. 'Well, I suppose. But Rudolph is—'

'The second choice. There had to be a reason for that.' Eleanor gasped theatrically. 'Gracious, though, I didn't mean to be uncharitable. Of course, he could have been filming some-thing big already, silly me. But no, that can't be right, otherwise he wouldn't have been free to step in at such short notice, would he?' She flapped a hand. 'I've no idea how these things work, you know. Where is Perry, by the way?'

Clara took a long swig of her champagne. 'Rudolph's not here. He doesn't do too many parties any more.'

'Tired of getting too much attention, is he?'

'Don't be ridiculous! There ain't no such thing when you're in the movies. Nothing works so well as letting ordinary folk see you in the flesh.' She grinned like a cat who'd stolen all the cream. 'Keeps 'em talking to everyone 'bout you forever. Immor-talises ya to them.'

Eleanor swept two more champagne flutes from the tray a passing waiter carried and passed Clara one. 'Then I don't understand why he doesn't do parties. He's not... golly, he's not thinking of retiring from making films, is he? At his age?'

Clara laughed maliciously. 'No, but he ain't really got much choice. The easing up on partying and the taking a break, I mean. Both are on account of seriously overdoing it, if ya catch my drift. I love Rudolph as a friend, but he's too soft for this business. Let's people get under his skin. Takes things too personally, if you know what I mean.'

Does he indeed!

Before Eleanor could press her any further, a scuffle a few yards away caught her attention. Up on the terraced balcony, Clifford paused in serving drinks and cast an anxious eye in her direction.

The row had broken out amongst some Americans and the group of artists she'd bumped into previously. Usually deep in what she assumed were artistic and philosophical discussions, they were now yelling and waving their fists at the Americans. Actually, she then realised, only one was. Eleanor winced as she recognised the passionate young chap with a penchant for lilac shirts.

'Oh, Augustine,' she muttered under her breath, 'what on earth are you doing?'

Those of his group who had been trying to restrain him fell back as he squared up to two Americans. 'You do not deserve to have art because you care nothing for its value. All that burns inside you is the love of money! And so you think to insult the creator and pay nothing for a great work!' He shoved the nearest in the chest, which given that he was way more slender, made little impression. He marched off, gesticulating and grouching loudly in French. Passing Clifford, he bumped against him, but seemed too incensed to notice.

One of the other artists went to follow him, but another of their group patted his shoulder. 'He has taken too much of the drink, this is all.'

The older Italian chap Eleanor had spoken to previously shook his head sadly. 'No, this not the reason. Always, Augustine shouts the passion for his art. And always cry over the price he get for his paintings.'

Floyd had clearly got wind that something was up and slid into the circle. 'It's a party, folks. What say we leave him to cool off and you all get back to what we're here for? I'll go check on him.' He walked after Augustine, pausing every other step, laughing and exchanging a word with guests.

'What a hypocrite!'

Eleanor spun around. 'Floyd?'

Clara shook her head. 'No, dummy. I was talking about that snivelling little French artist. I seen him shooting his mouth off several times, wailing that same old "poor me" song. It's pathetic saying us Americans are all caught up with money when every one of the French here are mighty keen to get their cheesy fingers on our dollars. Waiters, the manager and, definitely, all of them artists.'

'I suppose some people want money as recognition as to their worth. Or their art's worth. Some want it just so they can eat. And some care nothing for money, but just want fame and adulation. What about you?'

'Like it's gotta be either or! I'll take both. Fame and money. And I'm going straight to the head of the queue every time they're being dished out.'

Eleanor forced a laugh. 'It's great to have a reason to leap out of bed.'

'And to work your curvy behind off for too. Acting ain't no easy ride. It'll pop like a balloon if you don't do everything necessary to succeed.'

Clara spoke with such vehemence, Eleanor wondered just how far this ambitious creature was prepared to go. *As far as murder?*

'So I guess then that Perry isn't equally ambitious since he was taking a break from filming. And that he only agreed to do this film to help out the director.'

'Yeah right! And I'm an Eskimo! Rudolph *needs* this movie. His last starring one was a flop. And he was on a break only on account of his doctor making him.'

'He's ill? Poor chap.'

'Not exactly. Had a breakdown.' She turned her beautiful mouth down and jerked a disgusted shoulder. 'It weren't pretty, I can tell ya.'

'You were there?'

'Sure was. He just flipped out. Started crying and shaking. Movie company hushed it all up, of course.'

'Because of the investors?'

'Not hardly. His name's not Chester Armstrong, remember. And don't he know it too! But the hush up was 'cos of all the pills we were given to keep up with the crazy shooting schedule.'

Eleanor was appalled. 'You mean you were all given stimulants so you could keep working?'

Clara laughed again, but this time it sounded hollow. 'Don't dip ya toe in Hollywood, doll. Ya wouldn't last a second.'

'You might be right.'

Clara ran a disparaging eye over Eleanor's face and then stared at her fiery-red curls. 'Take my word for it.'

Running out of patience with this woman's arrogance, Eleanor took a deep breath. 'So, poor Rudolph had a breakdown because of all the drugs he was given?'

Clearly bored that the conversation wasn't about her, Clara clicked her fingers at a waiter. 'Other way around. He'd already had the breakdown, so he overdid it with the prescriptions he was given. Anyway, I'm going to dance.'

Eleanor decided she had to seize the moment or lose it forever. 'Do you know what caused it? His breakdown, I mean?'

'Sure. But it weren't a "what", doll. It was a "who".'

'Who?'

Clara grinned over her shoulder. 'Chester Armstrong, who'd ya think!'

26

'CUT! No. No. NO!' Truss yelled through his loudhailer, making Eleanor wince.

It was the following day, and she was once more on the film set on the pretext of auditioning for the director. She hadn't admitted it during Clifford's mischievous teasing en route, but the possibility that she might appear, however briefly, in a moving picture sent her stomach into paroxysms of nerves.

Truss dropped the loudhailer and threw his hands up at the two groups of soldiers facing each other across a stretch of the Egyptian desert. Even though the Chateau Beautour lay just behind him, 1920s southern France had been transformed into 1790s North Africa. An artful backdrop of the Pyramids combined with an impressive model of the Sphinx and the remnants of a battle-scarred village had worked their magic. The many tonnes of imported knee-deep sand also helped, as did the baking noon Riviera sun. Evidently, however, Truss' artistic expectations were far from being met.

'Come on, people! You're supposed to be highly trained foot soldiers. I'm watching this, not believing you could march through a paper bag! And French troops, remember, you're armed with sabres. They're made for killing the enemy, not waving around as if you're swatting flies!'

Sabres, Ellie!

She shook the image of Armstrong's body from her mind. She had a job to do. Truss took his anxious-looking assistant director by the arm.

'For crying out loud, Daniel, sort this out!'

'Take five, people!' Brockman called through cupped hands. 'Except foot soldiers. Stay for skirmish rehearsals from the top.'

Truss sprung up from his canvas director's chair and stomped over to the script table, where he mopped his brow with his handkerchief, looking up as Eleanor joined him. He eyed the proffered glass of water she held out with disgust. 'Couldn't have been a martini shot, huh?'

'Really? Is the desert battle scene so good that with one more take it'll be in the can and you can stop filming?' She was grateful that she'd remembered the slang Clifford had regaled her with over breakfast. He and her late uncle had picked up a smattering during their shared, if unorthodox, love of cowboy films while in America. A 'martini shot', he had assured her, was the most welcome cry an actor could hear. It announced that after the next take, filming was done for the day, and the bar was open.

Truss looked up, seeming to register she wasn't a member of his crew for the first time. 'Huh? Oh, it's you. Miss Gloria Swanson lookalike. I see ya been studying movie lingo. Credit to ya. But, to be honest, that scene was so far off we'll be at it all day.' He mopped his brow again. 'I could do with a martini, for real. Better yet, a fistful.'

'It must be hard,' she said sympathetically.

He frowned. 'What must be hard?'

'Well, how you take what's up there,' she said, pointing to his forehead, 'and communicate that to the actors and film crew. And in such a way that they can bring your epic stories to life.

And to such an extent, that all of us sitting in our seats at the picture house are instantly transported to wherever you whisk us away to.'

'You're damn right! And yet not one of these actors feels the passion like I do!' He spun round to her. 'You got children?'

'No... no children. Er, just a naughty bulldog.'

'Then you probably couldn't get it, either. Making a movie is like making a baby.' He jumped. 'Wait! No offence. I just mean it's like you first get a feeling that you wanna make this thing. For it to be a part of your life. And before ya know it, it's an obsession, like life won't be worth hauling outta bed without it. You long for it. Yearn for it. And all the while it ain't coming along, you feel empty. Hollow.' His expression took on an intensity she found unnerving. 'Then it comes together. You get confirmation your baby's going to be born. And, from that moment, all you can eat, sleep and drink is bringing that gem into the world to be the most amazing picture to ever hit the screen.' He shook his head slowly. 'It's a passion, alright.'

'But surely Armstrong must have shared your passion? And Perry? I imagine it was wonderful when you had both of them in your previous film. Two outstanding actors working together.' She peeped sideways at him to gauge his reaction.

He laughed. 'You really do want a shot at the movie life, don't ya? I ain't never met a kid who's done so much homework.'

She held up her hands. 'What can I say? But I'm always willing to learn more. Tell me, were Armstrong and Perry good friends?'

'No!' He stopped wiping his brow and shrugged. 'Oh, I mean, sure. It's all one happy, if exhausted, family when we're filming.'

She nodded. 'I'm certainly exhausted. Mind you, I think it's the Fitzwilliams' parties that have worn me out. Although' – she grimaced – 'I just hope Perry isn't going to get too caught up in all that partying and so forth after his, you know, difficulties. It's quite the chance you've taken, taking him on as the lead. Breakdowns can take a hideous time to recover from, after all.'

He laughed curtly. 'Not when the cause for the breakdown is gonna be six feet under soon enough.' An intense flush ran up his neck and struck his cheeks. 'What I mean is, it was on account of Chester that Rudolph... struggled. Chester was always shoving his nose into every part of the movie, always telling the other actors what they were doing wrong. Especially Rudolph. Oh, Chester was on his back all the time.'

'In front of the other actors?'

'Yep. And then he'd come complaining about him to me too, behind the scenes.'

'Gracious! Why do you think Armstrong did that?'

Truss licked his lips, glanced at the glass of water, and then turned his mouth down. 'Partly the perfectionist in him. But, honestly, the larger part is that, like so many actors, his ego was flimsier than that old spider's web in this crook of stone here.'

'Do you think some of it might have been... well, personal animosity?'

'What I think is that Chester had a—'

'Mr Truss!' a breathless voice called from the door. 'Sorry to interrupt, but Mr Brockman's got a problem.'

'Which means I got one,' Truss said wearily. 'The desert scene battle?'

'Sure is, Mr Truss. Only the battle is between Mr Brockman and those French extras this time!'

Without a glance at Eleanor, Truss shoved the man ahead of him and left the room.

Dash it, Ellie! You were so close to finding out why Armstrong seemed hell-bent on destroying Perry's career.

She shook her head, picked her way through the milling film crew and piles of props, and set off to leave. There was no point waiting to pick up the conversation with Truss; she could already hear him barking admonishments at the fractious extras through his loudhailer. And she'd heard Brockman telling a cameraman that Miss Spark had no scenes today and had taken off somewhere, while Perry would be in costume fitting and rehearsals until the end of the day.

'Oof!' She stumbled as she blundered into an unseen obstacle. An arm shot out and steadied her. 'Thanks!' she said. 'I'm so sorry, I walked right into you.' She straightened up and looked at a young man in a French foot soldier's costume, the gilt embossed buttons glinting in the sunlight, adjusting his evidently fake moustache. 'Wait, I recognise you, don't I? There's something familiar but I can't place it.' She stepped in front of him. 'Surely, it's Augustine, isn't it?' She frowned. 'But I thought you were an artist?'

Augustine coloured. 'I am an artist, but...' He cast his eyes down and shrugged.

Eleanor frowned. 'Then what are you doing on the film set? In costume?'

Like a man on the gallows, he hung his head. 'It is true, I am an extra.' He jerked upright. 'But nobody knows. Please keep my secret? It is no choice, I have. Everybody thinks I paint all the hours of the day, but even I must eat!'

'Ah! You need the money. Gracious, haven't you been able to sell many paintings recently?'

He laughed bitterly. 'I have no problem selling my paintings. The problem is the Americans pay me less than they feed their dog for each one!'

She blanched, remembering his argument with the Americans at the last party. 'I mean... er, perhaps you're waiting for someone to offer the right price?'

He continued. 'It makes me sick to my gut that I must sell them.' He spat on the ground. 'It is too little to live on and an insult to my talent.'

'But why do you need to be so secretive?'

He looked away.

'Ah,' she said gently, 'because you're working as an extra to make up the money you aren't being paid for your art?'

He nodded glumly. 'Now, instead of painting, I work for the Americans and their filthy dollar!' His eyes swam. 'I am no better than the street rat!'

Eleanor felt genuine sympathy for him. 'I don't see how that's the case. We've all done things we're not proud of in extreme circumstances. I'd say you're just doing what you can so you can keep painting.'

He gazed at her hopefully. 'Then you will help me? You will not say you see me here? That I am extra in this film?'

'Of course. Your secret is safe with me.' She scanned his face again. 'But surely one of the lead actors will have recognised you at the Fitzwilliams' parties?'

He scowled. 'Pah! These people do not see the dirt floor.' At her frown, he laughed without humour. 'Never they even speak to us, these American actors. Especially the one who plays Napoleon!'

'You mean Armstrong?'

He nodded. 'He was the worst. He never noticed my face. To him, I am like watercolour painting in the rain. No form, no features.'

'It's terrible about his death though, isn't it?'

He snorted. 'The only thing terrible is when he vanished, we were sent away with only half pay for that day!' He shrugged. 'Always he complained and made trouble. Nobody liked him.'

'Not even the leading lady?'

'*Non.*' He sucked his teeth. 'Mademoiselle Spark is same as others, but more. Everything about this woman is make-believe. She hated Monsieur Armstrong. No, not hate.' He thought for a moment, 'This man, she detested him.'

'Detest? Why would you think that?'

He tapped his ear. 'Because I hear her tell him this.' He

nodded. 'One afternoon, another extra gave me a cigarette. Oh, it is a precious treat, so I sneak away. And it is then I heard her.'

'But she didn't realise you heard because you were hiding?'

'*Oui!*' He looked horrified. 'If she knew I hear, then she'd get me thrown off the film! Mademoiselle Spark, she got two extras thrown off last week.'

'For what?'

He snorted in disgust. 'She said they look at her like a man should not. Her! This woman she plays with all the men like they are puppets, then' – he snapped his fingers – 'she tires of them and they are gone.'

'So, what did you overhear?'

His eyes darkened. 'I not know why but she made to Monsieur Armstrong the threat. I heard this very clear when I hid. They argued and then she said to him, "If you do, I swear I kill you, Chester!"'

27

Eleanor dropped into a cane chair on the lower balcony of Villa Marbaise. She stared out over the balustrade at the sparkling Mediterranean, the sun beating down from a cloudless midday sky. At her feet, Gladstone lay full-length on the cool tiles, panting.

'You know, Clifford, I think that's the main reason I feel like such a blunt brick in all this. It's all very well Damboise saying he needed my help because he doesn't understand Americans, but none of us gave a thought to the fact I don't understand actors! I have no idea who's telling the truth. Even Truss has spent a lifetime around them. He's probably able to pull the wool over my eyes as much as Clara Spark. Or Perry. In fact, I'm sure the dance girls could string me a... a... what's that expression?'

'"Spin you a yarn", my lady, I believe.' He flipped back a page in his notebook with a sniff. 'However, given the extreme minimum they seem to be permanently attired in, any yarn could be put to a significantly better use on their part. That aside, perhaps then we should start with the Fitzwilliams as they are not connected with the acting profession?'

'Good idea. I think out of our list of five suspects – six if you include Perry – we've learned something new about five of them since we last discussed the case: the Fitzwilliams, Truss, Clara Spark, and Perry. So, the Fitzwilliams. Their whole persona bothers me, but it's hard to articulate why. They're just too...' She scratched her nose. 'Too—'

'Perfect?'

'Yes! Spot on, as always. They've got the world in that they're impossibly attractive, impossibly wealthy, irresistibly generous and, to all appearances, irresistibly in love.' She shrugged. 'But as we said, something just doesn't feel right. There's an element of the manufactured about them.'

She paused as Gladstone raised his head as if he were going to take part in the conversation. The effort seemed to prove too much, however, as he lowered it once more and returned to panting. She ruffled his ears and carried on.

'And the Fitzwilliams admitted to knowing Armstrong in America. Kitty insisted they weren't friends, he was just someone who came to their parties. She was keen to make that clear. A little too keen. And I overheard Floyd say Armstrong's death was a "hiccup". So, if he was part of their operation or plan or whatever it is, then, it seems odd they should kill him. I mean, they would have been cutting their own throats as it were.' She blanched. 'Maybe I could have put that better.'

Clifford nodded. 'Perhaps. Nevertheless, it is accurate.' He looked thoughtful. 'There is always the possibility that they were forced to kill Mr Armstrong for some reason or other. Either way, the fact remains that his death seems to have been unwanted on their part.'

She nodded. 'So we seem to have found an *anti-motive*, as it were, for them killing Armstrong. While, in Clara Spark, we've found a bona fide motive.'

They were interrupted by Mrs Butters and Polly bringing

lunch. As Clifford left to fetch the wine, her housekeeper looked over Eleanor's face with concern.

'We do hope as you're alright, m'lady? Beg pardon for mentioning, mind.' She grabbed the food trolley to stop Polly ramming it into the table.

Gladstone shuffled reluctantly out of the way, eyes alert for titbits.

'I'm fine, ladies. Why would you think otherwise?'

'Well, Mr Clifford said as you would be wanting a light luncheon. Quite stumped Trotters. She said as she hopes what she's made is enough, but she's prepared double. Just in case.'

Eleanor smiled. 'Thank you, but I just don't feel very hungry at the moment. Whatever she's prepared will be perfect.'

And perfect it was. Clifford lifted the lid of the silver tureen to reveal a rich paprika-red soup of sea bass and snapper. He gestured to the accompanying basket of freshly baked rosemary and walnut bread with local olive tapenade.

'With a delicate lattice pastry ginger prawn tart served with honey-roasted lemon artichokes to follow. If that suits, my lady?'

'Absolutely.' She shook her head at the soggy slipper Gladstone reached up with in the hope of a juicy morsel. 'No thank you, old chum. That would be all robbery and no exchange.' She savoured several slices of the mouth-watering bread and black olive paste. 'Delicious, Clifford!'

'Most gratifying, my lady. I hope it won't spoil your luncheon if we return to discussing our suspects, with Miss Spark next, I presume?'

She enjoyed another mouthful before replying. 'Ah, yes. The manipulative madam that is Clara Spark.'

'Beginning with a character assassination, I see.' He hurried on at her look. 'Although there is, to be fair, much evidence against the lady. She left the film set not long after Armstrong and her car was seen in the hotel car park two hours later, giving her time to murder him. And we believe she may have been thrown over by Mr Armstrong in a most ungracious manner after, adding insult to injury, he was cheating on her with the entire dancing troupe.'

She laughed. 'Who's character assassinating now? It was only with one dancer. Or so I overheard. We've just speculated there might have been more.'

'I stand corrected. We do also believe, however, that Miss Spark was also treated poorly by Mr Armstrong prior to being thrown over, if Mr Tuttle is to be believed. And the hotel manager, disgracefully but helpfully, broke guest confidence by informing me Mr Armstrong and Miss Spark were overheard having a row of significant magnitude. Significant enough for the lady to be heard threatening Mr Armstrong that he would "go too far" and that "someone" would finally teach him a lesson.'

Eleanor finished her mouthful. 'So, was that someone Clara Spark herself? And what did she mean by "go too far"? Doing what? Sliding out of her bed sheets and into those of one, or more, of the dancers?'

He sighed. 'Perhaps, but if we might abandon any further voyages into unsavoury descriptions, my lady?'

'Ha! Don't pretend you're so horrified. I skimmed through your Voltaire novel yesterday. Rather liberal in his views in that regard, hmm?'

'Ahem, yes. "Enlightened" is the official term. Hastening back to Miss Spark...'

'Well, a new piece of information was imparted to me by one of the film extras and it might just answer those questions because...' She paused for dramatic effect and to savour a mouthful of the fish soup. 'Heavenly! Er, where was I? Oh, yes! One of the film extras overheard Armstrong and Clara Spark rowing as well. And our leading lady upped the stakes by threatening to kill Armstrong!'

Clifford, unusually, raised both eyebrows. 'So, Miss Spark wanted him dead?'

She nodded. 'And not just her, remember. Maybe Tuttle decided to do away with Armstrong, given how besotted he is with Clara? Maybe he believed he could slide into her—'

Clifford cleared his throat pointedly.

She tutted. 'All I was going to say was maybe he believed he could slide into her affections once Armstrong was out of the picture.' Under the table, she uncrossed her fingers. 'Mmm. And all of this definitely suggests Truss had a nightmare on his hands when Armstrong was in the picture. In fact, he told me it was worse than just Armstrong fighting with Clara Spark. This morning Truss said Armstrong was forever carping about all the other actors, though most pertinently...' She waved a coaxing hand.

'Mr Rudolph Perry?'

'Yes. To the point that in the last film they were in, Armstrong would pigeonhole Truss daily with a list of inadequacies he'd had to endure in Perry's acting that day. And even though Perry wasn't even in this current Napoleon film at the time, Armstrong continued attacking him.'

Clifford sniffed. 'Not quite cricket, my lady. Attacking a man when he's not even there to defend himself.'

'Precisely. And Clara Spark told me she believed Armstrong was entirely responsible for Perry's breakdown and enforced absence from filming. A break, by the way, Perry told me he'd taken voluntarily. And in Switzerland, not America as I'd thought.'

'That last piece of new information is very interesting, my lady.'

She shrugged. 'Interesting, but not much use. Even if we think Perry now has the strongest motive, he had no opportunity as he was in Switzerland when Armstrong was murdered.'

'Most inconvenient for our investigation.'

They paused while Clifford cleared the table. 'Yes, Master Gladstone.' He nodded to the wide-eyed bulldog. 'Her ladyship's leftovers would have been earned by your good self for near faultless conduct during luncheon. If, that is,' – he cupped his hand and pretended to whisper – 'she had eaten in a sufficiently ladylike fashion to have left any!'

''Tis alright, Mr Clifford.' Mrs Trotman arrived with a silver tray. 'I've brought Master Gladstone a specially baked chew as how I figured he might be coveting the mistress' lunch.' She threw Eleanor a conspiratorial smile. 'And to check just in case her ladyship was hungrier than first thought?'

Eleanor smiled back. 'Actually, I'm fine, Mrs Trotman. Lunch was ample, thank you.'

The jangle of the telephone bell made her jump.

Lizzie appeared in the French windows. 'Telephone, Mr Clifford, sir.'

Eleanor stepped beside her butler as he picked up the apparatus in the hall.

'Who is it?' she whispered.

'A certain policeman,' he mouthed.

'Hugh!' She grabbed the handset. 'Oh, Inspector Damboise, it's you again. No, forget it, I was speaking to Clifford. You've discovered what?' She frowned. 'He was where?' Her eyes widened. 'What! I just can't believe it... yes, yes, we'll meet you there at once.'

She spun round. 'Clifford, Damboise has found an eyewitness that swears he saw Perry near here five days before he was supposed to be in France.'

Clifford's brow furrowed. 'Which makes that—'

'The day before Armstrong was murdered!'

28

Eleanor's pulse raced as she waited for someone to get to the point. The strained atmosphere in the palatial office further fanned the flames of her frustration.

'*Mademoiselle*, all in the good time,' Damboise said quietly, his eyes sliding to Lessard signing papers at his desk.

She pursed her lips. 'Haven't you found that time is the one luxury you don't have in a murder case, Inspector?'

Lessard stopped writing and picked up the lid of his fountain pen. Having screwed it on just so, he adjusted his white whiskers before running a hand over his red silk sash.

'Mademoiselle Lady Swift, there is so much more of the English in you than I imagined. Particularly, wanting everything now, now, now!' He smiled thinly as he rose.

Clifford's cautionary cough halted the indignant reply burning on her tongue. She knew he was right. There was no sense in angering the most powerful man in the area. All she wanted was to be allowed to leave with her butler, his name exonerated of all charges against him.

Damboise took a respectful step forward. '*Monsieur le*

maire, permettez-vous?' Receiving a curt nod in reply, Damboise gestured for Eleanor to take a seat. 'And Monsieur Clifford, also. Please, it is better so I can tell you of the information I find.'

He then adopted what struck her as a courtroom pose, legs astride, hands behind his back, expression solemn. All very officious, but equally incongruous with his duck-egg-blue suit, loosely looped matching cravat and hatband. 'After you reported the body of Marcel Thibaud to me, I sent my men to make enquiries in the village of his lettings office.'

She raised a hand. 'Question, Inspector. You aren't hiding that Monsieur Thibaud was murdered then? Like you are with Mr Armstrong?'

Before the inspector could answer, Lessard tapped the table smartly with his finger. '*Mademoiselle* has misunderstood. We are not "hiding" the murder. No. No.' His eyes narrowed as he stared at her. 'We are protecting the interests of the people in my beautiful town. They will enjoy the chance for prosperity under my term in office. I have made the promise. And a Lessard' – he patted his chest – 'never goes against his word.'

'So, I understand, Monsieur le maire.' She turned back to Damboise. 'So your men were making the usual routine enquiries, Inspector?'

Damboise nodded. '*Oui*. In the case of Monsieur Thibaud we do not hide he is murdered because no one has reason to think there is a link between the two dead men. We do not say how Monsieur Thibaud met his end, though. Not outside of this room and my police station. So, my men asked to all the neighbours, the cafés, commerces and then to all the houses they knock. They also stopped the circulation.'

Clifford coughed. 'Circulation, my lady, is French for "traffic".'

'I knew that,' she muttered.

Damboise smiled. 'And we had good fortune. We stopped a driver in his van who said he know nothing of Monsieur Thibaud. But he liked to talk, this man. He leaned on his truck and chittle-chattled about where he went and what he delivered. The man told us he took a delivery to a villa in the hills above Bous, a village an hour from here. When no one answered the bell, he pushed on the gate and walked in. He thought to leave his delivery in the shade of the rear step by the kitchen. But as he walked past the swimming pool, he stopped with surprise. The man he saw asleep in the sun he recognised. A famous man.'

'Rudolph Perry?'

'*Oui, mademoiselle*. The man recognised him from the moving pictures he saw before.'

'And he is certain it was Perry?'

Damboise nodded.

She spun round to her butler. 'I totally messed up there, Clifford, believing Perry's story of needing a break and being in Switzerland. He can only have been in this area for one reason.'

'Most likely, my lady. That he knew there would be an opening for Mr Armstrong's role as Napoleon very soon.'

'Because he was going to make one!' Lost in her thoughts, she let her words tumble out. 'Maybe he was the person Truss was speaking to on the phone? They could have planned his murder together.'

Clifford discreetly mimed buttoning his lip.

But Damboise was already frowning. 'What is this, *mademoiselle*? You say nothing to me of this telephone call?'

'Didn't I?' she said innocently. 'We must have not had the time yet.' Quickly filling him in on the overheard call, she felt her shoulders relax. 'Gentlemen, this is such a relief. I was so caught up, I've only just realised why you called us both here.' She rose. 'My sincere apologies for doubting you, Monsieur le maire. With Mr Perry now safely locked up in the inspector's custody, I appreciate that you wanted to tell us in person. Clifford, we can leave.'

Her butler didn't move. She looked at him quizzically and then around the room. Damboise seemed decidedly uncomfortable. Lessard, however, merely held her gaze impassively.

'You haven't arrested Perry!' she gasped. 'What on earth?'

Lessard drew himself up. '*Mademoiselle*, this is France, not England. Matters we fix with a glove of velvet when they are most important.' He spread his arms wide. 'How can I allow the inspector to arrest Monsieur Perry without making the declaration to the world that Monsieur Armstrong was the victim of murder? And the culprit, like Monsieur Armstrong himself, a loved and venerated American film star? And what if we are wrong?'

Dread gathered in the pit of her stomach. 'Mayor Lessard, I mean, Monsieur le maire, you aren't saying what I think you are, surely?'

'This must depend on what you are thinking.'

'Well, in truth, I feel you are admirably serving the people of your town by trying to keep the Americans happy.' She held his gaze. 'But only at the expense of letting a possible murderer walk free.' At his silence, her eyes narrowed. 'Kindly tell me I am wrong.'

Damboise's eyes darted back and forth between them.

Lessard smiled thinly again. 'Mademoiselle Lady Swift, I think I have told you enough already. For the moment, there will be no bad news of Americans murdered – or arrested – in my town.'

Her stomach clenched in anger. 'So you would rather put Clifford back in jail than accuse Perry? Perry, the man who lied about where he was at the time of Armstrong's murder? The man who played second fiddle to Armstrong for years and then almost lost his career over a nervous breakdown caused entirely by Armstrong. The man who probably colluded with the director from the beginning to take Armstrong's role!'

Lessard rose. '*Non, mademoiselle.* Again, you misunderstand. America will not take as kindness that France has sent one of their own to the guillotine. And especially not if it is for the killing of their favourite film star. This they could never believe. Oh,' – he looked down his nose – 'those French police they do not like us! They frame the American! We will never go to that place!' He shook his head. 'This is all they will believe. And they will tell the world in their loud voices.' He sighed. 'It is not unknown to me that our police have not the best reputation outside of my country.' He glanced at Damboise and shrugged. '*Désolé.*'

The inspector shrugged and nodded in acknowledgement.

Eleanor fought to contain her anger. She stared helplessly at her butler, who stepped forward.

'Monsieur le maire, might her ladyship enquire if you intend to allow Inspector Damboise to call Mr Perry in for questioning at least?'

Lessard shook his head again. 'And what does your mistress suggest that I should ask him? It is not against the law that he is in France more early than he tells her.' He leaned forward. 'We have no evidence that Monsieur Perry is guilty. Not Damboise, not you, and not Mademoiselle Lady Swift. And if we ask the questions, he will taste the rat, *non*?'

Clifford cleared his throat. 'Smell, Monsieur le maire. The English expression is to "smell a rat". And if—'

Lessard strode past him. At the door, he turned around. 'Mademoiselle Lady Swift, you are free to leave with your butler. But understand this: even I can only keep the murder of Monsieur Armstrong a secret for a few more days. After that,' – he shrugged – 'someone must stand trial and take the punishment. It is up to you, who. Find me evidence, *real* evidence I can show the world that someone other than your butler is guilty of these crimes. Evidence they will not be able to doubt. And then, and only then, will Inspector Damboise make an arrest. And, yes, they will stand trial, American or not. Otherwise...' He shrugged again and marched out of the room.

29

The low purr of the engine and the rumble of the car's tyres on the pitted road surface were the only sound in the still, super-heated air of late afternoon. Even the occasional barking of a dog in the rambling stone hamlets they passed had faded as they left human habitation far behind. Eleanor had asked Clifford to go the long way back to the villa to give her time to think, but in truth her mind was blank.

Eventually, the switchback road that ran like a broken ribbon of tarmac high into the foothills of the Maritime Alps levelled out onto a bare, rocky limestone cliff. The view was dominated on one side by dense pine trees fiercely clinging to the near-vertical grey rock that rose to the sky. The other, by the twinkling waves of the Mediterranean far below, that lapped the horizon. Clifford pulled the car to a gentle stop and turned to Eleanor.

'My lady, I have failed in the duty I promised your late uncle on his deathbed I would carry out. For your safety, I cannot let you become embroiled in this distressing matter any longer. Please accept my abject apologies again.'

She fixed him with a firm stare. 'No, Clifford, I won't.' She raised a hand as he went to speak. 'I'm sorry, but on this occasion, you are wrong. Entirely wrong. You haven't failed in any of your duties. Ever. Quite the opposite, in fact. You go above and beyond every day for which I am eternally grateful. And there is something at the centre of Lessard's plan that *must* involve me. *You!*'

'Too gracious, my lady, but if I can entreat again—'

'Entreat all you like.' She folded her arms and cocked her chin. 'But I shan't budge. You'll have to carry me back to the house and lock me in a box to stop me.'

For a moment, as he ran his hands over his face, she thought she'd upset him. Then she realised he was actually trying to hide his amusement.

'Which is funny, because?'

'Apologies, my lady. Merely the peculiar sensation of being transported back in time to a particularly fractious summer when you were ten years old. You threw down the exact same ultimatum, if I remember correctly.'

She laughed. 'Gracious, yes! When you were trying to stop me building a rope bridge between the apple trees in the orchard because I'd already fallen twice and knocked myself out once.'

'Quite. Then, if you will allow, I will distract you with the lure of an impromptu picnic I took the liberty of asking Mrs Trotman to make, while I work furiously on another way to convince you to abandon this investigation.'

She tutted. 'You're a terrible man underneath your impeccable butler togs, you know. But even you cannot have anything persuasive enough hidden up your sleeve to change my mind. I, however, never need any encouragement to picnic!'

The view from the large flat rock they settled down on was nothing short of spectacular. The setting sun's orange fingers lazily rippled across the backs of the gently leaping white horses of the Mediterranean. In the distance, a yacht bobbed a lazy zigzag course towards destinations unknown.

Beside her, Clifford produced two glasses and several waxed paper parcels.

'Do you miss the sea, my lady? After so many of your formative years spent sailing?'

She smiled wistfully. 'I miss my parents' beautiful boat. And the smell of the sea at first light. Oh, and in my pyjamas, watching dolphins ride the waves beneath the bow, wondering what adventures they'd seen.' She shook her head. 'It amazes me that some lovingly crafted planks of wood and two strips of sail cloth carried us thousands of miles.' She looked down. 'And, as you know, I still miss my parents enormously, too.'

'Naturally.'

He held out a long slate of rock, spread with a pristine handkerchief, a miniature glass of brandy balanced on the end.

She laughed. 'Good to see even up here, and in trying circumstances, standards aren't slipping. Thinking back to sailing, though, after all these years, occasionally I still feel that I'm rocking slightly. Odd, isn't it?'

'Not really, since you do so when you are concentrating hard.'

'Gracious! Do I?'

'Only to the most observant eye. I conjecture, probably a hangover from your lessons taken at the cabin table?'

'Oh, my, I'd forgotten about that. You really are too perceptive, Clifford. Every morning, Mother and I would sit at our table in the main cabin and I'd try to stay still long enough to learn whatever she patiently strove to teach me.' She caught his amused look. 'Yes, I mostly failed. And we would give it up and go up onto the deck instead.'

'There are many ways to learn, my lady. Experience being the most educational, in my humble opinion.'

'And I'm still grateful for all those incredible experiences.

Isn't it funny, though? When you're a child, it's the trivial things that are so precious. I think what I loved most were the three shelves of books that made up the inside of the little door of my bunk. It was my secret world of stories and legends. If I close my eyes, I can still picture all the jacket covers. And, I remember now, I had a special wooden box with all my drawing pencils in which I absolutely loved. If you slid the lid one way, it opened up the main compartment. But if you turned the whole top sideways, it revealed a secret section, perfect for all manner of trinkets to be hidden away.'

'A collection of coloured stones plucked from the ground of many countries among them, no doubt?'

'Then lovingly washed and polished, yes.' She wrinkled her nose. 'Maybe I haven't changed much from that little girl.' She laughed at his look. 'Yes alright, if at all.'

'Happy days, my lady.'

The wistful edge to his tone tugged at her curiosity. 'Do you have a particularly abiding memory from when you were a boy?' She clapped her hand over her mouth. 'Oh, gracious, I didn't mean to pry. You're such a private man. My apologies.'

'No apology needed.' He stared out over the view. 'I do not miss the sea. Not surprising, however, as I spent a considerable part of my youngest years as far away from it as one can be in England.'

She held her breath, willing him to continue. Despite knowing him since she was nine, she knew nothing about his background or family. Nor of his history. And even less of his hopes and dreams.

Reaching for the waxed paper parcels, he slowly unpacked each one while talking. 'Most of my formative years were spent in the guardianship of Mr Gordon.'

'Oh, goodness,' she mumbled, having had no idea he had been orphaned. 'Was he related to you?'

'A good question. I have the impression that he may have been the brother of an aunt by marriage.'

'That would have made him your uncle, of sorts?'

'Indeed. But he was a singular gentleman and preferred me to address him as Mr Gordon.'

'But didn't you ever ask if he was related to you?'

'My lady, children never questioned their elders in my childhood years.' He arched a teasing brow. 'Much as they were not supposed to during yours.'

She shrugged. 'I missed that lesson. Now, Mr Gordon. What was he like?'

'Everything one might expect in a clockmaker, for such he was. Focused. Creative. And a master craftsman. A man of few words, unless it was about timing mechanisms.' He steepled his fingers. 'In fact, he was considerably more interested in the mechanics of time than finding customers for his exquisite clocks. In truth, I think he did not wish to let them go. But he was also fair-minded and generous in aiding me to continue my education in my own time.'

'How do you mean?'

'My apprenticeship with the gentleman began when I was eight.'

'But didn't you go to school?'

'Few children of my social class went to school.'

'Golly. But you're the most learned man I've ever met. How is that possible?'

He smiled. 'As Oscar Wilde reminded us, education is an admirable thing. But it is well to remember from time to time that nothing that is worth knowing can be taught. Mr Gordon made sure I had every book I wanted that I might indulge my natural desire to learn.'

'So you lived with him until you were an adult?'

'Alas, no. The gentleman suddenly passed away just after my twelfth birthday.'

'Gracious, Clifford.' She had to stop herself reaching to take his arm. 'You were... all alone in the world. At only twelve.'

His tone softened. 'One need never be alone if one chooses not to be. It is merely a matter of re-adjusting one's definitions. I simply needed a home and a reliable enough income, however small, that I might not go without food or shelter.'

'Mr Gordon didn't leave you anything?'

Clifford shook his head. 'As I said, the gentleman was more interested in making clocks than selling them. His workshop and our rooms above were taken over three days after he passed by another clockmaker.'

'And no one took you in? Clifford, I'm so sorry. That must have been awful for you.'

'The greatest lesson is in learning one need never be at the mercy of one's situation. However, in order not to be at its mercy, particularly at a young age on the streets, I had to occasionally resort to... unique actions and associations.' He neatly arranged nuts, cherries, figs and a selection of cheeses onto a small plate and passed it to her. 'So, if you will forgive my skipping over the detailed account of a few of the more, ahem... colourful years, we arrive at how I met his lordship, your late uncle.'

'Of course.' She shrugged sheepishly. 'Colourful enough to explain some of your more surprising and extremely un-butlery skills? Such as your incredible magician's sleight of hand and the ability to scale walls like a cat, render a man unconscious before he's seen you coming, and slot in seamlessly with people of any walk of life?'

'I really couldn't say, my lady. But, perhaps.'

She sensed despite his detached demeanour that those years had left memories he wished to forget. She hurried the conversation on.

'So, having achieved the most admirable feat of fending for

yourself from the age of twelve, how did you then meet Uncle Byron?'

He cleared his throat. 'I made my own way in the world for three years and then joined the army. I—'

'Hang on, Clifford.' She counted on her fingers. 'Surely you weren't allowed to sign up until—'

'Until I was seventeen?' He nodded. 'Those were indeed the regulations for being accepted into the ranks. However, regulations can be so restrictive on occasion.'

'Clifford! You pretended you were older than you were!'

'Not at all. Being of significantly above-average height and more sure of myself than many seventeen-year-olds given my... eclectic upbringing, the army recruiter merely assumed my age to be seventeen. And, ahem, I did not dissuade him.'

She peeped sideways at the man who she still felt was something of an enigma.

'I shan't ask, rest assured, but would it be too terrible of me to say that I hope amongst all of it, you found a very special girl. At least for a time.' At his silence, she hurried on. 'So you met Uncle Byron in the army?'

He nodded. 'Only two years into my army service, I was transferred to the regiment his lordship had also just been seconded to. As an officer, naturally. Unfortunately, his batman had been killed in a skirmish. I was temporarily assigned as his replacement. However, from the outset, your uncle and I got on famously, and I became his permanent aide until the day he gave up his commission and left the army.'

'I bet Uncle Byron pulled every string he could to keep you with him. He valued you as much more than just his batman. You were his confidante and his friend. Even as a child I knew that, if not the reasons why, seeing as you were supposedly employed only as a member of his staff when I knew you back then.'

He nodded. 'His lordship was as gracious, as ever, and

perhaps I might venture to add with the greatest of respect, also as unconventional as ever, when he asked me.'

'Asked you what?'

'If I would leave the army with him so that we might continue our association. As society forbade him taking me on in any higher capacity – certainly in public – he asked if I would become his butler. Naturally, I accepted the offer.'

'Clifford, that's the most wonderful story of friendship I've ever heard. And you can definitely stop trying to come up with any kind of plan, fiendish or otherwise now.' She waved him down. For a moment she stared out over the Mediterranean, her eyes picking out the lone yacht sailing into the setting sun. 'I... I've only ever had a few people who really cared about me, and most of them are gone. My parents. Uncle Byron.' She turned to him. 'All I have left is... you. And maybe Hugh.' Her cheeks coloured. 'But you're not going to be alone again, ever. Now it's my turn to do my duty. And nothing, and no one, is going to stop me!'

30

The rays of the setting sun licked around Chateau Beautour as if it were in flames. The colossus of a security guard frowned as he scrutinised the two cards.

'Okay, so both of you got a pass signed by the assistant director now.' Clearly disappointed, he thrust them back. 'Move along in, folks, though there ain't really nobody left inside. Filming's long done for the day.'

Eleanor felt a frisson of apprehension as they reached the far end of the enormous walled square, stacks of painted scenery boards leaning against the courtyard walls. The place did indeed seem empty. Anyone could—

She shook the thought out of her head and turned to Clifford. 'Time is definitely not on our side, so I'm going to ask Truss outright.'

'You'll have to be quick!' She jumped at the disembodied voice.

'Hello? Oh, Daniel, it's you.' His sandy hair bobbed up from behind a crate. She threw on her best winning smile. 'Erm, that probably sounded rather presumptuous of me, I imagine?'

'Presumptuous? No. Fearless, yes.' He disappeared again as he bent over the next crate. 'Where's that darn list gone?' He snapped upright, waving a sheet of paper. 'And fearless is what ya gotta be to get even a half shot at making it in the moving picture business.'

She laughed. 'According to my butler, that's increasingly become my middle name. Or is it foolish?' she murmured. She looked around her. 'Are you almost done filming here, then?'

'Yep! No choice. Rental period'll be up on this place in four more days.' He winced. 'And Herman can't ask the backers for any more money to try and talk extra nice to the owner. Besides, we got passage booked for everyone back to the States. We'll finish filming there in a month or so. It was amazing that Perry was able to learn all the scenes so quick though, huh?'

Amazing, indeed, Ellie. Almost as if he knew he was going to be needed!

He indicted the pile of crates. 'I gotta shift this lot before I return to the hotel. I'll drop you where Herman's finishing up on adjusting the set for the ballroom scene.'

'Then, Mr Brockman,' Clifford said. 'Allow me to assist while Lady Swift speaks to Mr Truss.'

'That would be swell.' He nodded towards the far door along the corridor. 'And, actually, Herman's only over there.'

Leaving them to it, Eleanor went in search of the director.

It hadn't occurred to her – and clearly not to Clifford as he continued helping Brockman – that the director might be alone. With the filming so close to finishing, she'd assumed he would be surrounded by at least a handful of crew. She stepped further into the empty ballroom, her footsteps echoing around the vast space.

The spectacle was no less impressive knowing the gold-relief walls inset with arched floor-to-ceiling French doors were actually nothing more than skilfully painted boards, comple-mented by fake chandeliers and plaster statues. Even the exquisite baroque ceiling fresco was an illusion, cleverly painted on lining paper.

A trumpet sound like that of an irate elephant made her heart stop momentarily. Through the floor-to-ceiling ivory voile curtains, Truss' back appeared. He was struggling with something as tall as himself.

'Need a hand with that?' Eleanor said, as if her being there was the most natural thing in the world.

'What?' His head swivelled around awkwardly. 'Hey, lady, you shouldn't be... Oh, heck, grab that end, would ya? Ain't heavy, just got a mind of its own.'

Together they manoeuvred what turned out to be a huge fake fireplace surround through the folds of the curtain and set it down on one side of the ballroom.

Eleanor ran her hand along the carved mantle top.

'It's remarkably realistic. And yet weighs so little.'

'Balsa wood. Amazing stuff. First time we've used it.' He ripped his handkerchief from the breast pocket of his crumpled white shirt and dabbed his forehead. 'Look, now ain't the time for a lesson in the movie process. And not for an audition, either. I know I promised you one before, but I got a tonne of finishing up here still. So skip on off home, okay?'

'Of course I will.' She folded her arms. 'Right after you tell me the truth.'

He rolled his eyes. 'Alright, I'll give it that ya got the tenacity for movie making. And the looks. So, yeah, if I'd had more time and less upheaval on this picture, I'd have given ya a shot at a walk-on part. Happy?'

'Actually, no. You see, what I don't understand is why you left it so late in the film's schedule?'

He threw his arms out. 'Left *what* so late?'

'Ensuring that Perry would be ready to step in the minute Armstrong died.'

His face paled. 'I... I didn't set nothing up.' Gathering his wits, he flapped her aside. 'In any case, how I run my movie is none of ya business.'

'True. You're absolutely right, it is none of my business.' She watched his face intently. 'However, it is the business of the French police. *And* your backers.'

He looked daggers at her. 'I don't know what your problem is, but I'm just trying to make a movie—'

'Ah, yes! The one where you decided at the very outset that Perry would be the leading man, Armstrong or no Armstrong.' At his grunt, she held up a hand. 'It must have been galling to waste all that film doing the initial scenes with him, knowing you were going to reshoot the lot once...' She paused.

His voice was icy. 'Once what?'

'Once poor Armstrong was dead, of course.'

He wiped his brow. 'How in God's name would I have known Chester was going to die? He just up and had some kinda heart attack.'

She tutted. 'Come now, Mr Truss. We both know it wasn't natural causes that took Armstrong.'

As the colour drained from his face, she nodded.

'It's a nasty business,' she said.

'The movies?'

'Murder, Mr Truss.'

His hand with the handkerchief curled into a fist.

She took a step back. 'My butler is waiting outside, along with your assistant, so I'd relax.' She smiled thinly. 'You can tell me the truth now. Or tell the French police if you prefer. And the Fitzwilliams were right. You really don't want to get mixed up with them. Do you know they still use the guillotine for murderers?'

He groaned, all the fight gone out of him. 'I've no idea what you've got to do with all this, but ya gotta believe me. Killing Chester was never part of our plan.'

'*Our* plan, Mr Truss? So the person you laid into on the telephone in that little tucked away booth at the Fitzwilliams' party was Perry? And you goaded him into helping you hide your dirty secrets by threatening to expose him. Only it wasn't his nervous breakdown you were holding him to ransom with, was it? It was his gambling habit.' She pulled a face. 'An unpredictable leading man with an obsessive addiction can't be a very appealing option for any film backer.'

Truss shook his head. 'Who are you, really?'

'Oh, just a Gloria Swanson lookalike with a strong sense of justice who doesn't like dead film stars turning up in the wine cellar of her rented villa.'

He stared at her blankly, jaw slack. 'It was *your* villa Chester was found in? What the hell was he doing there?'

'I have no idea. But once I've informed the police that Perry was not only in France before Armstrong was killed, but hiding out only an hour away...' She grimaced. 'I imagine they'll be here shortly asking you that very question.'

His face paled. 'But they'll think that I... that we killed Chester!'

'Wouldn't you, if you were presented with the facts? You and Perry cooked up a scheme to have him secretly on hand to take over from Armstrong *just in case* he passed away unexpectedly. Which, hey presto, he does! And then you're overheard blackmailing Perry into helping you cover up... what? Armstrong's murder? The man you never wanted in your picture and swore you'd never work with again. Makes perfect sense to me. Just as it will to the police, I imagine.' She winced. 'Have you ever actually seen a man executed by guillotine?'

'Alright, alright!' Truss' hand shook as he held it up in surrender. 'It was Rudolph I called that night. He and I had planned for him to take over from Chester, I admit it. But ya gotta hear my whole story. Rudolph was hiding out near here in the villa I rented on the quiet until... well, it was only a matter of time, you see.'

'Before what?'

'Before Chester pulled one prima donna stunt too many and I could go to the backers legitimately and get him out of my movie.'

'But every one of your cast I've spoken to has said Armstrong always flounced off for the best part of a day once or twice in every film?'

Truss' eyes flashed. 'Once or twice, yes. But eight or nine? That would have had the backers agreeing with me that we'd never finish filming on time. Or on budget.'

'And what would have caused him to do so that many more times, Mr Truss?'

'Me.' He groaned. 'Yeah, I wanted him out of my movie so bad I goaded him into it. And it was working except... except he never came back from the last time.'

'You mean, the tantrum Armstrong flew into on the fatal day was one you *engineered*?'

He nodded slowly. 'I did. And I sent Chester to his death. It's been killing me ever since that inspector showed up and told me Chester had been murdered.'

'If all that's true, why didn't you tell the inspector when he came to tell you Armstrong's body had been found?'

'Are you crazy!? It's like you said. When you lay out the facts, it looks too much like...' He croaked, 'Like I did it.'

Eleanor's brain was trying to process all she'd learned. 'Two more questions. What were you asking Perry to do when you threatened him on the telephone?'

'Only to keep his mouth shut tighter than a bolted barn door and bury any evidence that he and I had been in contact before Chester's death.'

'Where is Perry now?'

'He said he was going to the Fitzwilliams' party.'

She turned and started across the ballroom floor without a word.

'Hey, wait!' Truss cried after her. 'What happens now?'

'Now?' she called over her shoulder. 'Now I find out if you've been lying to me.'

31

As they stepped into the lobby, to Eleanor's mind the Hotel d'Azur's former grandeur was looking rather lacklustre. Even the musicians playing in the far corner seemed to lack sparkle. Half-empty glasses and overflowing ashtrays littered the tables. She wondered if the staff had given up or gone on strike. Maybe the manager had made good his earlier promise to quit?

Clifford scanned the lobby, lips pursed. 'It seems, my lady, that the Fitzwilliams have seen fit to finally set fire to decorum entirely.' He sniffed. 'Although, apparently, no one has the energy left to continue fanning the flames.'

She nodded. 'Something feels different. Party fatigue, do you suppose?'

Clifford sniffed again. 'Rather, the melancholy of having reached the pinnacle of dissoluteness and having nowhere further to go.'

Her skin prickled. She had the unsettling feeling someone was watching her. But looking around, her eyes only met with those of her relentless pirate admirer and trombonist.

'Hey, you!' He broke off playing, grabbed a hotel parasol

from the table behind him and mimed a swashbuckling sword fight with an imaginary partner across the marble floor.

She laughed. 'Hey, yourself. Have you seen Rudolph Perry?'

His shoulders sagged as he shook his head. 'No. When will the lady finally realise she can't resist the deliciously wicked fortune hunter in me after all? Movie stars are overrated, ya know.'

She shrugged. 'Sorry. Why the change of music tonight? It's not your usual jumping style.'

'Band's gotta play to the mood of the crowd. Floyd's conjured up some new coffin varnish, see?'

She didn't, but said nothing as he was still chattering on.

'Gotta hand it to that guy, ain't nothing Floyd can't lay his hands on when he wants it.' He caught his bandmate beckoning him with his drumsticks and waved back. 'Need to go blow my trombone again, but maybe I'll get a chance to walk the plank with ya later?'

She smiled. 'Don't shiver your timbers too soon on that one, Captain.'

Once he had rejoined the band, Clifford nodded sagely. 'Therein lies your answer, my lady.'

'Floyd's "coffin varnish", you mean? Whatever that is.'

'A colloquial term for alcohol mixed with various substances of lethal fortitude, I believe.'

'Marvellous.' She took the champagne he held out to her. 'One glass of fizz will do for me then.' She tapped the stem of the flute and looked around thoughtfully. 'Now, where am I going to find you, Mr—?'

'Here again, Eleanor, honey? Good on ya!' Floyd's long, well-built frame appeared in front of her. He nodded towards Clifford. 'Say, what's it take for Starchie Archie to give himself permission to loosen his buttons?'

Clifford tipped his head. 'Good evening to you, Mr Fitzwilliam. I am quite comfortable as I am, thank you.'

Floyd turned to Eleanor and chuckled. 'I love that fella. Just can't get him to bite. Somebody oughta cast him in a movie.' He looked around the room. 'Where's that director guy? I gotta suggest it to him.'

'I just left him at the film set, actually. But maybe you could suggest it to Perry instead? He was heading over here earlier.'

Floyd stared at her rather too intently for her liking. 'In with the movie set, too? Well, well.' His tone held a peculiar edge. 'I hope you don't got any more surprises up your fluted sleeves, Eleanor. Didn't your mama ever tell ya to keep a little mystique?'

'No, Floyd. She never got the chance. See you later.'

Leaving her host staring after her, and with Clifford dispatched to further question any staff left, she went in search of Perry. All she uncovered, however, were more party-goers in various phases of conscious or unconsciousness. Suddenly, she felt a jolt from behind. Spinning round, she found Clara Spark glaring at her.

'So you were with Herman, eh? Overheard you talking to Floyd. I shouldn't bother thinking ya might try out for the dance line.' Clara's lip curled as she made a show of adjusting the diamond bracelet on her wrist. 'Even the back row ain't getting away with having two left feet.'

Eleanor slapped on a smile. 'Then, dash it! There goes my dream.' She held the woman's stare, framed as it was by the most theatrical tower of coiffured blonde curls dripping with sparkles she'd ever seen. 'Thank you for the advice, anyway.'

'Only trying to save you the humiliation.' Clara flapped Eleanor out of her way with an imperious hand but she stayed where she was.

'Wait a minute. It must be my turn now.'

'For what?'

'Dispensing advice.'

The blonde crown leaned forward. 'Sugar, I ain't got no need for advice from the likes of you.'

'If you say so.' Eleanor shrugged as she stepped aside. 'Just seems a shame that people are saying those ugly things about you behind your back.' She glanced around the room as if the conversation were over.

Clara's smug look was replaced by a frown. 'What things?' She tossed her head. 'Not that I care, of course.'

'Of course. And neither should you.'

Clara caught her arm. 'Tell me,' she hissed, her grip making Eleanor wince.

With an effort, Eleanor shook herself free. It struck her that Clara's signature big blue eyes were an insipid version of their usual mesmerising lustre. Maybe she'd indulged in some of Floyd's special party additions this evening.

'It's about Armstrong.'

'And how is that of interest to me, since he ain't here no more?'

'About him and you, I mean.'

Clara rolled her eyes. 'For a grown woman, ya got a long way to haul ya skinny frame to reach the real world. Everyone has always talked about me. Sometimes it might have included him too, I guess, seeing as we were together a lot. Folk make up a truth they wanna believe.'

That she'd switched the emphasis to herself didn't surprise Eleanor, but something clicked. 'Only it was a truth you wanted to believe too, I think. Is that why you lied about his charms wearing thin to the point that you broke off the affair?'

'Lied!?'

'Yes, lied. Armstrong dumped you, didn't he?'

Clara's furious expression told her she'd probably guessed right.

'Talk about humiliation!' Despite the other woman's callous

attitude towards her, Eleanor felt a wave of sympathy. 'I'm sorry. Truly, actually.'

Clara laughed harshly. 'I don't need no sympathy from you. And *I'm* not sorry.' She ran her hands down her arms. 'I was just glad I didn't have to pretend any more.'

Eleanor's sympathy vanished. 'Really? Is that why you threatened to kill him?'

Clara's eyes widened in genuine surprise. Or so it looked to Eleanor.

'Threatened to *what*? Why would I do a thing like that? I didn't want Chester dead.' She bit her bottom lip. 'I don't now, either. Man was impossible but that don't mean I'd wish something that evil on him.'

'Well, we'll just have to let the French police decide. Once I've passed on what I was told, that is.'

Clara's manicured brows knitted. 'You should lay off the juice. Mind, I never did like riddles. Especially those that don't concern me.'

'Only it absolutely does concern you since you were overheard threatening Armstrong. But go ahead and carry on denying it if you wish. We both know the truth.'

'No you don't,' Clara snarled. 'It was advice, not a threat, I gave him. Only Chester thought he was king of the world. And that was before he was playing Napoleon!' She jabbed a finger in Eleanor's shoulder. 'I told him in the last film if he kept sniping to the director behind Rudolph's back, Rudolph would go to pieces. But then I realised that's what Chester wanted. On and on he went, forever carping. It was disgusting how he carried on. And then when he started up again on this picture, I'd had enough, so I told him straight.'

Eleanor frowned. 'He started criticising *your* acting?'

'No! Sugar, there ain't nothing to find fault with in the magic I bring to the screen. He was going off on Rudolph again. Day and night, like a darn stuck phonograph.'

'But Perry wasn't in this film until Armstrong passed away.'

'Sure wasn't.' Clara nodded, making her diamanté hair adornments swing against her flawless forehead. 'Didn't stop Chester from buttonholing Herman, though, and dredging up old whines about Rudolph at every turn. That night, I told him outright he oughta hush his ugly sour mouth or watch his back.'

Despite her words, something about the woman's demeanour didn't sit right with Eleanor. 'Strange for a man with such a large ego to spend so much time disparaging a lesser-known film star. Especially when he should have been too busy making eyes at you.'

Clara snorted in disgust. 'If ya really gotta know, me and Chester never had a fling at all. It was just the studio's idea to get extra publicity when we were in an earlier movie together. They wrote it into our darn contracts, so we had no choice but to play along.' She huffed. 'So, soon as it was known we were starring together in this Napoleon movie, the rumours started up again faster than dried grass kindling under glass in summer.'

'Tuttle doesn't think they were rumours.'

Clara blinked. 'Just who the heck's he?'

'For one thing, he's the man who was right about you never having even noticed he exists.'

'There's a lot of men in the world, sugar. Only a few of them worthy of my attention.' She looked across the crowded space at the drummer, who was banging his heart out. 'And the odd one who deserves the thrill just for kicks.' Clara clicked her fingers at a nearby waiter. 'You! Do I look like I got a drink? Get me a special. Now!' As the waiter hurried off, she glared back at Eleanor. 'So who is this Turtle person?'

'Tuttle. Walter Tuttle. He's playing Napoleon's second in command.'

She shrugged. 'Oh, yeah. That deadbeat.'

Eleanor bristled. 'He's quite sweet, in truth. Sweet enough

to be angry that Armstrong mistreated you when you were having a fling, which you insist you weren't.'

Clara sighed dramatically. 'Alright, sugar. Here's the real dirt, since I obviously ain't gonna shake ya off until you're satisfied. Chester was always trying to get me into a relationship. But he was mean underneath his chiselled movie-star face. Mean and rotten with it. Look what he did to poor Rudolph. Tipped him right over the edge just out of jealous spite.' She snatched her drink from the hovering waiter and took a deep glug. 'Despite his looks, I never wanted a piece of that man.' She pushed past her and headed down the stairs. Halfway, she stopped and turned back to Eleanor. 'Not every death is a tragedy, ya know. I might not have wished him dead, but he might just have got what he deserved!'

32

Clara's words were spinning through Eleanor's thoughts as she struggled to negotiate the tide of party-goers stumbling down the hotel's central staircase. Their gaiety was definitely sounding strained; every burst of laughter so close to hysterical, it was making her jumpy.

She forged on. If only the lighting wasn't so subdued, she might have made quicker work of scouring the blur of faces she came across, looking for Perry. As she backed out of the last door, she felt a hand slide around the back of her neck. Instinctively, she grabbed and twisted, preparing to deliver a disabling kick to the—

'Ow!'

'Oh, sorry, Kitty.'

Dressed head-to-knee in gold silk, Floyd's wife stood there, the soft glow of the wall light framing her with a halo effect. She pulled her arm away and massaged her wrist. For a moment, her eyes blazed and then the fire died and she smiled sweetly.

'Floyd said you were in and out of everywhere, Eleanor.'

'Just... just mingling. It's another great party.'

'I know. Every one is.' She purred. 'But you...' – she stepped forward – 'you've a whole heap more stamina than we anticipated.'

A cool wind blew along the corridor. Eleanor felt the prickle of goosebumps. Then she jumped as the balcony doors in the room behind her slammed shut.

'What's wrong, dear?' Kitty cooed, stroking Eleanor's cheek. 'Not feeling well?'

'Erm, no fine, thanks.' She pulled back. 'Just getting my bearings. This hotel is quite the warren of rooms and meandering corridors.'

Kitty laughed abruptly. 'And you never know what you'll find behind each door.' She ran her tongue over her bottom lip. 'You should try the third floor.'

'What's going on up there?'

'Whatever your imagination can handle. You might even find who you're looking for.'

She turned away and sashayed into the arms of two hovering men, who led her into another room without a backward look.

Alone, Eleanor frowned. How did Kitty know who she was looking for? Then she remembered. She'd asked Floyd earlier if he'd seen Perry.

The third floor looked in every way like the second, save for the choice of décor being an unfortunate palette of muted greys. The first two rooms had the usual party-goers in, but up here they were dotted on the settees or the floor, half obscured by the thick plumes of blue smoke they puffed.

As she came out of the second, she heard a familiar voice. She ducked back in and waited. Floyd appeared in another doorway down the hall with Perry. *Finally, Ellie!* Floyd patted the new leading man on the shoulder before strolling along the corridor towards her. She shuffled back a few steps out of sight. As he passed the door, he turned his head and winked at her.

Blast! So he had spotted her. She walked back out, but he had already vanished. Perry had disappeared, too. She crossed to the other room and peeked in.

As her eyes adjusted to the dim lighting, she could see the new leading man was still there. He was sitting on one of the blue sofas, tracing his finger around the raised fleur-de-lis pattern of the velvet upholstery.

'Evening, Rudolph.'

No reply. She watched him continue obsessively tracing the fabric's motif.

She frowned, unsure of what tack to try next. 'No roulette for amusement tonight, then?'

He looked up with a jerk. 'Lady Luck!' He rose. 'Just passing?' He cocked his head. 'Way up here on the third floor?'

'No, actually. I came to talk to you.'

His brow furrowed. 'Oh, see, the thing is, I should probably tell you—'

She flapped a hand. 'Don't fret. I haven't come to bat my lashes at you. Just as I was grateful you didn't with me at the casino.'

His relief was obvious, but was quickly replaced with a look of confusion. 'Then, I guess you'd better perch a moment.' He remained standing until she took a seat.

She looked around the empty room. 'Why are you hiding out up here, instead of holding court downstairs like the star you are?'

He looked away, tapping the arm of the settee.

She softened her voice. 'Rudolph, getting over any addiction is only to be applauded.'

He stiffened. 'I don't—'

She leaned forward. 'Especially if it was fuelled by a fellow actor.'

His hands balled into fists. 'I don't know what you're talking about. And I don't believe I want to hang around and find out! Won't you excuse me?' He half rose.

'Sure, I will. But the French police? Well, that's another matter.'

He slowly sat back down, his eyes wary. 'What have they got to do with this?'

'Rudolph, neither of us has the time, or the inclination, to make this any more difficult or protracted than it need be. You came to Europe to go into a sanitorium after the studio dropped you. Switzerland is renowned for its exceptional clinics, and when Truss contacted you to replace Armstrong as Napoleon, you thought you were ready.'

'I am ready,' he growled. 'And I'm doing great.'

'I know. Partly because you've had plenty of time to learn the entire film inside and out. After all, you and Truss planned that you'd take over from Armstrong *before* the filming even started.'

His eyes flashed. 'If you want to let that imagination of yours run freer than a wild stallion, might I suggest you take up writing novels 'cos everything you've said is pure fiction.'

She nodded. 'If you say so. Did you know, though, the French police have quite the penchant for that kind of fiction? And the mayor? He's probably the one to really be concerned about. He seems to be as powerful in this area in his own way as Napoleon was in his day.'

He scowled. 'I don't get what you're angling for, lady, but whatever it is, I ain't standing for it. Sounds too much like a threat.'

She shook her head. 'Not my style. It's simply the truth. And if you tell me the truth, Rudolph, I'll leave you alone. And so will the police. You see, I know you left Switzerland and came to France before Armstrong was killed. Not after.'

For a moment, she thought he'd walk. Instead, he groaned and rubbed his hands over his face.

'Alright. Alright. You win. What do you want to know?'

'Everything. The truth this time.'

He hesitated and then sighed. 'It started with Chester. He did everything to try and ruin my career because he was in love with Clara. And it ate him up.'

She scanned his face. 'What did?'

'That she wasn't in love with him.'

The final piece slotted into place. 'She... she was in love with *you*, wasn't she?'

He nodded wearily.

'But you... you weren't in love with her! That's what enraged Armstrong. He wanted her, but she only had eyes for you, which made him madly jealous. But then the fact that you had no interest in her must have battered his pride and ego even more. Which explains why he set out to destroy your career!'

He shrugged. 'Never understood why she fell for me. Stupid fool I was, though. I should just have enjoyed how it enraged Chester. But I was too busy fending her off and having to prove myself because of all the trumped-up faults Armstrong ran to the studio bosses with. Even though I'm every inch as good as him! And I've got one shot to prove it now.' He rounded on her. 'So why in hell did you rake all this up?'

She rose. 'I told you, I need to know the truth and I need to know it quickly.'

'I'll tell you the truth, alright.' He turned, his face uncomfortably close to hers. 'One person has already died, so maybe you should leave well alone. And by that, I mean me!'

She waited a moment or two after he had stormed out, collecting her thoughts. Then she left the room. At the top of the landing, it became clear the party-goers had spilled out of the rooms onto the stairs themselves, bodies and glasses littering the steps.

'It's wild! A staircase party!' a female voice shrieked.

Shaking her head, Eleanor picked her way down the first

flight to the second-floor landing before hitting upon the idea of taking the staff stairs. Before she could, everything went dark. For a second, there was silence. Then cheers, screams and laughter split the darkness. Someone knocked into her. Floyd's voice cut through the inkiness above her. 'Just the lights. Gotta be a fuse, folks. We'll all be safer downstairs until they come back on. Can't think why, but none of you seem that steady on your feet. Ha!'

More laughter followed, along with a collective shuffling in the dark as more party-goers tried to navigate the stairs. As she felt for the next step, someone barged into her. She stumbled forward so hard she fell into another body in front of her.

'Sorry!' She half turned to the person behind her. 'Slow up, will you? Then we'll all get down in one piece!'

The flicker of candles appeared as did, to her relief, the shadowy lobby. 'Move aside!' a firm but calm voice commanded from the steps below.

'Clifford?'

'My lady!' He pushed past the party-goers. 'Thank heavens you're safe.'

She tutted as he reached the step below her. 'Really, Clifford, you should take up being in moving pictures yourself.' She descended the last few steps to the lobby ahead of him. 'There's no need for such drama. I'm fine.'

'I am sorry to contradict, my lady, but I fear otherwise.' He whipped an embroidered cloth from beneath the enormous floral display on the central table like a conjuror, leaving the vase of flowers standing. He draped the cloth round her shoulders. 'The back of your gown—'

She sighed. 'Snagged, is it? I suppose I caught it when I was shoved. Not really a—'

'We must leave now!' He urged her forward.

'Oh, for goodness' sake!' They spilled out into the night air. 'Decorum in its place and all that.' She shivered. 'Golly, that suddenly feels cool. Yes, decorum and all that, Clifford, but it was dark. No one would have seen a tiny rip.'

Her butler took her arm and lowered his voice as he hurried her to the car. 'My lady, your dress is not ripped. Neither was it damaged by yourself. The back of your gown has been cut. And with a deadly sharp blade!'

33

'What am I missing, Clifford?' Eleanor tore her gaze away from the verdant view from the villa's rear terrace and took the cup of mid-morning coffee he held out to her. 'Enlighten me, please.'

Unlike the weather – a glorious sun had risen after the dawn thunderstorm – it appeared her butler's mood had failed to brighten. His exchanges had been uncharacteristically monosyllabic throughout breakfast. Gladstone, on the other hand, had been his usual vocal self, snuffling repeatedly while eagerly waiting for even the smallest morsel to come his way by design or accident.

Returning to the serving trolley, Clifford picked up a plate of oven-fresh apricot and walnut pastries. 'One can only hope it is not another round of "nine lives", you are missing, my lady. Since you most assuredly used one up on the staircase of the Hotel d'Azur. And, as far as I am aware, you are not actually a cat?'

She laughed. 'Meow!' At his grave look, she sighed. 'Alright, Clifford. I hear you. Last night's minor incident wobbled you.'

'Wobbled? No. Worried. Beyond all measure.'

'But whoever was trying to scare me off only cut my gown, no more. So, please. Enough worrying.'

'If you say so, my lady.'

A minute later, she realised he was still busying himself, smoothing the perfectly aligned seams of his white gloves.

'Clifford. Come on, say your piece. And don't bother beginning with all that "it's not your place, you know" business.'

'Very well, my lady. At the risk of souring your coffee with unwelcome drama, I do not believe the "incident" was necessarily designed purely to scare you off.'

Her eyes widened. 'Oh, gracious! You mean, they intended to kill me?' She thought for a moment and then shook her head. 'No, no, think about it. It would have been easy in the dark to... to...' She mimed stabbing someone in the back. 'You know, do a proper job, as it were.'

'Possibly. Nevertheless, only ignorance on the murderer's part saved you, I suspect. Your lack of practice at gliding elegantly downstairs in a floor-length gown and heels.' At her confused look, he nodded. 'I believe it is entirely due to the fact that you stumbled that you are sitting here now.'

She grimaced. 'Sitting here belatedly apologising for not realising how concerned you must have been all night. You can't have slept a wink. I'm so sorry.' She sighed. 'I can't say I agree with you, but something good did come out of it, either way.'

He arched a questioning brow.

'It means the murderer was definitely at the party. *And* we must be getting close enough to have put the wind up him. Or her.'

He topped up her coffee. 'You'll forgive my not sharing your elation, my lady.'

'I will. But...' She threw him a beseeching look. 'Truce?'

His lips quirked. 'Truce.'

The telephone bell interrupted them. It was Damboise.

Five minutes later, they were once more on the rear terrace.

Gladstone, having given up any hope of a titbit coming his way, had elected to stay where he was and, given the heat, sensibly snooze away the rest of the day.

Having respectfully refused to take a seat at the table, Clifford leaned down to peer through his pince-nez at the suspect list in her notebook. 'Yes, my lady, I can confirm that I too saw neither Mr Truss nor his assistant, Mr Brockman, at the Fitzwilliams' party last night.'

She nodded. 'Which suggests that Damboise's enquiries so far are correct. He rang to say two separate members of staff at the Hotel Le Blanc where the film mob are staying spotted both Truss and Brockman periodically throughout the evening. Which means they weren't at the party. I didn't see them and neither did you. In fact, given that Truss was in the hotel bar ordering a bottle of whisky early on, he must have left the film set shortly after we did and gone straight there.'

'And from your summation of the gentleman's state of mind, Mr Truss likely felt the need for several glasses. Straight.' His brows knitted. 'Although, since the bartender was told Mr Truss was not to be disturbed after room service delivered his whisky—'

She nodded. 'I know. Truss could have slipped out of a back door and driven up to Hotel d'Azur, then returned unseen later. But what's actually puzzling me is why Brockman wasn't at the party, either. He's always appeared, having the unenviable job of keeping everyone associated with the film from sliding so far into oblivion they are useless for filming the following morning.'

'Unenviable, indeed.' He frowned. 'Another absent actor, I believe, was Mr Tuttle, who also did not cross my view.'

'According to Damboise's inquiries, he'd retired to his room at the Hotel Le Blanc early with a debilitating migraine. If that was true, it's not surprising he didn't surface.' She shuddered. 'I'm so lucky on that score.' She grimaced. 'Unless I've overindulged in one of Mrs Trotman's home brews, I rarely get a serious headache.'

'Unlike poor Lizzie, who has frequent migraines, it seems. Her latest only cleared in the early hours when the storm finally broke, Mrs Butters informed me.'

'Then perhaps Tuttle suffers the same way.' She took a sip of coffee. 'So let's go with Damboise's assessment. He reckoned if Truss, Brockman or Tuttle had wanted to make themselves an alibi for last night, they'd have done a far better job of it than they did. So they are probably on the level.' She shrugged. 'It's the best we've got at the moment. So let's focus only on the suspects we know were definitely at the party and therefore would have had a chance to...' She mimed slashing a dress with a sabre again.

He nodded. 'Miss Spark, for starters, perhaps?'

Eleanor's nose wrinkled. 'Gracious, what a brat she is! Do you know, it took all my resolve not to descend to her level of condescension last night. Or bop her on the chin!'

'Bravo,' Clifford said drily. 'Instead were you able to pluck any pertinent facts from the lady?'

'Aside from her pointing out that I wouldn't even make the back row of the dance line on account of being so clumsy?'

He looked away. 'No comment. Did you, perhaps, learn anything of relevance I mean?'

'Well, she definitely has a thing for my pirate-cum-trombone player. She seems to think I snaffled him from her.' At his look, she rolled her eyes. 'What? It's not my fault. I haven't encouraged him.'

'Nor, ahem, heartily discouraged him since realising Miss Spark has her sights on him, perhaps?'

She shrugged. 'Maybe not. But she started it and he's only having fun flirting with me. Anyway, relevant to the case, you said. So, yes, is the answer. To start, Clara denied knowing who Walter Tuttle is, which I can believe as he's bemoaned the very same thing every time I've spoken to him. The most pertinent fact, though, actually made me feel genuinely sorry for Clara. She was adamant that the "affair" her and Armstrong were supposed to have had was nothing but a ruse. One dreamed up by the film company to create more publicity for the last picture they starred in. It was Perry who told me Armstrong was in love with Clara, but she wasn't in love with him. And to add insult to injury, she was in love with Perry who, apparently, had no interest in her.'

Clifford's brows rose. 'Very interesting and very relevant, my lady. I'd say Miss Spark is now a prime suspect. Because if she does love Mr Perry, then she might very well have decided to kill Mr Armstrong out of revenge. And, perhaps, to save the remains of Mr Perry's career and sanity.'

'Absolutely!'

'Moving on to Mr Perry, then?'

'Right. Well, I thought Clara was hard to read, but he's impossible. I can't fathom at all if he's telling the truth or just playing me along.'

'Might it not be possible that he is as he presents? A man captivated by the magic of film as opposed to one hungry for what the associated fame can provide?'

'I do love how you always manage to look at people without prejudice, Clifford. It's very endearing. Well, he definitely seemed genuine about not having any desire to slide into a relationship, or even under the sheets, with Clara.'

Clifford pinched the bridge of his nose. 'Any less indecorous observations?'

'Yes. He backed up what Clara said about Armstrong trying to destroy his career.'

'Mmm. I would say, my lady, that both Miss Spark and Mr Perry are now prime candidates for Mr Armstrong's murder. Possibly, they acted together.'

She nodded slowly. 'And, of course, they were both at the party last night.'

'As were our other suspects, the Fitzwilliams, seeing as they were the hosts.'

'True, but unlike Clara and Perry, frustratingly, we still don't have a motive for them wanting Armstrong dead.'

'My lady!' His white gloves muffled the sound of him clicking his fingers. 'That is precisely it. We have both repeatedly observed Mr and Mrs Fitzwilliam indulging, to all intents and purposes, as voraciously as their guests in all the substances freely available at their parties. And yet in the morning, we have equally observed, they seem unaffected.'

Her eyes lit up. 'And last night, they were both acting as if they had overindulged when I spoke to them. And Kitty was decidedly odd just before I went up to the third floor. Do you think they were putting it on in order to put me off my guard?'

'It is a distinct possibility.' He shook his head. 'One thing that still puzzles me about their parties is their mix of guests. That is, if they are a front for something else, as we surmised, the only loose connection seems to be the arts.'

'The arts.' She frowned. 'Then maybe what Damboise said as a throwaway comment on the telephone is more meaningful than he, or I, realised. Remember when I went to lunch at his house, he said all he'd discovered about Floyd's business was that he used to deal on the stock market? And that his practice had been rumoured to be rather sharp?'

'Sharp, as in buying low and selling high. Not illegal in itself.'

'Exactly. And then he seems to have given it all up and retired to Paris with Kitty. Living, one assumes, on his profits and indulging her passion for being a patron of the arts. But Damboise just mentioned that his latest information suggested Floyd had set himself up as a bit of a sideline art dealer while in

Paris. He apparently bought paintings and sold them on to America.'

'Again, not illegal if he is paying the appropriate duties. And not obviously connected to a murdered film star or a French letting agent?'

'Quite, as you would say.' She groaned. 'Oh, dash it! Why didn't I think of it before? When the lights went out, Floyd shouted for everyone to head downstairs. Perry might have been behind me because he had been on the third floor. But Floyd was also behind me!' She jumped up. 'To the car, quickly!'

34

'I hope Damboise's information is correct,' Eleanor whispered, looking around the spa's impressive Renaissance oval reception area. Ringed with scroll-topped columns, and hung with lavish gilt-framed mirrors, seven inset archways led to smartly tiled corridors symmetrically peppered with matching doors. 'Because I hadn't envisaged trying to question murder suspects dressed like this!'

She pulled on the thick collar of her robe, her hair twirled away inside a matching turban. Giving up trying to adjust it, she shoved her hands in the deep front towelling pockets.

Clifford, who was dressed as normal, tutted. 'Regrettable, indeed. All the more notably, since this is precisely the sort of establishment one had hoped a titled lady like yourself would be found in whilst visiting on the Riviera.'

She gave him a look. 'It is also the sort of place where a titled lady parades about in public in less than that which she normally reserves for the privacy of her bathroom, apparently!'

He winced. 'Granted, but I rather believe that is the entire point of a health spa.'

'Maybe, but right now, the entire point of being here is to

finally nail down just what exactly the Fitzwilliams are doing on the Cote d'Azur. I'll meet you back here when I have.'

'Look, Floyd! It's Eleanor!' Kitty's voice cut through the heated mist of the steam room. 'She's got her timeless beauty all wrapped up today.'

Floyd pulled his face out of her neck. 'Love the Grecian twist, Eleanor, honey. Botticelli should have put you in his *Birth of Venus* painting. Just like that in your bathrobe and fancy towel turban.' He frowned. 'He was Greek, wasn't he?'

Eleanor sat on the wide marble step across the narrow channel that served as a cool-off pool. 'Italian, actually. Funny, I had in mind that you'd have known that. Being, you know, an art lover.'

'Kitty's the real art aficionado. And spa aficionado.' His languid tone tightened. 'I don't recall seeing you in here before?'

She waved her hand airily. 'Oh, someone recommended it to me at one of your parties. Said it was a great place to unwind.'

'Absolutely,' Kitty purred. 'So you can wind yourself back up for the next one, darling!'

Eleanor laughed. 'There's no denying you're both the masters of that. But, there's one thing puzzling me. Everyone's told me that you were already the king and queen of partying in Paris. So why leave the very centre of it all and come down here to out-of-the-way southern France?'

'Oh, ya know,' Floyd said, casually stretching out his long tanned legs, 'better weather. Cheaper living.'

Not believing a word, she played along. 'Cheap enough to rent out an entire hotel for the whole summer. And fill it with guests at your expense too!' She swished her toes in the pool, feeling rather humid in her bathrobe. 'Must be hard, though. Being away from the Parisian scene.' She looked at Floyd. 'Surely your business would continue to flourish better there?'

His smile seemed a little cooler than normal, despite the heat of the room. 'I wrapped up my stocks business a while back. Got so as it wasn't much fun any more.'

'I meant your art business, Floyd.'

He flinched and glanced away. 'Somehow, Eleanor, I seem to have given ya the wrong impression. Not sure how, though, I don't recall saying anything about an art business of mine.' He turned back to her, his genial smile once more in place. 'But ain't that party conversations all over? When the band are banging out the tunes and everyone's getting stewed, it's easy to grab the cow by the tail 'stead of the horn, right?'

'I can't, in all honesty, say I've tried either. But, I admit, I'm now very confused. Here I am, eager to discuss purchasing some fabulous art works and you're the man to see, I hear, but apparently not.'

The couple shared a swift glance. Kitty adjusted the tie of her robe.

'Who did you hear that from, dear?'

'Oh, I can't remember.' She looked back at Floyd. 'But isn't that party conversations all over, too? So many faces. So many names.' A rivulet of sweat ran down her shoulder blades.

He scanned her expression intently. 'Sure, honey.' At her expectant look, he shrugged. 'Well, whoever it was got it wrong. Like I said, I'm not running an art business. But I do realise why it might seem that way.' Leaning over, he cupped his wife's face in his hands and nuzzled into her hair. 'You see, the thing is, Kitty here is a great artist. She's simply bursting with talent. And being a pure angel, she helped other artists back home, and then in Paris. Couldn't see no reason not to carry on doing like-wise down here, that's all.'

Eleanor scratched her nose, while surreptitiously wiping a bead of sweat from her forehead. 'Strange though. Now, it really makes no sense. Dash it, you've made me feel quite the blunt brick.'

'With those sharp pussycat-green eyes? No chance,' Kitty said a little too quickly.

'Well then, do put my curiosity out of its misery. If you didn't invite me to your parties in order to butter me up to sell me some paintings, why were you so keen to get to know me?'

Floyd shook his head. 'We were just being friendly, honey. Call it an American thing. We're not stiff about getting to know folks like you English. Say, speaking of stiff, where's Starchie Archie? I'd love to see him in one of them towelling robes!'

Eleanor's thoughts flew back to Brockman's words on the beach. 'Our host is as far from the giddy playboy he pretends to be.'

She shook her head. 'His name is Clifford, if I can remind you again. And you wouldn't want to see him bite.'

Floyd laughed, but it faded quickly as she nodded gravely.

'Trust me. But you intrigue me, Floyd. For someone like you who has made a decent fortune so early in life, it must become an unconscious habit. You must be forever assessing the business opportunity in everything, I mean?'

Floyd chuckled. 'Well, Eleanor, honey, to steal your cute phrase, I'd be the "blunt brick" if I didn't.'

He stood and slid his arms under Kitty's and lifted her to her feet. She threw Eleanor a thin smile, then ran a finger down his sun-kissed neck.

'You're many things, Floyd darling. But nobody could accuse you of that.'

He kissed the tip of her nose and turned to Eleanor. 'Been good seeing ya again. Now, we're all rejuvenated from this hot steam bath, we gotta go.'

'Shame. But of course you'll be getting ready for another party?'

'Not tonight,' Kitty purred. 'No party. Just in case you were thinking of showing up, darling. Wouldn't want you to be disappointed.'

Floyd hugged her into his side and led them towards the door, calling over his shoulder. 'Even we can't party every night.'

She watched them leave. *Well if things don't work out in the art business they insist they don't have, Ellie, they can try out for the moving picture world. They're always looking for good actors!* She stood up and went in search of Clifford, something gnawing at the back of her mind.

Having changed, she walked along the corridor towards the reception area where Clifford was waiting. Before she could tell him what the Fitzwilliams had told her, however, she overheard the receptionist calling to a tall, bearded man, dressed in a too-hot-looking blue suit.

Her brows knitted. Where had she heard that name before? After he'd left the reception desk, she hurried after him, ignoring Clifford's confused look as she passed.

In the car park, she called out, 'Monsieur Poudray!'

The man stopped and turned around, a confused look knitting his brow. '*Oui?*'

She smiled. 'I'm so sorry for stopping you, but aren't you the Napoleon expert from Marseille advising the American film company?'

The man shook his head. '*Non!* I am from the company that provide the uniforms and other Napoleonic paraphernalia, yes. But I do not advise this film company. Because,' he continued, drawing himself up, 'they do not want advising! They have not the interest in making the historical accuracy for one of the greatest Frenchmen who ever lived!'

Eleanor tutted. 'That's terrible. But as an expert on... everything Napoleon, you must have made sure as much as you could that everything you provided from your company was as authentic – and accurate – as possible?'

He glared at her. '*Naturellement, madame.* I am the foremost expert on Napoleon in all of France!'

She didn't know what she was expecting him to say – or quite why she did it – but she slipped the button out of her purse and dropped it in his hand.

'Then as France's foremost expert, you must recognise this?'

He gave it a cursory glance and handed it back. 'Yes. It is a military button. From, I assume, one of the uniforms we provide the film company. They pay for any damage, I make sure.'

'Of course. And as it came from Napoleon's uniform, it must cost more to repair?'

Poudray shook his head. 'This is not from the uniform of Napoleon. Again, what man you think I am? The uniforms we provide the film company are genuine, or identical to the original.'

Eleanor stepped closer, trying to keep her voice neutral. 'But it is an infantry button and Napoleon often wore—'

'The uniform of an infantry colonel. Yes, yes, this I know. But Napoleon as Emperor of all France – and Europe – had one small change made to the uniform. He had the normal infantry buttons, such as these with a crossed cannon, replaced with a crowned eagle. Even his troops may not see, but it is enough for him that it is so.'

Eleanor's heart skipped a beat. 'But the uniform – the one your company provided for the actor who played Napoleon – it had the buttons of a crowned eagle or crossed cannons?'

He gave her a withering look. 'Crowned eagles, of course! But I think no one notice in the film company, so why I bother, eh? Now' – he gestured to a car in the far corner – 'I must back to Marseille this evening.'

As Poudray drove out of the car park, she was aware of Clifford's presence.

'Did you—?'

'Yes, my lady. Only the latter part of the conversation, but enough to deduce that as the button you found in the wine cellar was not, in fact, from Mr Armstrong's clothing, then there must have been—'

'Someone else in that wine cellar with Armstrong, as we knew all along. The murderer.'

'Indeed, my lady. There is, however, another explanation.'

'Which is?'

'That Mr Armstrong and the murderer were both in the wine cellar, but the button came from neither. There was another person present, from whom the button came. Perhaps they lost it hiding.'

She nodded slowly. 'If so, then they would have witnessed Armstrong's murder and may be too scared to step forward.'

Clifford opened the car door for her. 'One thing *is* certain, my lady. If the murderer knows there was a third person in the wine cellar, then any more missing sabres may soon be put to deadly use!'

35

'Dash it, Clifford!' Eleanor pressed her hand to her forehead again.

Her butler looked sideways at her. Taking one hand from the steering wheel, he slid it inside his jacket pocket and pulled out a small folded-paper parcel. He dropped it into her lap.

She glanced down. 'Headache powder! Very droll. But given that we are already past the eleventh hour of needing to solve this wretched murder case, not particularly helpful.'

'If you say so, my lady. Then, I shall leave you to your musings.'

He drove on at his signature stately pace, taking the scenic route once again over the hills back to the villa. She'd hoped it would marshal her thoughts, but so far it had done no such thing.

She groaned. 'I am sorry, Clifford. I didn't mean to be testy.'

'Eminently understandable, my lady.'

Mollified she hadn't upset him, she lapsed back into thinking, which she quickly realised was a mistake. Her hand moved towards her forehead again, but she caught herself halfway and let it fall. 'Dash it! This is hopeless.'

'Uncharacteristically dispirited of you, my lady, if you forgive my observation.'

'I'm not dispirited.' She spun to face him and nudged his elbow, the force of her frustration causing him to swerve. 'Oops, sorry. Now, please, pretend to close your ears so I can break the rules by saying my wonderful butler is too... too precious to me to let discouragement get in the way. We need to extricate him from the predicament Lessard has so tightly woven on his behalf. And quickly!'

He took his hand from where he'd held it over one ear. 'For all of which, your butler is beyond grateful, my lady.'

'Not at all. I merely meant earlier that we needed to attack the problem from a different angle, that's all.' She stared out of the window, seeing nothing of the scenery. 'We've been faced with tricky conundrums when caught up in these things before, but for some reason, I can't make sense of my thoughts this time. I keep running over my conversations with the suspects. But they're as muddled with the additional information you've unearthed and everything Damboise has drip fed us as if I'd dropped the whole lot in Blendine the Blender. Honestly, Clifford, my brain is as thick as a raspberry soufflé, but greatly less enjoyable.'

'Continuing to force your thoughts will likely only result in increasing the blockage, my lady. A momentary diversion, perhaps?'

'There's no time. I feel as if my head is going to explode and go "pop!" like that champagne cork in the cellar.'

Clifford slowed the car. 'Kindly say that again. Word for word.'

'I said... erm... I can't remember exactly. I was just saying I feel like that champagne cork—'

He took a hand off the steering wheel and held up a finger. 'You mean as well as the button, you found a champagne cork in the wine cellar?'

She shrugged. 'Yes. So?'

He braked hard in the middle of the hamlet's narrow main street. She rocked forward, grateful the meagre population all seemed to be safe behind their shuttered windows and not in the road.

She stared at him. 'I'm sure it's a good idea to test the brakes occasionally, Clifford, in case we ever need them in earnest. However, do tell me you had another reason.' She spread her hands. 'Perhaps you've figured out who our murderer is?'

He shook his head. 'Would that I had, my lady, but regrettably not. May I ask, however, why you did not see fit to mention the aforementioned cork to me?'

She thought back to her examining the wine cellar soon after the discovery of Armstrong's body. 'Because, well, it's not an unusual place to find a spent cork, is it? I mean, I didn't mention to you that there were a few sprinkles of glass on the floor, or that there were wine bottles in the racking either.' She held out her hands. 'It's a wine cellar. It's what you expect to find down there. I assume that's why the police didn't mention it in their report either. They are not clues, like the button I found. Things out of place, as it were?'

He nodded slowly. 'I apologise, my lady. In the initial heat of the situation that may very well have been my dismissive reaction as well if I had been there. But it strikes me that it is, in fact, extremely unusual. One would only open champagne once it had been taken upstairs.'

She thought for a moment. 'Maybe the owner of the villa is a complete philistine in such matters? Or he employs a hopeless valet who has no idea of such things?'

He looked at her as if she had suggested he eat asparagus with a snail fork. 'My lady, any man who purchases a cold cupboard that can be set to a temperature of between eight to ten degrees – considerably higher than one would store food at in this climate – has but a single reason.'

'You mean, Rigobert the Refrigerator is really for champagne?'

'Quite. The champagne I catalogued in my aborted inventory is of excellent quality.'

'Then why is he drinking it in his cellar?'

Clifford's eyes were miles away as he put the car in gear and moved forward slowly, drumming his fingers on the steering wheel. 'Mmm. Inspector Damboise is convinced neither the owner nor his staff have been in France, let alone the villa, this year...'

'That may be, but someone was. It still seems odd there was no sign of a struggle.' She shrugged. 'Small consolation, but perhaps it was at least fitting that, being a film star, he died in luxurious surroundings. What I saw of Thibaud's place, it wasn't big enough to swing a kitten in, let alone a cat.'

Clifford stared at her. 'Why has that made me suddenly fixated on the difference in size between the two victims? Why indeed?' he murmured to himself.

'I can't help because you very thoughtfully stopped me from seeing Thibaud's body. I've no idea how he looked. What *was* he like?'

'Slight of frame, which likely measured five foot three to five foot four inches. Rounded of shoulders, of very limited muscular definition, early fifties. Loosely speaking.'

She shook her head at his unrelenting obsession with precision. 'Maybe we're on to something. You mean he was the opposite of Armstrong, who was positively strapping?' At his nod, she continued. 'And from your description, it sounds like I could have disarmed Thibaud with nothing more than my rusty Bartitsu training.'

Clifford nodded again. 'So how, my lady, did the murderer put someone as physically commanding as Mr Armstrong at his ease long enough to approach him openly with a sabre and run him through. For, as we have said, there was no sign of a struggle or disturbance at the scene.'

She opened her mouth to say she had no idea, but then his tone registered. 'Why didn't that sound like a question, Clifford?'

'Because it wasn't.'

Her eyes widened.

'Bear with me, my lady. Now, our killer meets Mr Armstrong at your villa. What Mr Armstrong was doing there, we don't know at the moment. Nevertheless, he was clearly there for some shady business or other and it seems it was concluded in the wine cellar. So, our killer offers a celebratory drink to mark the occasion. Naturally, being in France, only champagne will do. And as they are in France and Mr Armstrong is playing Napoleon, our killer shows him how Napoleon would have opened the champagne. By sabrage!'

'Sabrage, Clifford?'

'Indeed, my lady. Believed to have started in the Napoleonic era as a means of opening champagne with flair on the victorious battlefield.' He pulled over and seized a brandy miniature from the driver's door side pocket. 'Imagine this as a champagne bottle, which, like every bottle' – he ran a gloved finger along it – 'has a weakness inherent in the seam of the glass. And this,' he continued, pulling out his fountain pen, 'is the sabre. One tilts the blade like so, runs it swiftly along the seam and...'

She jumped as he made a loud popping noise with his tongue.

'The cork flies across the room,' she breathed.

He nodded. 'Along with the top part of the neck of the bottle.'

'And the murderer plunges the sabre into the distracted victim.' She leaned back in her seat, frowning. 'So, parking the fact that you are absolutely going to have to give me the full demonstration when we're back at Henley Hall – assuming we possess a sabre – do we believe any of our suspects would know how to... "sabrage", was it?'

He nodded. 'Sabrage, yes, my lady. But do I believe any of our suspects would know of it and be able to execute it proficiently enough so that it resulted in a clean break and only a few slivers of glass at the scene? No. I am forced to offer the view that in all probability, it would take a Frenchman to be so well versed. My theory does, however, also suggest the murderer need not have been physically strong, since the element of surprise was as much the weapon as the sabre itself.'

'Which puts Kitty and Clara firmly in the frame, then. But like all of our other suspects, they too are American. And if our button is to be believed, as neither of them wore any kind of uniform, though Clara would certainly have access to the costumes, they could not be the murderer. Unless the button did come from a third party who hid in the cellar and witnessed Armstrong's murder.'

He pursed his lips. 'Indeed. So maybe I am wrong.'

She sighed. 'Dash it again, Clifford. Having narrowed the field, why do I feel like we've just reopened the gate and sent the whole pack of horses galloping loose once more?'

'Because we are both too emotionally involved in the outcome of this case, my lady.' She swallowed hard and said nothing. He shook his head. 'I completely share your vexation at not being able to clear the mist shrouding my thoughts. Distressingly, however, I am overcome with the sense that when it clears, I will find that the answer has been staring me in the face all along!'

'Chin up, Clifford,' she said quietly. Letting her eyes rove anywhere but over his troubled features, she stared blankly out the window. With the light fading fast, there was little that caught the eye. But suddenly she froze. Winding down her window, she leaned out the top half of her body and scrutinised the tatty remnants of a large but long-forgotten poster nailed to a noticeboard. With a gasp, she stood up on the seat and leaned out even further.

He tutted. 'My lady, really. Must we fall short of propriety so repeatedly? Allow me to get the door for you.' He went to open his, but she raised a halting hand.

'No time!' She dropped back into her seat. 'And no time for tutting, either. Clifford, I've been an even blunter brick than I thought possible. Start the car. Go! Go! We may already be too late!'

The engine roared to life. 'Too late for what, my lady?'

'To stop another murder!'

36

'Oh, hurry, Clifford!' Eleanor slid against the door as the car swung round another of the inky black bends on the interminable twisty descent down to the coastal road. 'Can't you drive any faster?'

'Indeed. On the proviso, however, that you wish us to plunge into the sea. Which, one might feel, would be counter-productive.'

The headlights picked up a cluster of fallen rocks. He swerved around them, knocking her against her door again. She pushed herself back upright. He was right, but they had to try.

'But if we don't make it in time, it will be—'

'Out of our hands,' he said firmly, keeping his eyes on the road. 'And off your conscience, if you will allow it to be.' He glanced at her. 'My lady, we have made the best provision we could for a message to reach Inspector Damboise as expediently as possible.'

'But as there are no telephones or vehicles up here, that's not going to be very expedient, is it? Neither of us are very confident in that old chap with his donkey cart we gave the message to even getting it to Damboise. Let alone him doing so with enough urgency, are we?'

'In all honesty, no.'

'Exactly. To say nothing of the fact, we're not sure he understood, given that the poor fellow seemed rather deaf. And he didn't speak any English and our French is limited. And however much you don't want me to feel bad, Clifford, you can't deny it's my fault.' She raised a hand as he opened his mouth to reply. 'If I hadn't insisted we drove miles up into the hills on the way back to the villa, we might otherwise at least have been close enough to hare to the police station. Or the villa to use our telephone there. That is positively the last time I try to work out who the murderer is in the middle of nowhere!'

'Brace!'

She grabbed the dashboard as the car skidded around another bend.

'Apologies. Loose gravel.' He hunched over the wheel. 'Now, hasten I shall, since we have cleared the mountain road, but I will not risk your safety any further. Understood?'

'Understood.' She managed to stay silent until the next corner. 'Surely just a little faster couldn't hurt, though? We're talking about a life at stake here.'

Even with the road finally straight enough for Clifford to agree to speed up, it seemed a hideously long time before the monolithic silhouette her eyes were scanning the horizon for appeared.

'There, Clifford, the Fort of Antibes! If you remember, you told me the manager of the Hotel d'Azur thought he saw Floyd's car coming down the dirt track from it one evening.'

He snapped off the headlights and coasted into the seclusion of a thick swathe of trees flanking the perimeter of the high stone walls.

'We are at the western point of the star, my lady,' he whispered.

She paused in fumbling for the door handle. 'What star?'

'The fort. It is a remarkably impressive star-shaped construction of four bastions tapering from a central square quadrant.'

'Great. I don't suppose you happen to have a floor plan of this thing since it is approximately a hundred times larger than I anticipated?' At his look, she sighed. 'No, I thought not.'

He opened his door silently. 'Do not despair, my lady. Among the acres of passageways, rooms and towers – as well as the catacombs of the prison – the basic tenets of fortress construction will prevail here, I am sure.'

She shook her head grimly. 'I'll take your word for it.'

After a swift reconnaissance, Clifford detailed what he judged would be the safest route into the fort. There was no way to shorten the distance between the trees they were using for cover and the stronghold itself. They would just have to hope they were unobserved.

Waiting until the moon was briefly hidden by clouds, they ran for safety. Feeling dangerously exposed, she focused on calming her breathing and not simply charging forward blindly into more peril.

Reaching the outer fort wall, they flattened themselves against the stones, still warm from the day's sun. The thudding of Eleanor's heart was so loud, she was sure it would give them away. She tapped Clifford's arm. As he bent down, she cupped a hand to his ear and whispered, 'You mentioned before that Napoleon was imprisoned here?'

He nodded. 'Briefly, in 1794 during the French Revolution.'

'Then we need to head for the fort prison.'

He thought for a moment and then set off. She trailed behind him, staying as low and close to the wall as possible until they reached a small wooden door. The entire fort was in a state of disrepair, and the door was no exception. While she kept watch, Clifford soon had it jimmied open. With a quick glance behind to make sure they hadn't been spotted, she followed him into the darkness.

If the warren of unlit passageways had gone on any longer, Eleanor's fear that her usual resilience and courage would turn tail and flee might have been realised. However, Clifford's pocket torch finally illuminated an arched wooden door. He turned off the torch, produced his pistol, and indicated she should flatten herself against the wall. He then wrenched the door open and stepped swiftly inside.

'Empty.'

She joined him as he ran his torch around the room again.

'Wait! What's that?'

He shone the beam into the furthest corner. 'Another, if smaller, door, my lady.'

They inched across to it, both looking constantly over their shoulders.

'Locked,' he murmured.

There had never been a time when she was so grateful for her butler's lock-picking skills. After a few minutes of working silently, he turned to her.

'I know we are both hoping there isn't another body on the other side but, just in case, please wait until I have checked,' he whispered.

She realised this was no time to argue. 'Alright. But if I think you need help—'

His only reply was to wrench the door open and step inside as before. She saw the beam of his torch flash around the room and then the sound of metal on stone. A moment later, the flicker of an oil lamp lit the room beyond.

'My lady?'

She hurried forward. Her hand flew to her mouth.

'Clifford! I half thought we'd find a body – well dreaded that, actually – but I certainly didn't expect a room filled with... paintings!'

He picked up the lamp and together they examined the dozen or so oils. They were all simply framed and of various sizes. She shook her head.

'I don't know much about art, but even I know they aren't famous masters.'

'Indeed not.' Clifford held one up. 'They are all modern. And recently painted. One can only conjecture they belong to Mr Fitzwilliam.'

'*Non!*' They both jumped at the voice that answered from the dark of the doorway. 'They belong to me!'

37

They both spun around. A cry of pain and the clatter of metal on stone made Eleanor's breath catch. Clifford was holding his pistol hand, blood dripping onto the flagstones.

She looked up to see a fleeting flash of silver, then the sharp jab of cold steel in the side of her neck. Unable to move, she could only look on helplessly as their assailant slid Clifford's gun out of her reach with his foot.

'Leave the lady alone,' Clifford said calmly, though the tautness in his voice gave a hint of the pain he was in.

'It's over, Augustine,' Eleanor managed through her clenched jaw. 'The police are on their way. We know it was your button we found in my wine cellar. The button of a Napoleonic infantryman, or foot soldier, which is what you played as an extra. We checked the uniforms.' It was a lie, but she was sure it was correct. 'And we know now why you killed Armstrong.'

The sabre withdrew from her neck as Augustine stepped back and picked up the pistol. He laid it on a stone ledge.

'Say what you want, *mademoiselle*, it will make no difference.'

For a moment, there was silence as she tried to think of a reply. Meanwhile, Clifford wrapped two handkerchiefs roughly around his forearm. Grabbing the ends in his teeth, he jerked his head, pulling the knots tighter to stop the flow of blood.

Augustine raised the sabre again. 'You should not have come.' He sounded genuinely sad to her ears.

'I had no choice. Where is Floyd?'

His eyes flashed. 'Tied tight like a beaten dog. Waiting. I was there ready to give him all that he deserved but you interrupt me.'

Willing her voice not to show her fear, she waved a hand. 'No, Augustine. Floyd may be many things, but he doesn't deserve to die for any of them.'

His eyes flashed. 'He does! The cur lied to me.' He spat on the floor. 'He pretended to help me, but all he did was betray me and my art! Now, I will pay him back for his treachery!' He laughed darkly.

'What do you think Floyd lied to you about?' She already knew the answer, but needed to keep him talking. That way, she and Clifford would stand a chance. However slim.

He stared past her, his voice weary. 'It started in Paris. He pretended to buy my paintings to help me out because he knew I had not enough money to keep together body and soul. But he only paid me a pittance for each painting. But then I find out' – his whole body shook with rage – 'he was going to send them to America. And there sell them for a fortune to rich men of industry who care nothing for all my soul I had given to each painting. Stupid men who wish only to please their wife and their ego that they can hang on their wall what someone tell them they must have to impress everyone.'

'I agree that was underhand of Floyd, Augustine. But now you know your paintings are worth so much, you can sell your future work to a proper dealer who will pay you their true value.'

He shook his head wearily. 'It is too late. I don't paint to live, I live to paint. But I have been hungry for too many years.' With his free hand, he raked up his shirt, revealing painfully thin ribs and a hollow stomach. 'Inside me now does not work any more. My body, it is dying.' He let his shirt fall, his eyes darkening. 'And Floyd, he will do the same.'

Sensing that Clifford had stepped silently into the shadows – *let's hope he has a plan!* – she forged on.

'You never overheard Clara Spark threatening to kill Armstrong, did you?' She took his silence as confirmation. 'What you overheard was Armstrong telling someone on the film set that he needed their help to smuggle paintings out of France.'

He nodded. 'Armstrong was helping Floyd. He promised a member in the film crew who deals with the props that he pay him good money to help smuggle my paintings. He told the man that Floyd had found a "dumb French kid" who didn't know he had created art men would pay the roof to own.' He adjusted his grip on the sabre as he shoved his face forward. 'Now I show Floyd that I am not dumb!'

Out of the corner of her eye, she couldn't see Clifford at all. *Keep Augustine concentrated on you. With Clifford's arm injured, he probably doesn't see him as much of a threat.*

'So... so you also overheard Armstrong say what? That Floyd couldn't store your paintings at the Hotel d'Azur, I imagine. It was too risky that one of the staff or the manager would find them, wasn't it? Which is why he hid them out here, in this old fort.' The last of the pieces slotted into place. 'Which of course was built all those hundreds of years ago because this is a natural harbour. Perfect for sneaking contraband goods onto a smuggler's boat, perhaps? The thing I still don't understand, though, is why Armstrong was in the wine cellar of Villa Marbaise? My rented villa?'

Augustine grunted. 'Armstrong had not the time to drive all

the way to this fort from the film set without the other actors being suspicious. So, Floyd paid that cur Thibaud to store them in the wine cellar of Villa Marbaise as the halfway place. The man who owns your villa, he knew nothing about this arrangement.'

Just as he didn't know Thibaud rented the villa out to you, Ellie, and pocketed the money!

Augustine scowled. 'Armstrong was to pretend a tantrum. This was common for him, he was like the spoiled child. So, he pretended to be upset and stormed off the film set. But, really he went to collect my paintings from Thibaud at Villa Marbaise.'

Eleanor nodded to herself. That explains why Thibaud told Clifford we couldn't have the villa until later than we wanted. He had to make sure the paintings were gone first.

'Only it wasn't Thibaud who Armstrong found at Villa Marbaise. It was you, wasn't it, Augustine?'

His face lit up. 'Ha! For me, it was easy. I did not know where Floyd had arranged to have my paintings hidden yet, but I had some sabres in my little car because I stole them to sell at the flea market. They pay us film extras only a pittance each day. I needed only to wait until Armstrong started to act the angry child, then sneak to the office of Thibaud to make him tell me where Armstrong had gone.'

She shook her head in disgust. 'Then, after he told you, you killed him. In cold blood.'

'*Non!* This is not true.' His voice cracked. 'I planned only to get the key to the villa. Thibaud, he thought he was stronger than me because I am more thin than the abandoned animal of the street. He tried to take the sabre from me to kill me himself because he knew the man who owns Villa Marbaise, a gangster everyone fears, would otherwise discover what he had done without his permission. Then that man would kill him for sure.'

Eleanor heard a faint noise from the shadows. She raised her voice.

'So Armstrong arrived at my villa and didn't recognise you as an extra on the film. You said as much. Anyway, you distracted him by opening the champagne with a sabre to celebrate having fooled this "dumb French kid" and then ran him through.'

'Armstrong gave nothing to the world!' he hissed. 'Only he took. He thought he was Napoleon for real and could have the world. But he only acted for himself. Napoleon acted for La France, always for La France!'

'And at the party last night, in the Hotel d'Azur, on the stairs in the dark, it was you who sliced my dress. Only you weren't trying to kill me, you were aiming for Floyd!'

'True. He had more of my paintings I know, because I found only three in your villa but I sold twelve to him. He deserved to die for what he did to me. You do not, *mademoiselle*.'

Her heart skipped.

'But I have not the choice, so you will die.' His voice was tinged with genuine regret. 'And now.' He raised his arm.

Clifford's good hand flashed out to grab the pistol on the ledge. Augustine screamed and swung the sabre down, sparks flying as the blade hit the stone. For a sickening moment, Eleanor thought Clifford hadn't pulled his hand away in time.

He had. But he'd missed the pistol. It fell to the floor.

As Augustine lifted the sabre to strike again, keeping her upper body still, she struck violently upwards with one leg, striking the flat of the blade. It flew from his hand and clattered into the corner. He hesitated for a split second and then turned and scrambled for the fallen pistol.

'RUN!' Clifford shouted.

Out in the corridor, she heard Clifford hot on her heels. And then Augustine.

'Left. Right,' Clifford shouted. 'Stairs! Up one flight!'

Not daring to look back, she sped on, banging her head on the stone arch as she swung left, then grazing her knuckles on the wall as she sprung right.

But something was wrong. She powered on to the stairs, but with an increasing sense of dread. The footsteps had reduced by one. Either Augustine had stopped chasing them... or he knew the fort.

He appeared at the end of the corridor as she emerged at the head of the stairs. She flattened herself against the wall a split second before he fired. The bullet buried itself in the arch behind her.

She scrambled up another set of steps to the sound of another shot and sprinted along another passageway, now hopelessly lost. Even though she had no idea where Clifford had gone, she thought of doubling back to find him, but Augustine appeared in front of her again. This time, the fragments of stone dislodged by the bullet cut her cheek. She turned and ran up yet another staircase, the sound of more shots echoing behind her.

She stumbled out into the moonlight. It was the top of the fort. There was nowhere else to go. She heard footsteps behind her. Clifford? Or Augustine? Dashing to the nearest wall, she leaned over and stared down at a sheer drop—

'To the rocks of the sea, *mademoiselle*.'

She spun around. So the footsteps had been Augustine! His breathing was ragged, his hollow chest rising and falling.

Desperately hoping she was right, she held her arms out wide. 'It seems as though you've won. But there is one thing you should have brought with you.'

He shook his head and raised the pistol. 'And that is what?'

'More bullets.'

As he pulled the trigger, she deftly caught the sabre which javelined through the gloom to her.

'Oh, and the best butler – and friend – there's ever been.'

With a screech, Augustine threw the empty gun at her and ran. She ducked and sprinted around the other side of the stairs, cutting off his escape. Slowly she advanced on him, sabre outstretched. She nodded to Clifford, who had picked up the discarded gun and was awkwardly refilling it from his pocket. Injured, he was best guarding the stairs in case Augustine gave her the slip.

But Augustine didn't try. Instead, he backed away slowly from the sabre's tip until he was pinned up against the wall. A strange look had come over his face. He raised his hands.

'I ask only one thing of you, *mademoiselle*.'

She kept the sabre at the ready. 'And what is that?'

'That you see justice done.'

She frowned. *He's trying to trick you.* 'I intend to do just that. The police are on their way.'

He shook his head. '*Non, mademoiselle*. Not for me. For my art. Promise me you will make sure my paintings are not left in the hands of philistines.'

She held his gaze. Then she nodded slowly. 'I promise, Augustine.'

For the first time, he looked at peace.

'NO!' She dropped the sabre and lunged forward, but all she grabbed was air as he let his body fall backwards to the rocks below.

38

The hallway of the villa was a sea of trunks, cases and ribbon-wrapped gift boxes. And, to Eleanor's horror, a trail of earth-filled leather slippers. She gasped and hurried over to her bulldog.

'Gladstone, you monster! Clifford will have a fit, especially as his arm is out of action and we should be leaving in less than —' A halting cough from behind pulled her up short. 'Ah, too late, boy,' she whispered. She turned around to the uncharacteristic sight of her habitually impeccably suited butler sporting suit trousers topped off with a black cable-knit cardigan. It was buttoned to where his tie should have been and bore only one sleeve.

'We should, in fact, have already left, my lady. If you will forgive the correction.'

'We're all trying, Clifford.'

'Very.' He winked. 'Not something one might consider news, however.'

She laughed. 'You know, in your own way, you're every inch as mischievous as Gladstone.' She pointed to where the bulldog was now nestled against Clifford's legs. 'No wonder he thinks the world of you. I'm just so pleased you're in one piece. Look at you, finally some colour back in your cheeks. And who knew Mrs Butters could knit such a masterful piece of attire so speedily. And don't tut, you're very distinguished with one arm. Rather like Napoleon, in fact.'

'Most gracious, my lady, but perhaps there has been enough mention of that particular gentleman recently.' His eyes strayed back to the trail of slippers. 'Now if your diversionary tactics of flattery are quite finished?' He waggled his pocket watch at her. 'Lizzie can clean up this mess and join us in a moment with the other staff.'

As they stepped out of the villa, Garbonne sur Mer's mayoral Rolls pulled up. Lessard climbed out, resplendent in his signature red sash and a ceremonial jacket, judging by the loops of gold braid swinging from either shoulder. Inspector Damboise slid out after him. Lessard's white whiskers curled up as he beamed at Eleanor.

'Mademoiselle Lady Swift, the people of my town, our police and I, we are grateful to eternity for your assistance in catching Monsieur Armstrong's killer. And to Monsieur Clifford, also. But it is to you, I give...' He clicked his fingers impatiently. From the driving seat came the sounds of scrabbling and muttered panic. Pierre emerged holding a crimson velvet cushion, the tassel at each corner swinging as he scurried forward. Lessard waved a hand over the large brass key, decorated with red, white and blue ribbons, nestled on top. 'Mademoiselle Lady Swift, it is only the formality.' He held his hands up. 'Since there is no gate to my town, but to you, I present the key to Garbonne sur Mer. It is the symbol of freedom to come always as our guest. The guest of honour.'

'Gracious, thank you.' She took the key, feeling overwhelmed. 'But your dream for Garbonne sur Mer? The film company have already left.'

'Ah! But Monsieur Truss has persuaded his studio to open

the European showing of his film here, in Garbonne sur Mer! We will build a magnificent picture house for the occasion. And it will be the first festival of cinema here in my town. The first of many. And to think, you—'

She whipped her finger to her lips and gestured to her staff.

He lowered his voice. 'Ah, so sorry. It is to be the surprise that you are in the film, *non*?'

She nodded.

He nodded back and raised his voice again. 'It is because of you, Mademoiselle Lady Swift – and, of course, the good Inspector Damboise – that the film people have no reason not to bring their cameras to my town again. It is the tragedy that the man responsible for murder was a fellow of my country, but it means none of their American people fear our police. *Bon voyage*.' Lessard bowed.

As he settled himself back into the car, Damboise stepped forward.

'You are a lady of many surprises, *mademoiselle*.' He shook his head. 'Perhaps, too many. But please, teach me one more lesson before you leave? How is it that you came to know it was Augustine who was the murderer?'

She shrugged. 'Once we knew from Monsieur Pouyard that the button I found didn't come from Armstrong's Napoleon uniform, but from one of the other infantry uniforms, it narrowed it down. But even though Augustine was an extra, playing an infantryman, I still didn't really suspect him. I was focussed on the murderer being the director, one of the main actors, or the Fitzwilliams. In fact, though, it was Floyd who spelled it out for me. At one of his parties, he made the throw-away comment that "you can't spend if you ain't earning!" And it suddenly struck me that he was spending money faster than water, so he must have been earning somehow.'

He laughed. 'Surely faster than champagne?'

'That too! I remembered you'd told me of the rumours

about Floyd buying stocks low and selling them high. He was supposed to have been out of that game. But to keep up the lifestyle he was lauding so wildly with Kitty, to say nothing of their perpetual raft of guests, he had to still be doing the same. Only in another field. And what better field than one his wife is an expert in – art. Which is why when I saw a poster advertising an art exhibition, it suddenly clicked.'

He nodded. 'Now, this I have confirmation of, also. Monsieur Fitzwilliam made his money in Paris the same way. My contacts there sent me news yesterday. He bought the paintings of nobody-know artists and sent them to America. But recently the authority made it more hard and more expensive to export paintings. Also, we have a new law made this year that states that the original artist must be paid every time his art is sold again. No matter how many times.'

'Which is why Floyd and Kitty decamped down here, where it is easier to smuggle the paintings out by sea and avoid paying any taxes.'

'*Oui.* But they had good fortune suddenly. They passed Chateau Beautour, heard a film was being made and...' He waved a coaxing hand.

'And then found that the leading man was their old friend, Chester Armstrong. He owed them a favour apparently – so Floyd confessed when we set him free at the fort – so Armstrong readily agreed to help them. But they really didn't know he was coming here, Inspector?'

'After several hours of questions, Mr Fitzwilliam told me the truth and he insisted this is the case. They found out Monsieur Armstrong was in the film, they needed someone on the set, so they invited him to join their plan. He agreed and the rest,' – he pulled a face – 'well, you know how it ended for him, *mademoiselle.*'

She let out a long, low whistle. 'Normally, I love a coincidence, but I shan't applaud that one.'

He shook his head ruefully. 'So, I am the fool. I did not investigate properly the clue you found, the button. I made the wrong assumption. And the suspects I listed to you are all part of the film world, not the art world!'

'Don't blame yourself, Inspector. As I said, I was fooled in the beginning too. Augustine hid his tracks extremely well. So well, none of us thought to consider any of the artists at the Fitzwilliams' parties as suspects.'

He offered his hand for her to shake. 'It is my pleasure to tell to you, *mademoiselle*, that you will be the proud chittle-chattle of my police station for many years to come.'

'Well.' She lowered her voice. 'That is as much an honour as being given the key to Garbonne sur Mer. Perhaps more. Thank you, Inspector.'

'Please.' Damboise looked between her and Clifford. 'You will come again to lunch with me and my family another time? But I will lock away our slippers and get old ones for Monsieur Gladstone to hide. And Monsieur Clifford, perhaps he will allow us the honour of eating with us also?'

'We'll both be there, Inspector, I promise.' She glanced impishly at her butler. 'You will remember to pack my bucket and spade for slipper hunting in the garden though, won't you, Clifford?'

He bowed. 'If I might presume to be present for the delightful giggling that will inevitably ensue, then yes, my lady.'

Once Lessard and Damboise had departed, Eleanor took a last look at the outside of Villa Marbaise, relieved it was finally all over. Then she pulled on her leather gloves.

'Well, what do you say we move on to our next holiday destination?'

Her staff shared an uneasy look.

'Beg pardon, m'lady,' Mrs Trotman said. 'If it isn't rude to ask, where would we all be going?'

She smiled. 'Oh, Clifford's reminded me of a magical place.

Deep in the quiet, beautiful countryside and imbued with the spirit of one of the most wonderful, if eccentric, men who ever lived. With an endless supply of the most creative home-cooked food ever to grace a table. And, incidentally, some of the most creative – and lethal – home-brewed wines and spirits also. The cosiest, happiest kitchen anyone has had the privilege to party with their staff in, and,' – she turned to Gladstone – 'of course, a basket of slippers.'

The four women frowned as they stared at each other.

Polly raised a hesitant hand. 'But your ladyship, that sounds just like—'

'Home,' Eleanor breathed, suddenly feeling a prickle of hot tears. 'Would you all mind awfully if we went home?'

39

Before Eleanor could climb into the car, the sound of a bell rang out.

'Clifford, isn't that—'

'The telephone. Yes, my lady.' He cleared the steps in two long strides, unlocked the villa door once more, and disappeared inside.

Eleanor shrugged at the ladies. 'Shall we load ourselves in?'

Five minutes later, she ran her gloved hands over the steering wheel as Clifford took a moment to arrange himself in the passenger seat. His arm strapped beneath his clothing made it difficult to ensure the crease of his trousers was precisely so.

'Tradesman, was it?' She started the engine and slid the car into gear with only the minimum of graunching.

'No, my lady.' He stared forward.

'Clifford? I won't pull away until you tell me who telephoned.'

'Very well. Suffice to say, Mrs Butters will need to be prevailed upon to knit me another jumper. Only without a hole for my head. Unless she has found time to sew mine back on first, of course.'

Eleanor glanced at him, then swerved to avoid the edge of the cactus flower bed. 'I don't underst— Oh no! It wasn't?'

'It was.'

'Hugh! And he's found out?'

'Chief Inspector Seldon was rather surprised and extremely horrified on reading in *The London Gazette* about the murder of a famous American film star, one Mr Chester Armstrong. And that his body was discovered in the wine cellar of a nameless titled English lady, just a few miles from Nice. The very lady who helped solve the case.'

'Of which there could only be one. Me.' She groaned. 'Is he very, very angry?'

'No, my lady.' He winced. 'He is apoplectically furious. But only with me. For you, he has nothing but heartfelt concern and...' He tailed off, miming buttoning his lip.

'Clifford, please, I shall worry all the way home if you don't tell me.'

'If I might be so bold as to suggest, instead of worrying, we, ahem, spend the time getting our joint stories straight?' At her confused look, he continued. 'Straight on which details of the unpleasant recent events we will omit to mention to the chief inspector. We need to be ready for when the ship docks.'

'Why then?'

His eyes twinkled. 'Because the chief inspector has done the unthinkable and taken a day off to be free to collect you himself so he can be certain you are entirely unharmed.'

'But Hugh never takes a d—'

Clifford twisted in his seat to help wrench the wheel right with his one good arm as a long silver bonnet shot past.

They came to a dramatic stop on the side of the road. Slowly the dust settled.

'Hey!' two familiar voices yelled. The Fitzwilliams appeared beside her door, arm in arm.

'Eleanor, honey. We thought we'd missed you.'

'Well, Floyd,' she said, leaning out and peering along the outside of the car, 'this time I think you did.'

'Eleanor,' Kitty said in a more subdued voice than she had ever heard her use. 'We really wanted to see you to say, well, thank you. We learned a harsh lesson. It all turned out so badly, we couldn't help but confess to each other how our selfish behaviour played a part in the whole miserable affair.'

Floyd pulled his wife to his side. 'We're shipping out next week. Going back to the States. And, like you asked, we've passed Augustine's paintings on to the modern fine art museum in Nice.' He held up his hands. 'All taxes paid!'

Kitty nodded. 'The museum had ignored Augustine before, but now they know how much his paintings fetch in America, suddenly they see them as worthy enough to hang in their gallery of modern masters.' She looked down at the ground. 'It's a shame he'll never know.'

Eleanor thought back to what Damboise had said, 'to be alone after death is not possible'. She patted Kitty's arm. 'All Augustine asked me for was justice for his art. And somehow I think he'll know that's been achieved.' She shook herself. 'Well, safe travels and happy partying when you arrive.'

'No, the partying's scaling right down,' Kitty said. 'We're going home to set up as genuine patrons of the arts.'

'Yeah, Kitty'll find artists who need an ardent champion, and I'll help them sell their work for a fair price.'

'Good for you,' Eleanor said. 'But you'll still make a reasonable margin?'

He chuckled. 'Sure, honey, we all gotta help the American economy grow. But I swear the artist will get a decent share.'

Kitty patted Eleanor's arm. 'I think you're the strangest lady we'll ever meet. Which is a darn shame. I wish there were hundreds of you.'

'Me too, Kitten,' Floyd said. 'Eleanor, get out there and

spread that magic thing you've got with the world, won't you, honey?'

She was taken aback. 'I'm not really sure the world needs any more impulsive illogicality spread about.' She caught Clifford's lips quirking. 'What?'

'Fear not, my lady, "The true triumph of reason is that it enables us to get along with those who do not possess it." As the eminent Voltaire noted.'

'You total terror!'

Floyd roared with laughter and stepped round to offer Clifford his hand. 'I knew you had to have a wicked sense of humour hiding under that starched collar, Mr Clifford. It has been a pleasure. Take good care of this lady, for the sake of all of us.'

Continuing on their route, Eleanor mused aloud. 'I wonder in the future what it will be like when America, not England rules the world, Clifford. I mean, one day it's going to happen.'

He looked thoughtful. 'I concur that it is probably inevitable, my lady. They really are an irrepressible people. I can only conjecture that life will be rather loud, inappropriate and unexpected. Which,' he said with a cough, 'may not necessarily be a bad thing.'

She stared at him in surprise. 'Clifford!'

His eyes twinkled. 'All I meant, my lady, is that it would mean life would continue much as it has done since a young lady arrived at Henley Hall. And' – he gently steered her onto the correct side of the coastal road, the green hills to their left and the sparkling blue Mediterranean to their right – 'who would wish it any different!'

A LETTER FROM VERITY

Dear reader,

I want to say a huge thank you for choosing to read *The French for Murder*. If you did enjoy it, and want to keep up to date with all my latest releases, just sign up at the following link. Your email address will never be shared and you can unsubscribe at any time.

www.bookouture.com/verity-bright

I hope you loved *The French for Murder* and, if you did, I would be very grateful if you could write a review. I'd love to hear what you think, and it makes such a difference helping new readers to discover one of my books for the first time. I love hearing from my readers – you can get in touch on my Facebook page, through Twitter, Goodreads or my website.

Thanks,

Verity

www.veritybright.com

facebook.com/veritybrightauthor
twitter.com/BrightVerity

HISTORICAL NOTES

THE RIVIERA

A Winter Resort

The Riviera (or Côte d'Azur) in southern France stretches roughly from St Tropez to Menton near the Italian border. It encompasses the well-known resorts of Cannes, Antibes, Nice and Monte Carlo. Until the 1920s, the Riviera was almost exclusively a winter resort for Russian and European nobility, with hotels closing around May 1st, which is why Clifford was able to rent a villa at short notice and the American film crew shoot a movie with little interruption.

The Murphys

All of this changed when an American couple came down for the summer in 1922 and rented the Hotel du Cap (on which the Hotel d'Azur is based). They invited painters, writers and musicians –including F. Scott Fitzgerald, Picasso and Cole

Porter. They partied on the beach, dancing, swimming and sunbathing, much to the astonishment of the locals. Within a few years, Europe and America's most famous creatives flocked to the area and the glitzy, all-year celebrity playground we now know was born.

NOTE: The Fitzwilliams are entirely fictional. We are not suggesting for a moment the Murphys were involved in anything illegal or underhand. ☺

Sunbathing

Sunbathing was unheard of on the Riviera until the Murphys started the trend. To do so, they had to clear acres of seaweed off the beach and lather themselves in coconut oil. (If only Eleanor had known!) A couple of years later Coco Channel joined the trend and sunbathing became the new norm.

1920s INVENTIONS

Waterskiing

Eleanor is amazed at Floyd's waterskiing skills. Which is not surprising as the sport was brand new at the time. Ralph Samuelson is credited with inventing waterskiing in 1922, using wooden boards for skis and a clothesline as a tow rope. Water-skiing soon became a craze. Not to be outdone by all the young-sters taking up the sport, a few years later Samuelson used a giant flying boat to water ski at 80mph!

The Electric Blender

Blenders are all the rage today, mostly, it seems, for veggie and fruit smoothies. The original 1920s blenders were more often used for milkshakes and malt drinks (perfect for helping Eleanor drop off to sleep after a hard day's investigating).

The Refrigerator

The American's loved this new invention. The Delco-Light Company had sold over five thousand of its Frigidaire model in America by 1921. On the other side of the Atlantic, however, sales were slower. Most cooks, like Mrs Trotman, saw no use for such newfangled devices, arguing it hardly ever got hot enough in the UK to need one. Sadly true.

The Hairdryer

One wondrous appliance not in Eleanor's villa that she would probably never have seen before was the hairdryer. Prior to its invention, the 'modern' way for a lady in the 1920s to dry her hair was to use the, also newly invented, vacuum cleaner with a specially designed hose. Try it at your own risk. ☺

The Convertible

Like the newfangled inventions in Eleanor's villa, her French-made Delage rented car was equally up to date. It wasn't until 1922 that there was a practical convertible created. In that year Ben P. Ellerbeck designed a convertible Model T Ford and carefree, elegant motoring was born.

HOLLYWOOD

Not-so-Silent Films and Talkies

People often refer to old black-and-white movies of the 1900s as 'silent movies', which is something of a misnomer. Even though they did not feature the actors speaking, the whole film was commonly accompanied by a live pianist or organist. Often the musician would never have seen the film before and would just play whatever came to mind at the time. Later, the film studio issued books that simply said 'Fight scene', 'Love scene' or 'Chase scene.' Eventually the films were accompanied by live bands and even orchestras.

The Greatest Film Never Made

Hollywood never actually made a film about Napoleon. The French director Abel Gance made a six-hour epic in 1927 and the Russian director Sergey Bondarchuk produced the film *Waterloo* in 1970. (In one scene the British cavalry are shown wrongly attacking the French with curved swords – sabres – rather than straight ones. Had they asked Monsieur Poudray, he'd have put them right!) Its commercial failure forced Stanley Kubrick to abandon his planned film about Napoleon, often called the 'greatest film that was never made'.

THE ART SCENE

Droit de Suite

As well as tightening existing laws on exporting art from France, the authorities in 1920 introduced the droit de suite or 'right of follow' act. This gave the artist the right to be paid a percentage every time their painting was sold on. It was these laws – and payments – that Floyd was trying to avoid by smuggling the paintings he bought out of the country.

Buy Low, Sell High

Floyd applied this business mantra not only to his dealings in stocks and shares, but also art. In the 1920s foreign travel was much less common. Coupled with less sophisticated communications, it was possible for a smart dealer to buy art from unknown painters in Europe (or elsewhere) and sell them in America for many times more because the art market was booming and few people had any idea of the real worth of the paintings they were buying.

RIGOR MORTIS

Damboise states that Armstrong's body no longer showed signs of rigor mortis when examined. Some people tend to think that rigor mortis is a permanent state. In fact, it comes on around three hours after death and peaks at around twelve hours before gradually fading in the next seventy-two hours. This is why Dambois can ascertain a rough time for Armstrong's murder due to the lack, rather than presence, of rigor mortis.

FORT CARRÉ – ANTIBES

In the last chapters of *The French for Murder*, Eleanor and Clifford track the killer to an old fort on the Antibes peninsula. This is based on Fort Carré, built in the sixteenth century by King Henry II of France. Napoleon was briefly imprisoned there during the French Revolution, a scene that doesn't feature in Herman Truss' *Napoleon and Josephine*. (Unfortunately the rhinoceros scene also doesn't feature, as despite Daniel Brockman, the assistant director, being able to persuade Truss to include the scene, the new lead, Rudolph Perry, threatened to walk if it went ahead.)

NAPOLEON'S BUTTONS – AND WHY THEY MAY HAVE LED TO A GRATER DEFEAT THAN WATERLOO

Despite his grand title of Emperor of Europe, Napoleon actually dressed very simply. He often wore the uniform of a colonel in the light cavalry or a colonel in the infantry. The button Eleanor finds (or Gladstone does) is also from the Napoleonic Infantry, hence Damboise's initial judgement that it came from Armstrong's Napoleon uniform.

However, Monsieur Poudray was correct. Napoleon's infantry uniform differed in that it had gilt buttons with a crowned eagle, not two crossed cannons. Augustine, who was acting as an extra in the infantry, would have had such a button.

And how did such a small thing as a button defeat one of the greatest military geniuses the world has ever seen? Well, when Napoleon invaded Russia in 1812, the buttons on his soldiers' uniforms were made of tin. Unfortunately, unknown to Napoleon, in the extreme low temperatures of the Russian winter, the tin basically broke down into dust, leaving his soldiers with no means of doing up their uniforms and protecting themselves from freezing temperatures. Of 500,000 French soldiers who marched into Russia, only 10,000 returned, many possibly victims not of the enemy or disease, but of the cold due to their disintegrating buttons!

A DECENT RED

It may seem odd that there were no decent reds in the wine cellar that Eleanor rented, but, apart from the fact that Clifford is *very* fussy about his wine, on the Côte d'Azur, which is part of Provence, they tend to prefer rosé. In fact, around forty per cent of all the world's rosé comes from this area. Clifford's best bet for a decent local red to go with Mrs Trotman's beef daube would have been a bottle of Bandol (an area of Provence that *is* known for its reds) or any punchy pinot noir.

PROVENÇAL BEEF DAUBE

Beef daube, a rich French beef stew, was made famous in Virginia Woolf's book *To the Lighthouse* (1927) which is set between 1910 and 1920.

> ... *an exquisite scent of olives and oil and juice rose from the great brown dish as Marthe, with a little flourish, took the cover off. The cook had spent three days over that dish. And she must take great care, Mrs Ramsay thought, diving into the soft mass, to choose a specially tender piece for William Bankes. And she peered into the dish, with its shiny walls and its confusion of savoury brown and yellow meats and its bay leaves and its wine...*

The dish had become known in 1920s England as French cooking became more and more popular. Mrs Trotman, fine cook though she is, needs some local help!

Note: Like Mrs Ramsay's cook, you can take three days to make your daube.

Day one: marinade
Day two: cook
Day three: eat

And bonus!

Day four: stuff the leftovers into ravioli or have with gnocchi or pasta.

The most delicious daube I ever tasted was in a small family-run restaurant in old Nice where they cooked the beef for only (!) twelve hours.

ACKNOWLEDGEMENTS

Thanks to our editor, Kelsie, for her next-level editing and to the rest of the Bookouture team for making *The French for Murder* the best it can be.

Printed in Great Britain
by Amazon